ALSO BY EGAN HUGHES

The One That Got Away

LEAVE THE

THE

LIGHTS

ON

EGAN HUGHES

Sphere
An imprint of
Little, Brown Book Group
Carmelite House
50 Victoria Embankment
London EC4Y 0DZ

An Hachette UK Company
www.hachette.co.uk

www.littlebrown.co.uk

sphere

SPHERE

First published in Great Britain as a paperback original in 2021 by Sphere

1 3 5 7 9 10 8 6 4 2

Copyright © Egan Hughes 2021

The moral right of the author has been asserted.

Line from 'The Haunting of Hill House' © Shirley Jackson 1959,
renewed copyright 1987 by Laurence Hyman, Barry Hyman,
Sarah Webster and Joanne Schmurer

A CIP catalogue record for this book is available from the British Library.

ISBN 978-0-7515-7679-5

Typeset in Caslon by M Rules
Printed and bound in Great Britain by Clays Ltd, Elcograf S.p.A.

Papers used by Sphere are from well-managed forests
and other responsible sources.

To James, for showing me the pros and cons of rural living.

PROLOGUE

Last night, I dreamt the house tried to kill me. In the dream, I am standing on the dark landing, stricken with fear. A deep voice behind me calls my name and I can almost feel his breath on the back of my neck. My legs refuse to move. The paralysing terror roots me to the spot, despite my desperate urge to run. I often have dreams like this, when I'm frozen in shock instead of running for my life. I can't even cry out, and no one would hear me scream anyway.

A different voice comes through the darkness; the ghostly whisper I've heard before. At last, I'm able to run or at least stumble downstairs, lurching between the wall and the banister in the dark. Every step is fraught with danger, the house alive with hidden threats.

The front door is within reach and I lunge for it, claw at the handle, but it won't budge. No key, no chain, nothing. Blind panic closes in. I gasp for air but the blackness seeps into the edges of my vision. I shut my eyes, willing the nightmare to recede. For that's what it must be, a nightmare. I will wake in a fevered sweat and wonder how a dream could have felt so real.

One thing I've learnt from all this is that it's not just houses that are haunted. People can be haunted too: haunted by the past, haunted by their fears. Even before everything went wrong, home was no longer a haven and I was scared to turn the lights off. I try to wake up but nothing happens.

There is only blackness.

CHAPTER ONE

Two weeks earlier

There's a chill in the air as I lift the easel inside the house and kick off my trainers. The underfloor heating seeps through my socks and I close my eyes to the warmth. I never expected us to live somewhere so grown up. We could have found an easier renovation, but we'd set our hearts on this one. Once we knew Chilwood Cottage was ours, we celebrated with gin and tonics, heady with plans of how to make it work on our tight budget, and we've done it. We have a home and just need to settle in. Now the work is finished, I'm painting it to put our stamp on this dream come true.

I scroll through my playlist and activate the home audio by tapping on my chill-out mix. Music pipes through the downstairs space, stirring memories of bliss from my first holiday with Joe, our sunny week in Ibiza on the quiet side of the island where we swam from a sandy beach in a deserted little cove.

Basking in the warmth of the sun, Joe turned golden brown and looked even more gorgeous. We'd been together for three months and I already wanted to spend my life with him.

In the kitchen, I stand back and assess the canvas. Artistic licence has crept in with a dramatic sky in manganese blue above the slate roof, silver-grey as it catches the autumnal light. I'd wanted something soft and pretty, but somehow the colours have come out murkier, darker than intended. Painted branches reach towards the house like grasping bony arms with gnarled twigs for fingers.

Never mind, I'll soften it next time. The brick and flint walls are ready for warmer shades of sienna, which sounds too sun-baked for our little patch of Sussex countryside. It felt good to be out in the autumn air, trying to keep pace with the colours altering in the light. It's a welcome change, when earning a living from portraits means that I rarely choose what to paint, since commissions come first because we need the money.

It's nearly time for Dora's walk before dark. I'll add her to the painting later for some light relief, sunning herself on the front lawn. Dora's rich conker-brown coat will shine in the mellow light, and I want to capture her chocolate drop eyes and guilty dachshund expression. Animal portraits are my niche, commissions of beloved pets. I've even done a large-scale painting of a coiled green python in gold leaf for a Hong Kong businesswoman. Today though, I allowed myself time to paint the cottage.

I hum along to the music, cleaning paintbrushes in the kitchen sink. The colours merge and create a storm cloud grey that swirls down the plug. Joe doesn't know yet, but I'm painting the house for him as a Christmas gift. I could paint Dylan playing with Dora on the grass, to help him feel a part of things. He's Joe's son and we want him to be at home here, even if he prefers living with his mum. He might stay over now the work's mostly finished. That's what Joe hopes, after Dylan's troubles at school. It hardly seems like eight years since that cherub-faced five-year-old came into my life and we became a family of sorts.

The music jumps and then judders as if stuck. I dry my hands on my jeans, smearing water down the pale denim, and tap the screen of my mobile. The music stops and I press *play* via the app that Joe set up to control the sound system. It plays again, clear this time.

I'm not at home with technology, but technology is at home with us. It's built into the smoothly plastered walls. It can lock the doors at the touch of a button, and will turn on the oven when we're not home.

'You'll get used to it,' Joe said when he first showed me how it worked.

'We'll see,' I replied, because I'm trying to get used to it. We started the renovation eight months ago, but the smart features are more recent.

It began with him wanting a seamless sound system and has evolved into controlling all the gadgets via an app on our phones. Joe is in his element with the smart home. He loves the fact that we have audio everywhere at the touch of a keypad without visible speakers, remote controls or wires dangling down. As for me, I like to see the root of a thing, its origin. If you know its life-source, you can control it.

The paint is dry enough for me to hide the portrait in my studio out the back. Joe won't find it there. Then I go to the hall cupboard for my jacket and tighten a scarf around my exposed neck. I whistle for Dora and hear the clip-clip-clip of her paws as she patters across the tiled kitchen floor.

'Come on, little one,' I say, rubbing behind her ears. 'Let's walk you before it's too dark.'

Dora and I take the route round the edge of the field as dusk falls. It's cold now the sun has dipped behind the trees. The hills in the distance are a watercolour wash of muted grey-greens. It's a lonely place, but the surroundings make up for that. Night-times are pitch black out here. On a clear night, the sky is a midnight blue blanket of stars, but the nearest street-light is a mile away.

I skirt back round the woodland, Dora barely straying from my ankles. We make our way along the grassy track studded with flint rocks and chalky stone, towards our nearest neighbour's house. Mitchell owns an imposing property on three floors that broods over ours. Chilwood Manor looks grand from a distance, but come closer and you can see the flaking paint on the Georgian sash windows. The paint is the colour of bone. It must be cold in there in wintertime. A tangle of ivy creeps over his low garden wall. The place reeks of neglect, much like its owner.

We've had our run-ins with Mitchell over the building work. I catch sight of him in his garden, wearing an old olive raincoat.

He's stooped and battered by age but was probably tall and good-looking way back, with strong features and thick hair. He stands alongside a white stone statue of a woman with no arms. Another statue on a plinth nearby is of a female body cut off below the torso. 'Do you think they're women he's turned to stone?' I said to Joe when we first saw them.

'Doesn't bother me,' he'd said, passing it off as another of Mitchell's quirks.

Mitchell stares hard at me now, flanked by his dismembered statues. I hunch into my padded jacket and look the other way, but I feel his eyes drilling into me. Nearly level, I look towards him and attempt a stiff smile.

'That dog barks a lot,' he says, squinting past me as if he sees something that I can't.

'She doesn't. Not really.'

'I hear barking at all hours.'

'Must be another dog.' I keep walking.

Dora has a yappy little bark, but she's easily quietened. After years of city living, we're attuned to not hacking off the neighbours. Mitchell is easily hacked off, though. Dora quickens her pace now the cottage is in sight. I speed up too before the darkness spooks me. As a child, I had a night-light for years, unable to wean myself off its glow of reassurance. It wasn't until I left for art school at eighteen that I felt I'd conquered my fear of the dark, and even then, I was wrong. It was still there, lurking, waiting for the trigger. Now we use the app for mood lighting at home, but here in the quiet gloom, the gathering darkness leaves me exposed.

We reach home and I delve into my jacket pocket for the key. Joe calls me 'analogue' for sticking with a door key instead of tapping in the keycode. Soon after we moved in, I locked myself out and had to phone him for the code. He's always changing it and I struggle to remember pin numbers and passcodes. Before I can insert my key in the lock, the door swings slowly open without me touching it. No one's there.

'In the kitchen,' Joe calls through. 'I saw you coming.'

'Jesus Christ, Joe.' I come inside. 'Don't do that. It's like a haunted house.'

'All right, Morticia?' He comes through to the hall and kisses me, then he leans down to ruffle Dora's coat. 'And Cousin It.'

He's set the lighting to a soft lavender blue, and acoustic guitar plays in the background. We go in the kitchen and Joe pours his favourite Chablis into oversized wine glasses.

'Mitchell says Dora barks a lot.' I take a sip of wine.

'And Mitchell complains a lot. Rise above it, Dora,' he says to her. She cocks her head and wags her tail.

I go to boil the kettle for the steamer. 'How was your day?'

'Okay, thanks. Did you forget something?' He motions towards the tap over the sink.

'Oh yes.' Instant boiling water. Joe's embraced all the conveniences of our new home, but it's taking me longer. The traditional copper kettle looks good on the hob, otherwise it would have been banished.

'I've been flat out,' he says, 'getting ahead so I can focus on the tour tomorrow. You're here for it, yeah?'

'Sure.' Not that I'll be any use, but Joe's keen to show people around. He arranged it with our architect, something about best practice in smart homes. Joe's interest has taken over his life now that he's setting up a smart home business, using this place as the prototype. He's packaged it as a user-friendly system that anyone can operate. I tell myself this tour is his equivalent of an exhibition of my artwork for me.

'I'm dreading us having a power cut or something.'

A power cut would prove we shouldn't rely on the technology, but I don't say that. I won't trample on his love of technology any more than he'll rubbish my need to be creative. We cook linguine in a creamy garlic mushroom sauce, weaving round each other in our easygoing way. The acoustic guitar picks up pace with a Latin vibe and Joe takes my hand for some salsa dance moves. We sway and swirl in time with the music. The pan bubbles and he spins and dips me, and I can't help laughing.

When we're eating at the table, he asks what painting I'm working on.

'I'm starting a new one of a horse, for a couple in Harting.' I don't mention the cottage watercolour.

Later, we go to bed and Dora makes hers by scratching at her beanbag and turning in circles before flopping out. Joe's arms encircle me and he falls instantly asleep, as he always does after drinking wine. We should break the habit of alcohol on weeknights, even though he's keen for a drink when we start cooking in the evening. Booze or not, I sleep badly here. When we finished the building work, I thought the countryside would lull me to sleep, but it takes ages to drift off.

I wake with a start in the night. The bedroom light flickered on and off, jolting me awake, unless I dreamt it. My heart's racing. Joe's gone from the bed. The en suite's in darkness and I can't hear him anywhere. It's not like him to get up in the night. I turn on the bedside lamp and check the time on my phone. It's 2.57 a.m. The night is silent, and I go downstairs to look for him. He's at the kitchen table, hunched over his laptop and the only light comes from its screen.

'Joe?'

He looks up at me. Shadows fill the room and the stark light of the screen gives his face a haunted look.

'What's up?' I sink into the chair beside him and rest a hand on his shoulder. He closes the lid of his laptop and jabs at his phone screen for a muted grey light to fill the kitchen.

'I couldn't sleep.' He rubs his eyes and gives me a tired smile. 'And now I've woken you up. Sorry.' He reaches for my hand and our fingers entwine.

'Why can't you sleep?'

'Must be the tour today. I want it to go well. Be good to get feedback from people in the know.'

'It'll be fine.'

It's not like him to worry about something like that, but he's keen to move away from his property maintenance work for landlords. There's often someone ready to charge less, and we won't always have the stamina for hard grafting. We've talked about it, our plans for when we're old and grey, although we're still in our thirties. We used to live next door to an elderly couple who always went out together holding hands, the man

10

carrying the shopping bag. I want us to be like them, still holding hands in our old age.

Joe looks troubled, staring at the laptop.

'Is there something else?'

He clasps my hand more firmly. 'No, nothing ... it's just, I don't know, I guess I'm a bit worried about Dylan.'

'Oh, okay.'

'Since all that hassle with the school, I feel I can barely get through to him.'

Joe does his best with Dylan, including designing him a high-tech bedroom to tempt him to stay here at weekends. We fell into doing up properties when we couldn't afford a two-bedroom home, needing the second room for Dylan to stay over. We took on a complete dump of a flat with mould spreading up the walls, renovating it on a shoestring to make it habitable for the three of us. Dylan refused to stay over, so Joe said, 'Let's buy another wreck.' This is renovated wreck number seven and Dylan will be taller than me soon. He prefers sleeping in his own bed at his mum's place every night, but Joe hopes that will change.

I rub his back with one hand. 'You're on top of it. He knows you're here for him.'

He leans over to kiss me. 'Are you okay living here?'

'Of course I'm okay. I love it here.'

'It's just that you seem a bit on edge, as if you're scared of what's out there.'

Joe's eyes search mine. I don't like the concern in his face. My gaze drifts towards the garden and the dark silhouette of trees, their branches swaying in the October night. We don't have curtains downstairs because the smart glass function turns the windows from transparent to opaque. It cost a fortune but Joe wanted it. I don't turn the windows opaque now as it will prove his point, but anyone could be out there watching us and we wouldn't even notice. A tingle runs down my neck and I shiver. Joe reaches for his hoodie and helps me put it on. I tug the long sleeves over my hands.

'We're still settling in. Give it time. We're lucky to be here.'

'Love you.' He pulls me into a hug and nuzzles my hair. The first night we met, he hugged me and it felt so natural, as if we fitted together, which we have done ever since. 'Sorry for dragging you down here to find me. Let's go on up.'

We return to bed and Joe falls asleep again. I stay awake through the early hours, unable to forget him saying that I'm scared of what's out there. Maybe I am scared, but I won't tell Joe. He has enough to worry about.

CHAPTER TWO

In the morning, Joe makes the place presentable for the tour. He's obsessive in the detail, needing everything to be faultless for showcasing his packaged smart home solution. He sets the robo-vac to clean the floor. When we first got it, we tried coaxing Dora to take a ride as it buzzed around, but she just runs and hides.

The robo-vac trundles around the open-plan space. The study and lounge area at the front leads into the kitchen and dining space at the back, where we're clearing away the worktop clutter. When the kitchen was first installed, we put everything away in its proper place, but we're more relaxed now about leaving out the coffee pot, the stoneware storage jars and assorted everyday things. Minimalism doesn't suit me, but clearing the clutter means our visitors can focus on the sleek look of the house.

I take a moment to savour the perfect calm of our pristine home. We'll take photos before the tour to go on the blog for Joe's fledgling company and show the property looking at its best. I jump at a movement outside. Someone's out there. A man in a dark fleece walks past the kitchen window.

'It's only Kev,' Joe says. 'Come to fix the outside light, a week later than he said.'

I recognise him now from the salt-and-pepper dusting of his scruffy hair. Joe lets him in through the back.

'Doorbell's not working,' Kev says, holding his electrician's toolbox and wiping his feet on the mat.

'Are you sure?' Joe goes through to check.

'Mate, I rang the bell and nothing happened.' Kev's either cultivating designer stubble or hasn't bothered to shave for days. 'All right, Lauren?'

He follows Joe. 'Must be a connection problem.'

'It's a good connection.' Joe sounds rattled. 'Maybe it's the sensor.'

'The wiring was fine when I did it. Might be an *IT* issue.' He says it in a snippy way.

We're used to tradesmen passing the buck and blaming whoever else touched the job. Joe and I shoulder most of the renovation work, shovelling rubble, shaking plaster dust from our hair, but we leave the electrics to Kev.

The two of them work on the doorbell and the app connected to it. We can see who rings the bell through our phone screens, and talk to them via the sound system whether we're home or not. The control panel of the doorbell and intercom lies discreetly against the wall. It lights up when you approach the door and then fades back once it's been used. Give me a basic doorbell that actually works and I'd be happier, but I don't say that, especially not today. I make Kev tea with two sugars, and they get it working again.

'I'll do the light outside the garage,' Kev says.

'Not today,' Joe says, 'not with the visitors coming, but can you check everything else is working?'

Kev takes the mug that I hand him. His face is pasty, probably from fast food, judging by the burger packaging that piles up in the front of his van. I haven't seen him for a month or so. I tend to leave Joe to deal with him while I'm in the studio. He used to be in good shape, but now his fleece strains over his ample stomach. Joe said his wife left him in the summer, so maybe he's not adjusting to single life.

'It's nothing obvious with the doorbell, so you'll have to call your *IT lady*.' He takes a gulp of tea. 'All that money to turn up with her laptop. I do the hard work with the cabling and she presses some buttons and charges a fortune.'

'She didn't charge a fortune,' I say. She didn't charge anything because Joe and Nicole are in business, combining her computer skills with his property experience.

I met Kev seven years ago, after we'd sold our first flat and had a loan to buy a vermin-infested house. It took several attempts before I could go inside without gagging. Kev pulled up in his white van. The digger partly blocked the drive, so I jumped in and reversed it to give him space to park.

'Not bad, for a woman,' he said when I climbed off the digger. I should have hated him on first sight.

A few weeks later he showed me the spotlights he'd fitted in the kitchen.

15

'Not bad, for a man,' I'd said. It's been an in joke between Joe and me ever since. *Not bad, for a woman*, Joe will compliment me with a wink. Then he'll grab me and plant kisses on the ticklish part of my neck until I squeal and slap him away. Joe likes Kev's workmanship and he doesn't charge a fortune, so I leave them to it.

I turn to go. 'I'll be in the studio.'

'Half day, is it?' Kev says. 'Off to do your drawings.'

'Paintings. I'm working on a commission for a client.'

'Yeah, your pet pictures. Can't pay much, can it?'

He's such an idiot, the things he comes out with.

'That's where you're wrong, mate,' Joe says. 'Her daily rate's higher than yours.'

He looks sceptical.

No wonder his wife left him. I walk away since I can only take so much of Kev. Dora trots outside after me. The wind's fierce but it'll be okay in the studio. My first-ever artist's studio is a summerhouse in the garden, positioned for the natural light. The upside of being in the country is more space and better quality of light. It's raised, with four steps leading to the door, and my heart lifts every time I come inside.

I laid the reclaimed brick floor, and chose the slate tiles beneath the quirky little wood-burner to match the roof tiles. The walls are painted in my favourite shade of Prussian blue. My latest watercolour waits on the easel. The paints and brushes are laid out with photos of the sleek black horse, resplendent beside its stable with lush summer foliage behind.

I mute my phone and press *play* on my CD of The Sundays.

It reminds me of my childhood, Mum playing indie music like The Cranberries, and my brother strumming his guitar. Joe has our music online, but the CD player is all I need out here. Low tech suits me. I've drawn the line at some of his innovations. When he set up the voice activation, he demonstrated how it changed to a soothing tone at night-time. A woman's voice whispered 'lights out' and a cold shiver went through me.

'Joe, that's horrible,' I'd said.

'Really? I like it.'

'A whispering voice? It'll give me nightmares.' We agreed to ditch the disembodied voices, thank God.

I wrap myself in the homely nostalgia of the music and work on the horse painting. People like Kev assume my 'pet pictures' are a hobby I make money from, but it's so much more. I see each animal through the owner's eyes, capturing their affection. Sometimes I imagine myself as the animal, inside their skin; in this case, standing proud and powerful. If I paint birds in flight, I imagine how it would feel to soar and swoop in the air. I love the times when it's just me and the painting and it comes together. When I'm immersed, there's no space for anything else. But today it's difficult to get fully in the zone when the visitors are arriving soon.

With an hour to go before they arrive, I lock the studio and return indoors. Kev's gone and Joe is using his spirit level app to check the big canvas print in the living area is straight. I go out the front to clear rotting leaves and fallen petals from the crimson velvet roses. I'll get up early tomorrow to finish the painting, since it's better in natural light, and it'll be dusk when the tour's over. I bring in the wheelie bin from the road and yelp in shock. A windswept man appears from behind a hedge as if lying in wait. It's Mitchell in his stained raincoat and mud-caked wellies.

'Why is your bin out here?' he snaps. His thatch of grey hair looks even wilder than usual.

'It's bin day.' I pull it in front of me, as if warding him off. 'You scared me.'

He keeps glaring. 'They were emptied hours ago.'

'I've been working. Why are you standing out here?'

'This is a public highway. I'll do as I please.' He cranes his neck past me at our garage that he complained so bitterly about, even though it blends with the house and he can't even see it from his place.

'Jeez.' I turn and march the bin round the back, my heart pounding. If it weren't for our visitors arriving, I'd have left it out there to annoy him.

I don't want to be unkind to Mitchell because he lives alone and it's isolated out here. If he wasn't so hostile, I'd look in to say hello and check if he needed anything. He introduced himself as Mitchell when we first met him. We thought that was his surname, but when he objected to our planning application, the documents named him as Mitchell Unsworth. His letters of complaint to the council slowed down the already sluggish bureaucratic process. Our renovation plans stalled because of his objections, combined with probate hassles and drawn-out land issues over who owned what.

I go inside and tell Joe. 'Does he talk to you like that?'

'No. He complains about the garage. He was probably having another nose around to check we're not building anything else. I'll swap you the garage complaints for the bins. They're easier to deal with.'

'I don't want to talk to him about anything.'

'Don't then. You can't reason with him.'

My heart still hammers in my chest. *It's okay*, I tell myself. *It's only Mitchell. He doesn't mean any harm.* Joe and I are returning to how it used to be, or that's the plan. We even talked about going back to Ibiza, which wouldn't be a big deal for most people, but I'm not quite ready.

I call up the CCTV on my app and tap the screen that shows the doorstep and drive. Mitchell's gone and no one's there. Joe installed CCTV outside to keep me safe, but foreboding creeps over me when I check it on my phone. It always looks ominous, as if I'll see something bad if I stare for long enough.

CHAPTER THREE

We're ready for the house tour visitors, who are due to arrive any minute.

'Isn't Nicole coming?' I ask Joe.

'It's not her thing,' he says. 'She'd rather do the technical stuff and leave me to deal with the people. She thinks the older punters won't take her seriously, since she only looks about eighteen.'

'She'll gain confidence as it progresses. How old did you say she is?'

'Twenty-three.'

I don't blame her for leaving it to Joe. It's his brainchild and he has the majority stake. Nicole has agreed a thirty per cent share in return for the IT development.

A pair of black Range Rovers pulls up, driven by our architect and his business partner, and filled with the visitors. They'd met at the architects' office for a car share. Joe lingers in the entrance hall.

'Are you going to let them in?' I ask.

'I'll do it through the app. I want them to use the door entry system.'

When they ring the bell, Joe releases the lock so the door opens in a smooth motion to an appreciative audience. *Load of bollocks*, I think, pasting on a smile and standing back for him to welcome them in. I nod 'hello' to everyone and shake hands with the two architects.

Joe leads them to the utility room to show them the home hub, even though it's the least interesting part of the house. I hang back as there isn't space for us all. They stand with their backs to me while Joe explains the set-up to the nine of them, all men.

I'd expected the architects to invite property developer clients or people wanting their own smart home, but judging by the impressed murmuring over the smart hub's touchscreen, they're techies. Shame that Nicole isn't here, in that case. I stand against the wall, uneasy about these men looking over the control panel for our home. But I'm being silly when Alistair knows them all.

Joe's in his element, showing the place off, his boyish enthusiasm shining through. He deserves some recognition for all his hard work. He's smiling a lot, his cheeks dimpling. Nicole's not the only one who looks young. Joe could pass for ten years younger than his actual age of thirty-eight. He's nervous and keeps running a hand through his short chestnut hair, his usual comfort gesture, laughing at every little thing, trying to keep everyone onside.

21

They emerge into the kitchen and I give Joe a smile of re-assurance. He makes everyone hot drinks with the instant boiling water on tap, having hidden the kettle in a cupboard. I could do it, but he likes demonstrating how easy everything is.

'No more boiling kettles for you,' a man in a black anorak says to me.

'I'm the tea boy round here,' Joe says. 'I know my place.'

The men snicker. I show willing because Joe asked me, otherwise I'd have left them to it. I take milk from the fridge and reach into the cupboard for the sugar. Joe fires up the hob via the app, and taps again to turn the smart glass opaque on the patio doors.

'Ready for bed?' a woman whispers in a low, seductive voice.

There's more snickering at her words, and I stiffen at the whispering voice that I'd objected to earlier. Joe didn't mention turning the voice activation back on. The man in the black anorak gives me a lascivious glance, as if I'd been the one saying 'ready for bed' in a suggestive voice. I grit my teeth.

Joe takes them on the patio to demonstrate the smart glass from the outside. When they come back in, I keep my smile pleasant and turn my gaze from Joe to admiring the deep blue ceramic vase on the windowsill. Sunlight spills onto it and reflects off its shiny glaze. We bought it at a potter's studio in the summer. He hands round the drinks and gives me a mug of tea.

Joe hits his stride, showing them his favourite toy: the sound system. I don't blame Nicole for staying away, although she'd get a kick from the interest. The technology is seamless and user friendly, and Joe's set it apart from the competition with some clever features.

'. . . It can be piped through the whole house or just selected areas,' he says, tapping his phone. Soothing classical music begins to play. It's not his usual choice, but the gentle piano melody resonates around us. Everyone agrees that it's perfect sound quality.

'It's a guy thing,' one of them says to me, a hint of pity in his voice. I raise my eyebrows in response and sip my tea.

'Lauren loves the sound system too,' Joe jumps in. 'I can be listening to my playlist out here and she could be in the bath with an audio book.'

It's not true, since I don't listen to audio books, but for some reason, I picture myself alone at night, scaring myself with a supernatural thriller. The man in the black anorak looks at me with a furtive leery expression, possibly thinking of me in the bath. I return his stare, and he looks away.

Joe shepherds them upstairs. 'Anyone can have multi-room audio, but we wanted to show you this system because it's seamlessly integrated in one user-friendly app. The hub is out of the way and there aren't clunky speakers and wires, or remote controls.'

'What advice would you give someone wanting this system?' Alistair prompts him.

Don't bother, I nearly call after them. What's wrong with me? Maybe I'm tired from being awake half the night. I love Chilwood Cottage more than anywhere I've ever lived. It's a world away from the dump of a flat we first bought to do up, but Joe's right about me being on edge. I need time to settle in. We've only just finished transforming it from a building site to a home over the last eight months, living in it the whole time, with most of our belongings in storage. It kept costs down and pushed us to make it habitable. Now I'm becoming used to it as a home instead of the latest cycle in our renovate-and-move-on way of life.

I click the blackout icon to reinstate the clear view of the garden. It won't be long before the sharp cold brightens the landscape and turns it crisp with frost. I'll grow veg next summer and we've talked about keeping chickens, both of us keen to collect warm eggs, fresh from the hens.

Dora's come out of hiding now the robo-vac is back in the cupboard and she's had time to satisfy herself it won't make a reappearance. She flops on her bed with a heavy sigh. I hear the men's voices overhead and go to clear up the mugs.

A shiver runs through me. *Someone's walked over my grave.* My mum used to say that. A movement catches my eye: a man darts into the utility room. I go to investigate. The Anorak Man is back at the smart hub. He's either studying it or fiddling with the switches. I avoid moving closer, not wanting to be in a confined space with him. Even with a house full of people, my instinct is to back away from a man I don't know. I hear Joe answering questions upstairs, punctuated by his nervous laugh.

'Can I help you?' I ask the man.

He stiffens and turns to me with rabbit in the headlight eyes. Then he rearranges his face. 'I couldn't resist another look.' He points to the control panel. 'Fascinating, isn't it? I've never seen it done so well.'

Someone must have cracked a joke as they all laugh upstairs.

'Sounds like you're missing out.' I tilt my head towards the stairs. 'Why don't you go on up?' I wave a guiding arm along the hall.

He goes back upstairs and I check the control panel, not that I'd notice anything out of place. Minutes later, they troop downstairs, talking animatedly about the 'sensory experience' in Dylan's bedroom. The cuboid space-age room is fitted with fibre optics, lights that slowly change colour and a floor-to-ceiling glass tube of swirling white bubbles. Plus his Xbox, of course. To my relief, Joe opens the front door to let them out.

Alistair, our architect, is the last to leave. 'You've done a beautiful job, Lauren.' He holds my shoulders and kisses me on both cheeks. 'I bet you don't know yourself, settled here.'

He leaves with his car loads of visitors, and Joe and I are alone again.

'How did it go?' I ask.

'They seemed to like it, but my phone was buzzing the whole time. There's some crisis at Hawthorn Grove.'

I want to tell him about the man in the anorak, but he kisses me and rushes out to deal with his property maintenance work. He's my counterbalance. Solid, dependable Joe, the voice of reason. He'll say, *don't worry about the man*, and he'll be right. He's always right.

CHAPTER FOUR

Joe comes home later and catches up with work emails while I grab some more painting time. When daylight fades, the portrait is more detailed and Joe is visible in the kitchen, talking on his mobile. Dora goes into the garden to pick up wildlife trails and I check on the shrubs we planted last month when the earth was still warm from summer. When I go indoors, Joe's FaceTiming Dylan.

'But I don't like her touching me.' Dylan's voice comes through, awkward and petulant at having to explain himself.

'I know,' Joe says. 'She likes you though, and she's only little.'

'She doesn't like me. She likes playing on my tablet.'

'What if you sit at the table with it?'

'It's too noisy. *Peppa Pig* drives me mad.'

'Earphones?'

'She pulls them off.'

When I first met Dylan, he was an adorably dimpled little

version of Joe and I would want to scoop him up in a cuddle. He shrugged away any attempts at touching. Sometimes I'd forget and nudge against him or touch his arm to point something out, and he'd stiffen or recoil.

'Can you remind your mum about turning down the volume?' Joe says.

'I'd like to turn down Harper's volume.'

'You can't really do that with a three-year-old.'

I steer clear, not wanting to encroach, but I picture Dylan in a huff, his long dark fringe covering half his face; the fringe I always want to reach over and brush from his eyes. He has lovely eyes, not that you'd know. He's big for thirteen but seems younger when he talks.

'Dylan, I hope you're not using it on your own in your bedroom? You know you're not allowed to do that.'

'I don't have a choice.'

'Dylan, we agreed—'

'You don't know how annoying she is.' His fraught voice becomes a wail.

'Listen to me—'

'Stop picking on me.'

He's getting louder, but Joe stays calm and rational. 'I'm not picking on—'

'It's not my fault!' he shouts.

'Okay, Dylan, let's calm things down. I'll speak to your mum and we'll talk again tomorrow.' Joe knows he won't achieve anything when Dylan's wound up. 'Love you.'

Dylan logs off in a huff.

Dora prances round my feet, wanting to be fed. I grab her bowl and add a measure of dried food. 'How's Dylan?' I ask.

'Forever on his computer.'

'Where does he get that from?'

'Tara's still letting him use the tablet in his bedroom. The toddler tries to play with it if not, and we all know Dylan's *particular* about his stuff.'

'It's a tricky one, blended families. The younger one takes all her mum's attention, so Dylan gets to hang out in his bedroom.' Blended families are tricky for me too, namely the other woman in the scenario. Joe's ex-wife struggles with Dylan, who's on a different wavelength. She struggles with me too, so I stay out of it.

'We can't risk him getting in trouble again,' Joe says.

'Are you still monitoring it?' He downgraded Dylan's laptop to a tablet and has remote access to everything he does online after Dylan shocked us by hacking his school's mainframe. It was one of the few times I've seen Joe lose his temper with Dylan, prompting a monumental meltdown, but Dylan had to learn that hacking could land him in serious trouble.

We knew he liked online escapism, and Joe thought he was gaming. We worried that he might be an easy target online for anyone shady, so Joe once set up an internet pseudonym and tried to befriend him. Joe went to all the trouble of setting up a fake avatar to appeal to Dylan, but he refused to engage. I felt uncomfortable at the trickery, but Joe insisted the online persona would teach him 'stranger danger'. As it turned out, we didn't have to worry on that score, unaware back then that his solitary activities stretched to illegal hacking.

'It's not the same as being there,' Joe says. 'For all I know he's got a second internet source. He could be up to all sorts.'

'Do you think he would? He knows it's not worthwhile, not since the fallout from what happened.'

'I've talked to him about black hat hackers – the online criminals – and the white hats who try to stop them. I'm hoping he'll want to be a white hat.'

'Now I'm picturing hackers wearing black or white hats to show what side they're on.'

Joe rubs his face tiredly. 'Why's life so difficult?'

He turns away to take a call and I put Dora's bowl on the floor. I carry the laundry basket up to the bedroom and fold clothes to put away in drawers. I'm halfway through the pile when I hear Dora growling in Dylan's bedroom. She must have wolfed her food and now she's playing 'growl and pounce' with a chew toy, abandoned since Dylan last played with her in his room.

He hasn't stayed overnight yet, but he chose the duvet and the paint colour, and Joe installed the sensory effects in the room. When Dylan comes for the day, the two of them lie on the bed and play Xbox games. It doesn't fit the tranquil vibe but so long as Dylan's happy.

Joe designed the smart home with sensory features to be calming for people with conditions like autism and anxiety disorder. It's only installed in one room because of the cost, but he added a reclining chair so I can relax in there. The bubble tube is turned off now, but I'm often mesmerised by its luminosity as the soft lighting changes colour. The dreamy swirl of bubbles is like the lazy ripples of a jacuzzi. It's nearly enough to lull me to sleep. Joe is aiming the smart home at families with special needs or people who want somewhere peaceful to de-stress.

I finish putting the clothes away with a strange sensation of being watched. I turn from the chest of drawers but no one's there. No one can watch us through the smart home because Joe only installed CCTV outside. We agreed to no cameras indoors. The room's turned cold, more like the outside temperature. I shudder and zip up my hoodie.

When I go downstairs, Joe's finishing the call and Dora's pushing her bowl round the kitchen, licking every last trace. I stop in my tracks. My mind had wandered and I'd forgotten about her playing upstairs just a minute ago.

'Has Dora been down here the whole time?'

'Yeah. Since you put her food down.'

'But she was upstairs, growling.'

'I don't think so.'

'I heard her when I was in the bedroom.'

'Where was she?'

'In Dylan's room.' It doesn't make sense. Even if Joe didn't notice her coming upstairs, I'd have heard her trotting down before me, her claws tapping on the wooden floor. 'Was she growling down here?'

'No. She hasn't made a sound, apart from crunching kibble.'

'Joe, this is weird. I heard her upstairs.'

'Maybe it was an animal outside.'

'It was Dora. I know her growl.'

Come to think of it, it was more of a fearful growl than

a playful one. I should've investigated, but I'd thought nothing of it.

'Is there something weird going on with the sound system?' I keep on.

Joe shrugs as if it's one of those things, so I let it go.

CHAPTER FIVE

The next morning, Nicole taps away at her keyboard in the utility room. She stands beside the control panel working on enhancements that Joe had delayed until after the tour. Her white blond hair is in a ruffled pixie crop that suits her heart-shaped face. I can picture her as a quiet, geeky child, her luminous emerald eyes lighting up at computer coding, the same as mine would from a box of paints.

'Joe should be back soon,' I say. 'He's catching up on some maintenance work after spending time on the smart home tour yesterday.'

'No problem.' Nicole keeps tapping. I hardly know her, since Joe took ownership of the high-tech stuff, but she arrived early. She has long eyelashes and light freckles sprinkled over her face. No make-up; she doesn't need it. I imagine her as a cat person, since she ignores Dora.

'Is it hard to update because the IT is hidden away?'

'Not really. We've made the tech seamless, but it's

controllable. It's the right approach for somewhere this beautiful. You don't want speakers and wires spoiling the effect.'

That's the upside Joe sold to me. We might have gutted the place, but we kept the original fireplaces and features, putting it back together with elegant, clean lines, reclaimed oak floors and neutral heritage paint on the walls.

'The tour went well,' I say.

'Oh yeah. Cool. Joe emailed me.'

'You might have liked it. They were enthusiasts.'

'It's not my thing.' She wrinkles her nose apologetically. She's a good ten years younger than me, but I could be friends with her. 'I'm better behind the scenes. It's a great side hustle though.'

A side hustle. It's the same for Joe, fitted around his day job since it's not making money yet.

'I look so young that people think I'm doing work experience. Joe's the front person. He can refer to me as the IT team.'

'It doesn't matter how old you look. You know your stuff and you're enthusiastic. That's important in business.'

She deserves more than staying in the background, not that I'm in a position to lecture, given my own reluctance to be around other people since my confidence was knocked.

'I heard something strange last night,' I say.

She looks expectantly at me and I tell her about hearing Dora growling in the bedroom when she was downstairs with Joe.

'I honestly don't know how that could happen,' she says.

33

'I was kinda hoping you'd tell me the growl was recorded and played back.'

'There's not a function for recording sound and playing it back, so you can't activate it by accident. Perhaps there's weird acoustics here and the dog was growling somewhere else but sounded closer.'

I shake my head, because that's not the case. Her phone lights up with a message, which she instantly checks, taps out a quickfire reply and returns to the job in hand without skipping a beat.

'How are you finding it out here? It's a bit remote.' Nicole looks as if she suits an urban environment. She's in a battered khaki utility jacket and boyfriend jeans with chunky boots.

'I like the peace. We've been working up to a home like this for ages.'

'See that massive spider in the corner?' She eyes it dubiously.

'Ha! That's the downside of living in the country. The first house we bought was rat infested, so we're used to sharing with the locals.'

'I couldn't live somewhere this remote. Doesn't it creep you out?'

'A little. I couldn't live here alone.'

'That weird man stood out there staring at me.'

'What man?'

'Some shabby old guy with wiry grey hair.' She waves her hands around her head to indicate our neighbour's unruly thatch of hair.

'Mitchell.'

'What's his problem? He was standing in the road. I slowed down and he moved over, then I opened the window to see if he needed help and he gave me this death stare.' She looks pained. It's not just me he has that effect on.

'He's complained about our planning applications.'

'Why?'

'To quote him, "You do know this is a national park? You can't swan in and do as you please. There are laws to protect the natural beauty against your sort."'

'He's a charmer.'

'I expect the building work shattered his peace and quiet. I feel sorry for him, rattling round on his own.' I don't tell her how he unnerved me by conducting our first conversation over my head, looking beyond me. 'As if I'm beneath him,' I said to Joe afterwards. Then Mitchell had turned and walked away mid-sentence, with a slight limp on one leg.

'And what's with the armless women?' she says.

I almost smile at us sharing the same opinion. 'The statues?'

'Yeah. With the missing body parts.'

'Joe calls them the naked ladies.'

'At least he hasn't got any heads on sticks.'

'Yet.' I smile.

'So he's your only neighbour for what, half a mile?' Nicole looks unimpressed.

'Yup. Chilwood has a population of three on this side of the woods.'

'Wow. What if you had an emergency?'

'I wouldn't go to Mitchell, that's for sure. But talking of

random men, there was this guy on the tour yesterday ... he broke off from the group and came in here to check out the control panel.'

'Really?' Her face clouds. She might look young, but she's serious about her work. Her eyes are vaguely familiar when she scowls. Maybe she reminds me of someone from my student days. 'Did he touch anything?'

'I don't know. He was peering at it and then he looked startled when I challenged him.'

She checks it over. 'That's not good. What did Joe and Alistair say?'

'I didn't mention it in case I seemed paranoid.'

'Why would you think that?' She looks at me and tilts her head.

'He gave me the creeps, but he was probably harmless.'

'I find it helps to listen to your gut instinct if you have a spidey sense about someone. If a guy gives me the creeps it's because he's creepy. I'm on Tinder so I know all about sketchy guys.'

Dating apps make me glad to be married. I'm lucky to have Joe, but I don't tell Nicole that. Nor do I say that Joe thinks I see problems where they don't exist, so I haven't mentioned the Anorak Man. It's hard to trust your instincts when they've been on red alert from the harm people can do.

'Tinder doesn't sound much fun.'

She blinks and smiles. 'They're not all bad.'

'What are the good ones like?'

She shrugs. 'We have fun. They're like me, I guess ... my

age, into *Star Wars* and your basic nerd stuff.' Her fingers patter away on her laptop keyboard. 'Joe says you've been doing houses up for a while.'

'Eight years as a couple. This is the first we've bought to actually live in. What about you? Did you always want to work in IT?' I don't mind that Joe isn't here as I like chatting to her.

'I've always been fascinated by how things work. Soon as I sussed out how to use a computer I wanted to know how it worked.' She looks at me with bright-eyed enthusiasm, and then goes back to her keyboard. 'I liked taking apart electronic toys and games. That led to coding at school and college.'

'Great that you found a way to make a living from it.'

'It wasn't always great. Being obsessed with computers isn't exactly the road to popularity at school. Nobody got it. They had me tested for autism at one point.'

I like her tomboyish stance. When I was small, I preferred building Lego houses to playing with dolls. Now I can bash down internal walls and lay bricks with no problem at all.

'I'm useless with technology,' I say.

'It's worth knowing how everything works. Do you have the passcodes?'

'For the smart home? No.'

'I'll reset them and give them to you as well as Joe, because you should have them too.' She gives me a sweet smile. 'It's good to know your way around the system if Joe's not here. It is your home, after all.'

'My brain's not wired for technology.' She spurs me on to make an effort, though. I need to learn how it works.

'You can do stuff,' she says. 'When I was setting up, you were digging the patio out and laying slabs.'

'I like seeing things take shape, but technology's different. You can't see what's going on.'

She nods vaguely and keeps tapping and frowning at her screen. Joe doesn't make it home before she leaves in a rush. He must be tied up with work, otherwise he'd be discussing the finer technological points with Nicole and updating her after yesterday's tour. She's inspired me to get to grips with the smart home. It's part of our lives so I'll embrace it. Well, maybe not *embrace* it, but I'll make an effort.

I'm about to go into the studio when the doorbell rings. Not expecting anyone, I open the door to the man in the black anorak from yesterday's tour; the one who lurked round the control panel.

'Hello again,' he says.

'Hi.'

'I think I dropped a key here yesterday.'

'We haven't found it.' I keep a tight hold on the door.

'Can I come in and have a quick check?'

I look back over my shoulder. 'Um, no ... sorry, I'm working.'

'That's okay. I won't disturb you. I'll retrace my steps from yesterday.'

'It's not convenient.'

'It won't take long. I need my key back.' A smile plays on his lips, as if it's a game to win me over. 'So, um, can I come in?'

'If it turns up we'll give it to Alistair.' I close the door, not wanting him back in here. There's something about him I don't trust. It wouldn't surprise me if he never dropped his key in the first place. Anyone seeing me would think it an overreaction, but my heart pumps fiercely.

He rings the bell again. I go upstairs to the bedroom window, clutching my phone. I call up the CCTV on my app and tap on the image of the front door.

He lingers, hands in pockets, and peers through the thick glass in the door. Then he goes to his car and drives off. I come closer to the bedroom window. His brake lights flash red outside Mitchell's house. Mitchell's there and the Anorak Man stops and lowers his window. They're talking and he motions back towards here. Mitchell shakes his head. The man drives away again, leaving me with a sense of unease. What were they saying?

CHAPTER SIX

I suspected early on that the smart features wouldn't suit me. Joe had raved about how you can walk through the whole house and the lights come on room by room as if by magic. Alone here for the first time after dark, I walked into the living area and the lights came on. I settled down with a book. Minutes later the lights went out, plunging me into darkness.

Did someone turn them off? Heart in mouth, I fumbled for my phone and realised I'd left it somewhere else and couldn't use the app to turn the lights back on. Cursing at the thought of feeling my way through the dark, I stood up and the lights came back on.

When Joe came home, he told me that the sensors detect movement. 'They thought the room was empty. If you'd had your phone to hand you could've turned them back on.'

'Joe! It freaked me out. I don't want the lights turning themselves off and scaring me in the dark.'

He adjusted the settings so it didn't happen again, but

when I'm alone, I still half-expect the lights to turn themselves off.

When Joe comes home he gives me a bunch of old-fashioned roses in soft peach. I once told him I thought scented vintage roses were the most romantic flowers, and he's bought me them from a florist ever since.

'What's the occasion?' I breathe in their sweet, delicate scent.

'I thought you'd like them. It'll make the place more homely.'

'I love them.' I fill a sage green pottery vase with water. 'Nicole did the updates you wanted.'

'Oh yeah, she messaged me.'

'You didn't find a key someone dropped after the tour yesterday?'

'Nope. A house key?'

'Don't know.' I snip off the string tied around the stems. 'Someone who did the tour came back to look for a lost key.'

'Did he find it?'

'I wouldn't let him in. It seemed a bit off, the way he was acting.'

'Oh ... okay.' Joe looks carefully at me as I pull the lower leaves from the roses.

'Ow!' A thorn pricks my finger. I pluck it out and suck the pinprick of blood. 'Did you get an alert on your phone when he rang the doorbell?'

Joe shrugs and looks at his phone. 'Don't think so.'

'He came back a couple of hours ago.' I call up the CCTV playback on my phone and scroll back. 'Let me show you.'

He looks over my shoulder. 'I'll send Alistair a screenshot. He'll know who it is.'

Except Anorak Man's not on the CCTV. I scroll back and forth but can't find the playback of him. There's nothing other than the usual static view from the front door.

'He's not there.' I try to sound normal and double check the footage, but he's not on it. How can that be? I look more closely for clues that he's been edited out.

'Maybe it stopped working,' Joe says, 'like the doorbell yesterday.'

I scroll through Joe coming and going, me setting out with Dora, the postman's delivery and Nicole arriving and leaving, all roughly where they should be on the timeline. My eyes hurt from staring at the screen, so I leave it for now.

'Nicole said that as a child she took computers apart to see how they worked. She was tested for autism, but didn't have it. She just liked electronics.'

'Oh yeah?'

'It makes me think of the way Dylan likes seeing what goes on behind the scenes, so to speak.'

'That's a polite way of describing it. If only it can be channelled into something constructive. By "constructive" I mean legal.'

'Maybe we can introduce them. She could be a role model.'

'Maybe.' He's checking messages on his phone and not really listening. 'I'd better crack on and get back to work. I won't get much done tomorrow with Dylan here for his inset day. I'll be back by seven.'

I take Dora out before dark and we follow the path along-side the woods. I never go in there alone. No one else is here, but I clasp my mobile with my personal attack alarm attached to it. Deeper in my pocket is a small red Swiss army knife. If I ever have to explain why I carry it, I would say I used it for cutting garden twine, or something like that. Black crows caw overhead, like bad omens circling. My mum used to call them harbingers of death.

It's a relief when we get home and come inside. The hall light senses the dark and comes on at dusk. I make sure the door is locked behind us and use the app to turn on the lights. Another few taps turn the windows opaque so no one can see in. I grimace at the thought of that man erased from the CCTV. It's quiet without Joe, so I distract myself in the kitchen and play the soundtrack from a favourite film to drown out my edginess.

Fergie and Will.i.am finish 'True' and UB40 plays 'Every Breath You Take'. I go to the sink and then stop, tilt my head. The music has distorted, the guitar an eerie twang and the vocals a slow-mo drunken drawl. The bass drops to a thick-ened low pitch. It reverberates through me, each note creepily drawn out.

What's happening? I instinctively check around, as if some-one's watching me. *Don't overreact*, I tell myself. *You're safe*. But am I? I kill the music, my heart thudding.

Just then, Joe's car sweeps into the drive. I clutch at my chest, my heart still pounding through my top.

He walks in and his face drops. 'You look like you've seen a ghost.'

'The music's gone weird.'

'How?'

'It warped and slowed down like it's possessed; scared me half to death.'

'Come here.' He wraps his arms around me and hugs me tight. We stay that way for several moments and my heart rate slows to something approaching normal.

'Let me check it out.' He puts his playlist on and tilts his head. 'Sounds okay to me.'

I call up 'Every Breath You Take'. 'It was warped like an old cassette.'

We both listen. It's fine.

'You must have your own force field,' he says.

'It's my sheer magnetism.' I force a smile.

'Kev's coming back to do the outside light. He can have a look.'

There'll be a rational reason. Kev did the electrics, so he'll know. The man in the anorak made me jumpy, that's all.

'Kev'll say it's a dodgy connection,' Joe says.

'Or he'll blame Nicole.'

'It's probably just settling down after she worked on it earlier.' He reaches over and tucks my hair behind my ear. 'It's okay. We'll sort it out.'

I can relax now Joe's back, making everything seem better.

'Do you think you're spending too much time on your own here?' He has that look of concern again. 'You said you wouldn't hide away when we moved to the country, but you've disappeared more into yourself—'

'I'm not hiding. We're settling in and I've got paintings to do.'

'You don't want to go anywhere.'

'Just not crowded places. I'm working on it. Give me time.' I know what he's getting at. I might be a functioning adult of thirty-four who earns a living and climbs scaffolding, but I can't go to the supermarket on my own or meet a friend in a bar.

'You're safe now. He's gone.'

My breath catches. It's an unspoken rule that we don't talk about *him* directly. We don't use his name, since neither of us wants the reminder.

'When things were bad,' Joe says, 'I wanted to help you, but I couldn't.'

'That's behind us now.' I give him a look of reassurance so he doesn't think I'm slipping backwards.

'Of course it is,' he murmurs into my hair. 'We just have to stick together, right?'

We agreed that after everything that went on and the emotional fallout, a move to the country would be good for us and help us recalibrate. Joe's right. We do have to stick together.

CHAPTER SEVEN

By the morning, Joe's rational thinking has rubbed off on me. I was spooked, that's all. Maybe the system went jumpy after Nicole's modifications yesterday. Even if I can't explain Dora growling upstairs when she was chomping kibble downstairs, I'm prepared to write it off as a random glitch, along with the music warping. The Anorak Man is probably harmless although I sensed something off about him. I meant to email my friend Brooke, since she's good at plain-talking and will rationalise it. I'll send her a message later to catch up. Meanwhile, Joe hasn't noticed anything amiss.

'I'll go and pick up Dylan,' Joe says. 'Kev's coming to fix the sensor light.'

We chose this location to be within easy reach of Dylan, who's a twenty-minute drive away in Clanfield. When Joe's out, Kev turns up and stands on a stepladder outside the garage, taking the light apart. I bring him a mug of tea, warming my hands on it until he's finished. It's late morning but more like dusk in the gloomy grey light.

'How you finding it here?' He comes down from the stepladder and drops his screwdriver in the toolbox with a metallic clunk.

I hand him his mug and look at the hills in the distance. 'It's lovely.'

'Bit different to where you've lived before.'

'Yeah, I've never lived anywhere without streetlights.'

'Getting spooked, are you?'

'No. It's just different out here.'

'Rural houses look good during the day when you view them. It's something else entirely on winter nights. The light's got a motion sensor, so it comes on when anyone drives in, or you can set it to turn on before dark. Shall I check out the audio? Joe said it's playing up.'

'Please. It sounded wonky yesterday.'

He follows me indoors. 'Interference?'

'No, the music slowed down and warped.'

Kev asks me to put some music on, so I go back to 'Every Breath You Take'. We both listen to the playback in the kitchen. It's fine now, but in my mind it's tainted by the warped sound.

'Stalker song!' Kev says.

'Excuse me?'

'"Every Breath You Take". We had it at our wedding for our first dance. From *50 First Dates*. It's the ex-wife's favourite film. Then my mate said it's about stalking.'

I didn't know it was about stalking. I feel the blood drain from my face.

'She chose it. Not me.'

I go to shut off the music.

'No, leave it running,' he says. 'Where else did you hear it distorted?'

'Only in here. I haven't played it upstairs yet.'

He goes to the utility room and peers at the home hub control panel.

'Do you know much about the multi-room audio?' I ask.

'Not this one since I didn't install it. I only did the cabling. You'll need to check the warranty.' He must still be prickly that Joe didn't choose him to install the smart home.

'What if there's a fault with the cabling?'

'What you described isn't a cabling fault. It's digital, and the sound might stutter or cut out, but the cabling won't make music go warped. How are you getting on with the smart appliances? Do you turn things on remotely?'

'It's not my thing.'

'You have to be careful with artificial intelligence,' he says. 'It's the future, but I'm not ready for robots at home.'

'Can it be dangerous? Like ... can you be electrocuted if someone messes with the appliances remotely?'

'There's safety features to avoid that sort of thing. Why? Are you worried about the appliances rising up and taking over?'

'Not really.' I don't want him to know it's bothering me in case he uses it as a put-down.

Still in the utility room, I hear a car pull up outside and doors slamming. Within a minute or two, Joe and Dylan come in.

'Here's the main man.' Kev goes out to the hallway. He nods

to Dylan who stands mutely behind Joe, avoiding eye contact. 'All right, mate?'

'Hey, you two.' I smile at them both and go back to painting in the studio. After Dylan's fractious session with Joe on FaceTime, it'll do them good to spend time together. And Joe can take over with Kev.

I return indoors at lunchtime to Joe making toasties. Given the choice, Dylan would have toasties every day. He sits on the floor petting Dora.

'She likes you doing that,' I say, and grab a bowl to mix ingredients for his 'special' pancakes, which are normal pancakes with chocolate sauce in a dish on the side and a row of raspberries, none of them touching. I bought a square plate specially to make it easier to line up the raspberries. 'How's Kitty?'

'Fine.'

'Does she like to play with you?'

'No.'

'Why's that?' Joe asks.

'She doesn't like being touched.'

'Some cats don't like being touched. I'm sure she likes you.' I beat the pancake mixture.

'Kev's finally fixed the light,' Joe says. 'It's paired with the app so we can turn it on and off.'

'Great.'

'Dad, shoot Dora.'

Joe stops what he's doing and points at Dora with two fingers in a trigger gesture. He makes the sound of gunshot. Dora keels over with her legs in the air to play dead. Dylan collapses into hysterical laughter and Dora leaps up to do a mad victory lap around him. I've seen the routine many times, but Dylan's infectious laughter makes me laugh too. Affection surges through me. It's lovely when he's happy, and Joe prefers having a laugh with Dylan to laying down the law.

After lunch, they go back to the Xbox. I'll have a game with them next time, but not today since the natural light is good enough to keep painting. Dylan taught me how to play games on the Xbox a few years ago when Joe was laid up with flu. I drove him home afterwards and we talked about superpowers.

'If I could choose a superpower it would be to fly,' I'd said. 'Spread my arms and take off into the sky. Wouldn't that be amazing, Dylan?'

'Yes,' he said in his flat voice.

'What superpower would you like?'

He looked out of the window for ages and I didn't think he would reply. 'I'd be invisible.'

'Cool. Why's that?'

'So I can disappear.'

I kept my eyes on the road ahead. 'What's good about disappearing?'

He wouldn't be drawn any further, and it gave me a pang of upset at the time. He'd been bullied at school not long before and I'd fought the urge to stand guard at the playground fence to keep him safe. I didn't realise until then how protective I'd become of him. Kids are kids, but how could they be mean to him? Not everyone can be a popular child at school and he's easy prey for bullies. We try to compensate so at least he fits in here, but Joe worries about his ability to cope with what life throws at him.

I told Joe about the invisibility when he'd recovered from the flu. 'Do you think it's related to the bullying?' I asked. 'It's sad, isn't it, that he wants to disappear?'

'You're reading too much into it,' he said. 'I'd like to be invisible too. I loved *The Invisible Man* when I was a kid.'

CHAPTER EIGHT

Joe comes home after dropping Dylan back. 'Sure you're okay about me staying at Chris's tonight?'

'Yes.' *No*, but I can't tell him that.

'Because I can cancel.'

Joe needs a social life and I have to stay rational. He goes snowboarding with friends and he's been on stag weekends. But we lived in flats or terraced homes back then, surrounded by neighbours. Tonight he's staying at Chris's after their drinking session for Chris's birthday, and they're taking Chris and Ava's son to play football in the morning.

'I'll be fine. You go and have a good time. Tell him happy birthday from me.' I can hardly stop him celebrating with his best mate. I don't say that I'm dreading all those hours of darkness on my own. I want the old me back, who loved a night alone bingeing on the reality TV shows that Joe hates.

He catches up with work admin in the kitchen and gets in the going-out mood by playing 'I Gotta Feeling' by The Black

Eyed Peas. It reminds me of the early days when we went clubbing. I'm stabbed with regret that we've lost the shared buzz of partying. Does Joe miss it too? I want him to be happy, it's just that I'd like to be the one making him happy.

He points to a bottle of wine and a bar of Dairy Milk on the kitchen counter. 'Thought you might like these when I'm out tonight. Why don't you bring in some of your favourite pieces from the studio? Make the place more homely.'

I'm more at home in cosy rooms but we agreed that a sleek, open-plan approach would flow better. Joe loves the expansive living area, which is a transformation from the poky, dark rooms here when we moved in. The studio is filled with my colourful pots and miniature sculptures, and it is a bit cluttered. I go and fill a cardboard box with some pieces and find homes for them indoors.

Joe brings down a couple of soft fawn throws that we'd packed away until the building work finished. He drapes them over the side of the sofa. 'You can hunker down and watch a film.'

It's more homely with the throws and my favourite pieces from the studio. The roses look pretty on the table, filling the air with subtle fragrance. Cast in warm light from the smart settings, the place is beautiful, and my heart lifts with a small burst of happiness that this is our home. The fear of being alone subsides, which is just as well when I need to get over it.

'Let me show you something.' He takes my hand and leads me upstairs. He's wearing a soft aqua-coloured T-shirt that I bought him ages ago, thinking that the shade would look good on him. It's faded now, but he's still gorgeous in it.

He leads me to the bathroom where he's placed candles round the bath. 'For you to light when you're in the tub later.'

'Aww, thanks.' But I'll be leaving the lights on.

It's my turn to lead him now, into the bedroom where I kiss him deep and his hands tangle in my hair. He eases off my jumper and I put his phone out of reach, so it's just us. Without saying a word, we slide under the covers to kiss and touch. It feels right, just the two of us. A photo of our wedding day hangs on the wall facing the bed. We're barefoot and happy on a Californian beach in a relaxed black-and-white shot, taken by my sister-in-law, Kim, who's a keen photographer.

Such a beautiful day, six years ago. No stress, no seating plan, just the four of us at our beach wedding when Joe and I stayed with Kim and my brother, Dale, at their place in Santa Monica. I didn't even buy a dress as Kim had a white halterneck in floaty chiffon that fitted me. That was my something borrowed. Joe looked so handsome in a crisp white shirt open at the neck, showing his suntan, his ink blue trousers rolled up at the ankles. Marriage suits me. We're so close that he can read me. My friend Brooke says we should be over the loved-up stage by now, but Joe's easy to love.

He leaves me to take a shower and then goes out at around six. After a moment of listening to the silence echo round the house, I head downstairs to the kitchen. If I knock back the wine, I'll have a better chance of sleeping. But I'm just opening the fridge when I hear a noise behind me. I swing round. A darting motion outside catches my eye. *Just a rabbit*, I tell myself and rub at a pinch of pain between my shoulders. Every little thing spooks me, from the chilling sense of being watched, to shadows in my peripheral vision that disappear when I look straight at them. I never outgrew my vivid imagination, still scared of the dark at thirty-four.

I press the blackout icon for the smart glass and go upstairs to run a bath. When I unbutton my shirt in the bedroom, a shiver runs through me. I stiffen. Nothing's there, but the room's turned cold again and I can't shake the feeling of being watched. I close the bedroom door behind me and have a soak in the bath with aromatherapy oils.

Then I pull on my soft cotton pyjamas, fresh from the bedroom radiator, and watch *The Other Woman*, helped along with chocolate and a large glass of white wine with rich honey tones. The film is carefully chosen for enough of a diversion without scaring me, especially as Joe installed surround sound. I don't want the dramatic sound effects of a tense film pulsating around me, freaking me out. When the credits roll, I stretch and remember his idea of sending Alistair a screenshot of the man in the anorak. The man came on the tour, so I could look it up on the CCTV.

I scroll back to the time of the tour, expecting to see footage of the two carloads of visitors arriving. I go back and forth but nothing's there. I inhale sharply. Joe and I are coming and going at the right times, Kev leaves in his van and I bring in the bin after seeing Mitchell. Then there's a static view out the front around the time the visitors arrived and departed.

What's going on? The man isn't on the footage for either of his visits. It can't be a coincidence that he's been wiped both times. I scroll ahead a second time to Nicole's visit and see her arrive and leave. The Anorak Man rang the bell not long after. My eyes strain from staring at the screen. He's not there.

Dora distracts me by wanting to go in the garden before bed. She has a dog flap, but unless she's alone she wants us to let her in and out. I follow her through to the kitchen and pull back in shock. I'd switched the windows to opaque earlier, but now they're transparent with a clear view outside. Anyone out there can see in. Did I switch it off without realising, tap the wrong setting, or has someone tampered with it?

My heart pounds and I feel a sharp prickle from the hairs on the back of my neck standing up. I can't be scared, not tonight on my own. Dora's whining at the door. The outside light illuminates the patio and walnut tree, bare from fallen leaves and sculptural in the light. The shadows beyond merge to total darkness in the murky starless night.

Dora shoots off to bark at something in the bushes at the end of the garden. I stand jittering by the door, hoping she comes back under her own steam so I don't have to go out there. The cry of a woodland animal pricks at my nerves. Eventually, the glint of Dora's eyes come into view as she returns from night patrol.

If Joe were here, he'd say it's nothing to worry about. I must have touched the transparent setting by mistake after turning them opaque. It's early days, and I'll get used to the remoteness and IT glitches. I push the CCTV malfunction from my mind and take the stairs two at a time, singing the words to 'I Gotta Feeling' under my breath until Dora's on her beanbag and I'm in bed.

My first night alone here and I'm off-balance, still not entirely at home. I haven't slept well since we finished the house. I often lie awake, unable to drift off to sleep the way Joe does. The air feels charged with a strange electricity. I leave the hall lights on and tuck my mobile under the pillow.

CHAPTER NINE

I wake to Dora growling. This time it's not coming through the sound system. She's trembling beside me on the bed, growling at the bedroom door that's ajar. It's dark. Someone's turned the hall light off. Beyond Dora's low growl is another sound downstairs. I reach for the bedside lamp. Has Joe come home drunk? *What the*— I jump at a sudden crashing sound from downstairs. Dora butts her tiny quivering body up close to me.

I grab my phone and call up the CCTV in a frantic blur. Is it Joe? The cameras cover the drive, the front door and the back. I zoom in on a shadowy man loitering on the patio and catch a glimpse of his face. *It can't be* ... I'm struck with a bolt of recognition, blindsided.

In the piercing terror, I scoop Dora up and call 999.

'Which service do you require?'

'Police.' I make it to the en suite and bolt the door with shaking hands.

'What's your location?'

I can hardly speak but manage to give her the address and postcode. She transfers my call and I huddle on the bathroom floor. The white heat of fear sears through me.

'What's your emergency?' a different woman asks.

'Men ... in the house ... broken in.' My voice shakes so badly I'm not sure she'll understand me.

'Are you alone?'

'Yes. I'm in the country. It's remote. There's at least two of them. Someone's downstairs and one's outside, he's ... he's ...' I go to say I know who he is but break off.

'Where are you now?'

'Upstairs. In the bathroom at the back of the house.' I grab Joe's razor and the nail scissors as makeshift weapons. I should have brought the Swiss army knife from my jacket pocket. 'They can kick the door in. Is someone coming?'

'We're getting an officer to you. Stay on the line.'

I crouch on the floor, Dora burrows into me, her claws digging into my thighs. I clutch the scissors and listen for footsteps, too terrified to look at the CCTV.

'The officers will be with you within ten minutes.'

Ten minutes? They could kill me before then. I put the operator on hold and call Joe.

'Yeah?' His voice is groggy with sleep.

Thank God he picked up. Tears spill down my face and I tell him what's happening in a choked whisper.

'Shit. The police are coming, yeah?'

'Yes. They're on the other line. Can you get a cab?'

'Be there as soon as I can.'

Still crying, I flick back to the operator. She asks routine questions and I answer in strained whispers. It must be a way of keeping me occupied.

'Can you still hear someone inside the house?' she asks.

I pause. It's silent. My hysteria ramps up. What if he's crept upstairs and is coming for me?

'They're nearly with you,' the operator says. I hope she means the police.

Braver now, I call up the CCTV. No sign of the intruders, of *him*. I enlarge the front view of the drive. After what seems like ages, car headlights swing into range. It's the police. I don't know if the burglars have left the front door gaping open, so I unlock it through the app, still too scared to come out.

A man calls out 'Police' and I'm faint with relief. The phone operator confirms it's an officer and tells me to open the door. She rings off, and I come out of the bathroom as the man in uniform reaches the top of the stairs. He has the burly physique of a rugby player and looks a bit older than Joe. I'm so glad he's here that I nearly dissolve with relief. The next few minutes are a haze of him checking rooms upstairs and me following behind. We come downstairs. It's exactly as I'd left it. No sign of a break-in, nothing out of place.

'Shall we have a cuppa?' he says.

Confused, I drop teabags in two mugs and fill them with boiling water.

'What noises did you hear down here?' he asks.

'Banging. Crashing. Like they were trashing the place.'

'Inside or outside?'

'Inside. There was someone in here and a man outside. I saw him on the CCTV.' I weigh up whether to tell him I know the man outside. But I need to tread carefully.

'Is it recorded?'

'Yes.' I fish my phone from my bathrobe pocket and scroll through the playback. I have to see his face again to prove it to myself. The officer peers over my shoulder. There's nothing but the empty patio.

'What time did you see him?'

'Just before I called 999.'

'The call's logged at 03.27.'

I scroll back to 03.24 and play all three CCTV screens in real time for five minutes. The officer takes over the tea-making and places two steaming mugs in front of us. There isn't so much as a mouse scuttling past in the playback. We establish it's set at the correct time. He goes out front and waves at the camera. We play it back. It's him waving at the right time.

'Any CCTV inside the house?'

'No.'

He looks intently at me. 'Do you think you had a nightmare?'

Burning with humiliation, I open my mouth to protest. He holds up a hand as if to say *hear me out*.

'And you woke up, heard strange noises, because you do hear really strange noises in the countryside.'

But I didn't dream it. I didn't.

'I'd be spooked out here on my own.' He stands against the sink, drinking his tea.

'I didn't imagine it.'

'In this line of work, we deal with the facts and the evidence. There's no evidence of a break-in. I'm not saying you didn't hear anything, but there's no sign of the place being trashed, which was what you thought you heard.'

I wrap my arms around myself.

'Did you drink any alcohol last night?'

What? I'm suddenly aware of the empty wine glass in the sink, too delicate for the dishwasher. He's seen it too.

'Just one glass.' At least I didn't swig it all. 'I'm not drunk.'

'I'm not saying you are.'

I open the fridge and lift the bottle from the door to show my restraint in leaving most of the wine, and it's not as if I'm slurring.

'You said your husband lives here. Just the two of you?'

'Yes. He had a night out. He stayed over with a friend.' I pick up the mobile. It's on silent. Joe's already phoned and texted to say he's on his way.

Are you ok? his text asks.

Yes. Police are here.

I take a sip of tea and wince at the syrupy taste. It's loaded with sugar.

'I've checked the whole house,' the officer says. 'No sign of any disturbance or forced entry. There's no one else here. All the entry points are locked. I locked the front door on the way in. When's your husband due back?'

'He's on his way.' I'm longing for Joe to walk in and somehow make it okay.

'Do you have someone else who can sit with you? A neighbour?'

I shake my head. No way am I asking Mitchell to come over. 'If you have to go, I'll tough it out till my husband's back.'

By the time he's ready to leave and we're at the front door, a car pulls into the drive. Joe hops out of the front passenger seat. Chris's wife, Ava, waves to me from the driving seat and reverses back out. At least she doesn't come in to witness my humiliation.

Joe shakes hands with the officer. I'm flooded with relief that he's home.

'Looks like everything's under control here,' the officer says to him.

'What about the break-in?' Joe asks.

'Appears to be a false alarm.' He gives me a kind smile.

'Thanks for coming.' I cringe inwardly and retreat inside, expecting Joe to follow me in, but he and the officer keep talking. The officer's voice is lower and I can't make out what he's saying, but I can hear Joe.

'. . . she suffers from paranoia. It's triggered by stress. She used to have a stalker and it set her off.'

Mortified, I double back to the front door where I can hear better.

'She can't be in confined public spaces like lifts or trains. Crowded places scared her – shops, restaurants, anywhere really. I thought she'd be better out here.'

'What about the stalker?'

'A man latched onto her a while back. He caused her a lot of grief.'

'Was any action taken?'

'We involved the police when it became clear he wasn't giving up, and again when he set up a revenge porn web page.'

My heart plunges at Joe's words.

'Revenge porn?' the officer asks.

'It wasn't her. He used a photo of her face superimposed on porn images of women. It affected her, though. Every time we went out, she thought she saw him in the crowd, but it wasn't him.'

My face heats with shame. I can't bear Joe excusing it away as a figment of my imagination. What he's saying isn't even true, or not entirely true. I never thought I saw the stalker. I was scared I *might* see him.

I go through to the kitchen, fighting back tears. Joe means well but it leaves me feeling deficient. I pace around to absorb the shock and confusion until he comes in and holds me close.

'Christ, Lauren, I'm sorry.'

'What for?' I bury my face in his shirt and breathe in his warm, comforting smell, overlaid with his best aftershave and a hint of beer from his night out.

'For leaving you. I never should've gone.' He thinks it's in my head and I'm slipping back to imagining things, like before, when I was scared of the stalker lurking in every crowded place. It overwhelmed me, the crippling fear of seeing him, of what he might do. My world reduced and I stayed safe at home.

'I know you're uncomfortable with the smart home,' he says softly. 'Is it because of the revenge porn? Is that why you're struggling with the technology?'

I pull away and tip the syrupy tea down the sink.

'It's okay.' He follows me to the sink and rubs my back. 'We'll work it out. We'll keep things stable.'

I catch a movement outside, just the wind in the shrubs. My gaze drifts over my reflection in the window and the vivid mental image of Karl Winter comes back to me. The man who stalked me was outside, looking no different to last time. I picture his relentless gaze and hollowed cheekbones and I step back. Is he out there watching me?

'Lauren?'

'We can't stay here.' I choke out the words. 'It's not safe.'

He hugs me again, tighter this time. 'I'm here. We'll get through it, okay?'

I nod into his neck and shoulder, not wanting to let go. 'I'm not imagining it—'

He pulls back to look at me, our faces close. 'We need to look after you, sweetheart. Stop it flaring up again.'

'This isn't like before. There was a break-in. Dora heard it too. She woke me up growling. She was shaking from the noise downstairs.'

'She might've picked up on your fear.'

'When I was asleep?'

'Did she sense you were nervous before you went to bed? What if you had a nightmare that scared her? Your waking nightmares are pretty freaky.'

'The noise woke her. She was freaked out looking at the door, not me. And I saw a man out there.' I nod towards the patio.

'What did he look like?'

I can't tell him it was Karl Winter. He'll take it as confirmation I imagined the whole thing. It happened, and I need Joe more than ever. He'll doubt me if I tell him. 'I only caught a glimpse of him on the CCTV, and I heard someone else down here.'

'Same as you heard the audio distorted, and Dora growling upstairs when she was down here with me?'

'You think I'm imagining it.' I bite the side of my lip. We both know the paranoia is triggered by stress and emotional upheaval. I've been careful to guard against it and I stopped going out much to keep it at bay.

'You've done really well to keep things under control.'

'But?'

'I think you need help. Let's book an appointment with the doctor.'

'I'm not imagining it. I absolutely know what I heard.'

'Tell me everything that happened, from when I went out.'

We sit at the table and I go over it all, about feeling on edge before going to bed, leaving the light on, and then what happened when Dora woke me. Joe listens carefully until I finish telling him and cover my face with my hands.

'You know I always look for the logical solution,' he says.

'Which is?'

He pauses to consider his words. 'I believe that you think it happened.'

'But you think I'm paranoid.'

He's mindful of not upsetting me, but he told the police officer about the paranoia and how it's triggered by stress.

'Honey, the police say there's no evidence of a disturbance and nothing on the CCTV. Let's run it past the doctor, to be on the safe side.'

It's dark and silent outside. I'm torn between Joe's steady voice of reason and knowing that I saw Karl Winter. But it's impossible for him to be lurking outside, because Karl Winter is dead.

CHAPTER TEN

We went to bed in the early hours and Joe's sleeping late this morning. When I hear him moving around upstairs, I feel safe enough to go outside and look for evidence. Dora snuffles in the garden, and I check the ground surrounding the cottage in case the stalker and his accomplice left anything behind. I breathe in the damp morning air. Mist hangs over the landscape and there's no sign of the intruders on the wet ground. Joe's buttering toast when I come in.

'How are you feeling?' he asks.

My mood lifts a little because at least I have him. 'I'm freaked out about last night. How are you?'

'I'm worried about you.' He takes a big bite of toast and munches.

'What happened was real. It wasn't in my mind.'

He nods and looks at me with soulful eyes.

'Which means someone's out to get me.' My voice trembles.

His quiet watchfulness makes everything worse.

A lump forms in my throat. 'Just because there's no evidence, doesn't mean it didn't happen.'

'I know.' He gives me a sad look and comes towards me. His face says he's worried that my paranoia is back, which means he doesn't believe me. His arms encircle me, muscles strong from digging trenches and hauling building materials.

'Listen,' he says, 'I've got a site meeting. Come with me. We'll talk on the way.'

'No, I'm okay now it's daylight. I'll paint in the studio.'

'If you're sure. You can call me and I'll come straight back.' He hugs me a little bit tighter and then leaves, shoving the rest of the toast in his mouth.

The real reason I don't mind staying is because I emailed Annette while he was sleeping this morning. I haven't had a therapy session in two years, but I need a perspective from someone who's not involved. I don't tell Joe, not yet, because he might want to join us and make it about the paranoia. He's only trying to help, but he doesn't understand. I remember the paranoia, and this is different.

My email to Annette said just enough to register that I need her help and to arrange a convenient time. She's already replied and we've set up an 11 a.m. session. I lock myself in the studio, away from the smart home weirdness, and I'm logged in to Skype when she calls.

'Lauren, good to see you,' Annette says in her calm way. She looks the same as I remember, with wavy silver-blond hair and eyes that crinkle when she smiles. She's settled into her big, padded computer chair, looking contentedly at me as if ready to watch her favourite box set. 'How are you?'

'I'm struggling, and I need to talk about what's going on.' I force the words out, not wanting to talk about it, but she helped me before.

'How are you struggling?'

'Well, we've moved into a new home and things have turned strange.' I tell her about the smart home with its warped music, the CCTV, Dora growling upstairs when she wasn't there, and my mounting sense of fear, leading to the disturbance last night.

'Can't you just turn it off?' she says.

'What? The smart home?'

'Yes. Sounds like you need to disconnect.'

'I'm not sure we can. I'll ask Joe.'

'From what you say, this is Joe's baby, but it's also your home and you need to feel safe. So turn it off.'

'Okay.' Stupid of me not to think of it, but the home hub is so much a part of the house, it didn't occur to me. 'Joe thinks I'm spending too much time at home and that's affecting me somehow.'

'Do you think you're spending too much time at home?'

'I walk the dog and go to clients if they're nearby. I go places with Joe, but not alone, so yeah, I'm home a lot.'

'How does that work for you? It sounds restrictive.' She tilts her head, her blue-grey eyes taking me in through the screen. I guess she's easing me back in, talking about this thing I hate talking about.

'Joe and I work together on the developments. I do a lot, but I only go to public places with him, and even then, I don't like going out.'

'How does it affect your relationships?'

'Well, I only have my relationship with Joe.'

'Does it affect your relationship with Joe?'

'He handles it really well. No one wants a millstone dragging them down, so I make sure we're a team. We're a normal couple in other ways. He wants me to go out more, but I don't like pubs and restaurants. He goes out with his friends instead.'

'And your friends?'

'I have friends but not nearby. My closest friend is in Australia – we email and phone. I'd rather not have local friends than be forced to say, "I can't come to the wine bar on your birthday."'

'Is there a way you could go to the wine bar?'

'I don't like car parks. Or taxis. I don't walk down city streets. I'm always looking over my shoulder, can't relax if it's outside my comfort zone. Why do it if it makes me feel bad?' It's draining, having to explain myself when this isn't the life I want. I cover it up so most people would never know. 'I'm not some recluse. I earn a living. I'm just mindful of where I go.'

'You mentioned your comfort zone. What does that mean to you?'

'Staying safe.'

She nods. 'What would happen if you went to a bar with your friends?'

'I'd want to cancel on the day. If I had to go, I'd do risk

assessments in my head, watching everyone in the street, in the bar. It's no fun for me or whoever I'm with.'

'Do you have any friends you can meet at home for a coffee?'

I sigh. 'It doesn't work out. They ask me to go places, then I have to explain why I don't want to, and they try talking me into it and take offence when I say no. I get that, I just don't want to go places.'

'Bring me up to date on your family situation. How are things with your brother?'

'No change.'

Dale is my only family since Mum died – my dad left before I was born – but I haven't seen him since my wedding. And we haven't spoken since the argument between him and Joe.

Even though Dale and I weren't that close, the wedding felt special. I'd had visions of seeing them regularly, perhaps even going on holiday as two couples. But then on the last night Joe stayed up drinking with Dale.

I'd gone to bed, since we had an early start the next day. But not long after that I'd awoken to shouting in the kitchen. After we'd left, Joe said he'd encouraged Dale to get on the property ladder, since he has always rented. Dale never liked anyone telling him what to do. It escalated pretty quickly and ended with Dale calling Joe a capitalist pig. We left without saying goodbye and when I messaged Dale and Kim after we came home, they didn't reply. I followed up with a card to say how special the wedding had been and it wouldn't have been the same without them, but still I received nothing and I haven't heard from them since. I avoid mentioning them to Joe, who was stung by his

72

exchange with Dale who, Joe claimed, had a nerve to criticise him when his wife works for a tech start-up.

'So you've no one nearby but Joe?'

'Joe and I are close. We've been through a lot together. I have contact with my clients and people who work on the developments, and my Aussie friend, Brooke. We chat online.'

'That's good, Lauren.' She stares through the screen at me. 'You say if you went out, you'd be watching everyone. What are you looking for?'

'The stalker.'

'The stalker who died?'

'Yes.' God, I hate this. Bringing her up to speed is worse than I expected. I avoid talking about it, but I'd rather pick up with Annette than explain it to someone new.

'Remind me how he died.'

'Accidental death.' My rigid jaw makes it hard to talk, everything feels rigid, but my mouth is my only moving part. The more she delves, the worse it feels and I loathe the messy truth. 'He fell in a river after a heavy drinking session and drowned.'

'Ah yes. I remember. What was his name?'

'Karl Winter.'

'So, you don't go out socially because you're fearful of a man who stalked you. That might be sensible if he still posed a threat, but Karl Winter is dead. Do you think it's helping you to stay home?'

'I feel safer this way.'

She nods and says nothing.

'I haven't told you the strangest part.'

Annette stares into the screen, waiting for me to go on.

'I caught a glimpse of the man outside on CCTV ... it was Karl Winter.'

She looks gravely at me. 'That must have been terrifying.'

She's taking me seriously. Tears of relief well up and I fumble in my pocket for a tissue. I'm still in bits over last night and it's worse if no one believes me. I blot my eyes with the tissue.

'Take your time, Lauren. Remember to breathe.'

'The whole thing terrified me. It nearly scared me to death that someone had broken in, and then to see the stalker ...'

'You said that he drowned. Was his body identified?'

'There was a body, an inquest and a funeral. I don't know who identified him.'

'It's usually the next of kin.'

'What if he didn't die? What if his family identified a different man who'd fallen in the water, someone bloated from death, with them not in their right minds? What if a homeless man drowned instead, with no one to report him missing?' My voice wavers and I clutch the damp tissue in my fist.

'How sure are you that it was Karl Winter on the CCTV?'

'It looked like him.'

'Even if he didn't die, why would he leave it all this time to come back?'

'Perhaps he was lying low,' I say. It's not plausible, but Annette goes along with it, her brow furrowed in contemplation.

'If it was him – and it might not be – what do you think he wanted?'

74

'To scare me.' A shiver runs through me. I look over my shoulder at the empty garden.

'Why would he want to do that?'

'Revenge.'

She looks at the screen, waiting for me to elaborate.

'Because Joe threatened him the night he was supposed to have died,' I say in a choked voice.

'What happened?'

'Joe saw him in a pub and warned him off. There was an altercation. Joe left and came home. Witnesses say that Karl Winter downed spirits at the pub. Then he walked home alone along the river. He fell in.'

I recount it like a police report, as if distancing myself will make it easier to bear. It doesn't. The whole thing was a mess, from when I met him at a mental health unit after Mum passed away. I struggled with the grief but didn't want to go back on medication. My doctor referred me to the out-patients unit in case the paranoia flared up. *He* was there too, Karl Winter. He latched onto me.

Annette looks through the screen, her face neutral.

'Joe didn't push him in. The police established that. They said it happens that people walk home after having one too many and sometimes fall in the water.'

'It happens,' she agrees mildly.

'They said it's more likely to be men. Women tend not to walk home alone, so there's someone to help them out. It was a cold night. His body could have seized up in the cold water so he drowned before he could get out.' I bite my lip. 'It was awful ... he was getting help when I met him, and it turned out so badly.' Fresh tears fall, and I pause to mop them up. It's a strange thing to feel sorry for the life he lost, even though he tried to ruin mine.

'It is awful. He stalked you for a long time, didn't he?'

'Three years, but not constantly. I kept thinking he'd given up and then he'd start again.'

'How did it affect you?'

'It started out quite harmless. He was friendly, wanting to tell me how he was getting on. But he turned intense and I backed off, expecting it to burn out if I kept my distance. I was dating Joe, but Karl acted as if he had a claim on me. Joe intervened and told him not to contact me again. A few months later, I'd had a drink in town with a friend and walked back to my car alone. I saw him standing in a doorway, lying in wait. I was terrified he'd overpower me, drag me into an alleyway. But he just stood watching me and I panicked like crazy and locked myself in the car.' The memory still makes me shudder.

'Your response was entirely understandable. Any woman would fear going out in those circumstances. Did you contact the police?'

'Not at first because he hadn't threatened me. I tried ignoring him, but eventually they spoke to him. Joe did too. He stopped following me and set up the revenge porn. The police warned him off again, but there wasn't enough evidence to charge him. I stopped going out. Or if I did go out, I'd panic and want to come home. It wasn't psychosis, it was the fear of what he might do. Even now, I feel safer away from prying eyes.'

'How long ago did you say he died?'

'Five years.' Five whole years. 'I hate that he still has this hold on me.'

'Trauma doesn't have an expiry date. Did he look the same as you remembered? Any older?'

'I only caught a glimpse on the CCTV before the footage was wiped, but he looked the same.'

'Okay.'

'I don't know if he's really alive. I just know what I saw last night.'

'Do you still have a police contact you can ask? You can check on who identified the body. That might help put your mind at rest.'

'I could get in touch with the police. I don't have to tell them I saw him. They won't believe me anyway. No one else does.' I stare at the wet tissue balled in my hand.

'You had a traumatic time. In those moments after you were woken by the disturbance, your subconscious might have flashed an image of Karl Winter in your mind.'

'Why?'

'Because you associate him with fear. The mind plays tricks on us all.'

I prefer that to the more sinister option that he's back from the dead, and I only caught a fleeting glance.

'It strikes me that you were already isolated when we spoke last. And now you're more so by thinking that no one believes you.'

I murmur in response.

'It all comes back to this smart home of yours. Do you think someone could override the system?'

'Can that be done?'

'I have no idea. It seems the main source of your anxiety comes from unanswered questions about the technology in your home.'

She's right.

'Joe thinks I imagined it because I spend too much time alone out here. Something happened, I'm sure of that, but ...' I shake my head, not making sense of it. 'I don't know what's worse, that I'm paranoid, or that someone's trying to get at me through the smart home.' I look away and swipe at a tear trickling down my face. If someone doctored the CCTV, they could have superimposed Karl Winter's face on the footage, just as he superimposed my face onto porn images. Is it someone who knows of the revenge porn, giving it a sick twist?

'You had a terrifying experience last night. It's important you look after yourself. When we worked together in the past, you were taking medication.'

My jaw tightens.

'How are you feeling, Lauren?'

'Not great, actually. And no, I haven't taken medication for a while. Joe's making an appointment with the GP, so he'll put me on a load of pills.'

'Pills can help you through difficult times. I believe you when you say you've seen and heard these things. And I understand why you're scared of what might happen. It's important to keep the doctor's appointment so you can have a medical diagnosis.

I'm here for you, so we can talk some more to understand what's going on.'

'Thank you. I'll see what the doctor says. And I'll talk to Joe about disabling the smart hub.'

'That's good, Lauren.'

Annette wraps up the session. Talking to her brings everything into sharp focus. It leaves me wanting a conversation with Joe, since turning off the hub would lift a weight from my mind. In the aftermath of Karl Winter's death, I still worried about seeing his face in a crowd. My mind went into overdrive and now the smart home is reactivating all the hardwiring in my brain. If we sort out the external factors, then my mind will calm down.

Did I really see him on the CCTV? That fleeting glimpse was enough to recognise him, but Annette says the mind can trick us. I play it back in my head, the eerie image of him in the shadows, staring through the window. It wasn't distinct enough to judge whether he's aged or if he's frozen in time.

Could I have imagined it in some kind of waking nightmare, and transferred my fear to Dora? I think of Joe and the sad certainty in his eyes when he implied just that. Is it possible for the mind to play such an elaborate hoax? Annette seemed to think so. But then I remember Anorak Man from the tour, who vanished from the CCTV even though I spoke to him. I didn't imagine it. A gathering sense of resolve convinces me that I'm right about this.

CHAPTER ELEVEN

Annette suggested I contact the police, but I'm not ready after the officer visited last night, especially if he's put it on record that I'm paranoid. Times like this, I long for a friend nearby to meet for a coffee. Brooke and I go back to when she lived here several years ago and admired a racehorse portrait I'd had on show. Now she's the other side of the world, with ropy internet 'in the bush' where she works on a ranch. I send her an email asking about her news and filling her in on the strange happenings.

The conversation with Annette has urged me to research the smart home weirdness. I do an online search and the screen fills with headlines and videos about the alarming ways smart homes can turn against you. One catches my eye:

ARE YOUR SMART DEVICES SPYING ON YOU?

My heart rate increases and I recall the strange sensation of being watched in the bedroom. I grimace and turn away from the laptop to focus instead on my latest portrait. Painting soothes my mind and keeps me grounded. My horse painting in progress is further along than I remember. Sometimes I'm so deep in the zone that I lose myself and work in some kind of trance. It's a strange term, to lose yourself, but it's similar to watching a film and jumping in fear when something scary happens, even though it's not real.

Dora comes back in and I set to work layering more detail into the painting. A while later, Joe arrives home and strides across the garden to the studio. I unlock the door.

'Am I disturbing you?' He kisses me and makes a fuss of Dora.

'It's okay, I'm due a break.' I stretch my arms above my head.

'Oh, wow.' He looks in awe at the painting of the horse. 'Your paintings take my breath away.'

'Thanks. It's nearly there.'

Joe says I'm talented, but I've always been drawn to painting and put in the hours to hone my skills. He's kind about my artwork, right from the night we first met at an art show where I had some pieces on display. He knew the gallery owner and dropped in for a quick drink on his way to see a film. I'd been standing around making stilted conversation and trying not to neck all the wine.

When Joe came and introduced himself, everything changed. He had the loveliest smile and bright amber eyes. Three hours later, we were still talking and he'd missed the film. The memory blankets me with warmth. *You're so lovely*, I thought, there must be a catch. It turned out that he shared a home with his estranged wife. He'd stayed on in the spare room to be close to Dylan. His home life took some sorting out, but we've come a long way since and his gorgeous smile still has the same melting effect on me.

'How are you feeling now?' he asks.

'Not great, but so long as I can still paint.'

'You can certainly still paint.' He studies the picture, his face rapt. 'The client will love it.'

'Hope so. Let's go indoors.' I go to close the internet search from earlier.

'What's that?' Joe sees the search page on smart home malfunctions.

'Oh, that … I was looking up what weird stuff might be going on in the house.'

I lock the studio behind us and huddle into my jumper. The headline stays with me about smart devices that can spy.

'I phoned the surgery,' Joe says when we're in the kitchen. 'They gave you an emergency appointment for Monday at 9.50. The doctor might want you back on the meds before things flare up.'

I ignore his assumption that I need medication. 'Could someone be watching us indoors? They might be watching us now, waiting to get me alone.'

'Honey, there aren't any cameras in the house.' He rubs his stubble and gives me a pained look. 'We've only got cameras on our laptops.'

But suspicion has taken root in my mind and I spin round, looking for hidden cameras in the light fittings. 'Someone's watching us, they must be. They know when I'm alone. They recorded Dora growling and played it back when I was alone upstairs. They knew you were out last night.' It comes out in a breathless rush.

'Hey, let's slow down a bit.' Joe stands in front of me and holds my shoulders. 'No one's watching us in here. There aren't any cameras, are there?'

'But the sound system . . .'

'Even if someone wanted to take that amount of trouble, there aren't microphones. No one can record Dora indoors. I've asked Kev to come back and check it out. Why don't we try and relax over the weekend? If anything strange happens, I'll be here and we'll work it out.'

'I had a session with Annette earlier.'

'Oh.' His tone changes to pleasant surprise. 'How did it go?'

'She got me thinking. Can we turn the smart home off?'

His face drops. He expected an admission that I need help, not a prompt to dial down the smart home. 'It's part of the house. We can't turn it off.'

'But we can disable it.'

'It's working okay now.'

'Yeah, but all the weird stuff is coming through the smart hub – the sound, the CCTV.'

'But we'll lose all the features. Everything's connected.'

'I'm asking you to turn off the hub, not sever an artery.'

'No need to put it like that.' He looks hurt. 'I'm just saying it won't help.'

Annette's right that we need to disconnect. I put up with

Joe's smartphone obsession and the way he geeks out over gadgets. This is something else entirely.

'Annette said this is our home and if it's making me uneasy we should turn off the hub. Then I can work out what's real and what's not. If we eliminate what might be causing it, there's a better chance of getting a handle on it. That makes sense, right?'

'Okaaay.' He rubs his jaw in contemplation.

'We're not turning it off forever. Just for now.'

'Yeah.'

'I'll feel more settled if I'm not listening for woo-woo stuff from the sound system.'

He scratches his head. 'Okay. I'll ask Nicole how best to do it. Staying out last night was a mistake. I already knew you were struggling.'

'I'm not a child who can't be left. I was fine until the intruders woke me. Anyone would be freaked out by it.'

'Intruders steal. They ransack, but nothing's gone. Nothing's damaged. What reason did they have to be here?'

'To scare me.'

We lock eyes.

'Do you believe me?'

'Of course I believe you,' he says. 'I feel bad for you, that's all. This is meant to be a stable base and it's having the opposite effect.'

'What if it's not a stable base? What if it's doing me harm?'

Joe pulls back and rubs his forehead in frustration. 'Then we'll deal with it.'

I go and grab Dora's lead. A walk will clear my head and prove I'm still a functioning adult. I power walk around the field, filling my lungs with cold country air. I keep checking over my shoulder, one hand on my panic alarm and phone, but no one's following, not even Joe, who I half expected to come after me. Even though it's daylight, I don't feel safe after last night. Whoever came here might still be hanging around.

I can't let this get the better of me. Moving here is our fresh start and I need to venture out more. It's crystal clear that Joe isn't thrilled about turning off the hub, but he'll come around. He wants us to ride this out, like we did with the stalker problem and handling Dylan's issues, and the stumbling blocks when we bought the cottage. That's Joe all over, to keep going and let everything settle down.

We could have a break and go away, but my painting deadlines can't be put off. Everyone on the waiting list wants their portrait in time for Christmas, and we need the money coming in. I walk back up the garden path, the wooden gate swinging shut behind me. Joe opens the door, by hand rather than remotely. He rubs Dora's damp paws with her towel.

'I've turned off the voice commands,' he says, 'since that might be triggering something in you.'

I shrug off my jacket. I don't use the voice commands anyway. 'What about the multi-room audio?'

'I'll check whether we can turn it off, but in the meantime, this is our home and if something's going on, I want to witness it. I won't leave you again overnight, not unless you feel safe. Let's take it a day at a time. Deal?'

'Deal,' I say, because I want him to witness the strange happenings. At least he's trying to address it. We have to stick together and work out what's going on. I'll handle it so long as we're in agreement and I'm not alone here.

CHAPTER TWELVE

Instead of finishing the watercolour, I'm researching smart home malfunctions, scrolling furiously on Joe's laptop at the kitchen table. He's organising his electric tools and work supplies in the garage, and I fall down an online rabbit hole on the ways a smart home can kill you. A bunch of geeks on an internet forum pick apart how artificial intelligence can override human commands.

> The AI can turn the hob on remotely. If the inhabitants have left papers or something flammable on it or nearby, it can cause a house fire.

My gaze darts to the hob, checking we haven't left the post beside it.

One of them talks about a mass market AI home assistant with a random creepy laugh.

It's only supposed to respond to voice commands, but the
laugh goes off when it's not activated.

I shudder. That's worse than Joe's whispering woman and
Dora growling when she's not there.

An email reply comes through from Brooke.

Hey, Lauren,

Wow. Just wow.

What the bloody hell's going on? It seems to me that
you're protecting yourself from harm by not going to public
places. And now your world's reduced, but the problem has
found its way inside your home. You're not seeing the stalker
in a crowded street, he's on the patio. What do you think?

I think I'm screwed.

It's like someone is trying to freak you out, unless the
place is haunted. Would you rather it was a ghost from the
Haunted Woodland, or a real person? I'd rather a ghost.
Ghosts only scare.

Joking aside, I doubt anyone's going to harm you
because they've drawn attention to themselves and now the
police are involved. Someone's mucking about, but who?

I'm worried about you stuck in that weird house. You
need to get out more in the big bad world, since it can't be
worse than what's going on at home. You should defo have
words with Joe about his 'smart' home. Doesn't sound

very smart to me. Tell him he's dreaming if he thinks it's
a safe bet.

Here's a photo of my passion fruit pavlova. Get on the
next plane and I'll make you one.

Brooke xxxxxx

It would take a dose of Valium to get me through Heathrow
and on a long-haul flight with a bunch of strangers, but her email
cheers me up.

I jump as a figure appears on the patio. It's only Joe, who
comes indoors. Tiredness is making me nervy. At least he's here
tonight and I should sleep better. I click away from my emails
so he won't see Brooke slagging him off. I can almost hear her
twangy voice saying, *What the bloody hell's going on?* The forum
page on abuse by smart home is displayed instead.

'What are you looking at?' He comes closer to the screen.

'Smart home malfunctions.'

'It's not malfunctioning. It'll be fine if we let it settle. By
the way, when you're finished can I use the laptop? I promised
Dylan we'd FaceTime.'

I log off. When Joe's busy with Dylan, I go to the studio
with an urge to phone Alistair about the smart home tour, since
he'd arranged it. I can't shake off the feeling that the man who
came back for his key was involved in last night's disturbance.
Alistair will know him. Joe's concerned look just now stopped
me saying I wanted to call Alistair. It might lead to me saying
the Anorak Man gave me the creeps, and Joe already thinks I'm
slipping back to the aftermath of the stalker.

I call Alistair's architect practice and he answers on the third ring.

'Hi, Alistair, it's Lauren.' My free hand toys with a tiny bronze sculpture of a woman, made by an old friend on my art course at Central Saint Martins. We've lost touch, but I could drop her a line to say hi and see if she wants to catch up.

'Hello, Lauren. How's my favourite client?'

'I bet you say that to everyone.'

'I can assure you I don't. It was good of you to put up with us the other day. The house looks amazing.'

'Thank you.' I stand at the studio window and stroke a finger over the dainty bronzed limbs of the sculpture. 'I wanted to ask you about a man from the tour. He came back looking for his key. I should've taken his number, but I was distracted.'

'Who was he?'

'He didn't tell me his name. He broke away from the tour to have a closer look at the smart hub. He's about forty, short hair, receding hairline, not that tall. He wore a black anorak both times he was here.'

'Not sure who that could be. Did you find his key?'

'No.'

'I can't really help, I'm afraid.' He sounds perplexed.

'Um . . . I thought I'd get his details in case the key turns up.'

'Oh, right.' He's dubious. No wonder when I'm making a total hash of it.

'Could you email the people you invited?' I ask.

'I could, but we're not allowed to share email addresses now.

Against the law. Bloody annoying, especially as I get as much junk mail as before.'

'Can you ask whoever responds to email me?' Since I don't want the man turning up again.

'Never fear, if anyone replies I'll point them your way.'

Good old Alistair. I like his genial old school ways. 'Thank you. Do you know much about our smart hub?'

'I'm not an expert, but Nicole's done a super job. Are you happy with it?'

'We've had some teething problems.'

'Ah, well, teething problems are to be expected. Nicole will sort it out. Will you get the hang of it? I know technology's a pain sometimes, but it's amazing what it can do, and Joe knows his stuff, so you're allowed to be a technophobe.'

'Yes, well. Thanks for saying you'll send the email.'

We wish each other a good weekend and I ring off. Alistair's wrong. Being a technophobe leaves me open to exploitation. I'm glad he doesn't know what's been going on. I crane my neck towards the house and see Joe talking to someone via his laptop, Dylan probably. I message Nicole.

Can I FaceTime you?

I lean back and assess the nearly finished horse painting. Joe's right, it does look good. My phone comes alive with a video call from Nicole. That was quick. I accept the call and she appears, all sparkly eyes and platinum spiked hair. She gives me a cute wave.

'Hi, Nicole, how are you?'

'Hey, Lauren, all good here. How can I help?' Her voice is high and soft.

'You know how there are reports of AI home assistants doing weird things?'

'Like ... malfunctioning?'

'The creepy random laugh.'

'If it's sold in big enough volumes, a tiny proportion will go wrong, and it makes headlines.' She leans towards the screen, resting on her elbows. 'You don't have one, do you?'

'No, but have you heard of our system malfunctioning?'

'In what way?'

'Is it possible the CCTV doesn't record the whole time?'

'Um, run that by me again.'

'Remember that creepy guy I mentioned from the tour? I went to show the CCTV to Joe, but the man wasn't on there.'

'Sure you got the right time on the playback?'

'Yes. Other stuff's on there, including your visit, but not him.'

'There might've been a break in service. We set the system up to avoid that, and there are no dead spots in the house that the smart home can't reach, but the connection can break without you realising, or the motion sensor isn't picking everything up.' She nods to herself as if that's the most obvious solution. 'What time was it? I'll take a look remotely.'

I give her the rough timings of the Anorak Man's two visits. I like conversations with people who don't question my sanity. And a dodgy motion sensor would explain not seeing the man on the playback. But it doesn't explain the chilling footage of the intruder, which disappeared from the playback, and I saw

Anorak Man on the CCTV in real-time before he drove up the track and spoke to Mitchell.

'Is it usual for the sound system to go warped?'

'Warped, how?' She looks confused.

'I played a song that sounded warped. The notes and words were drawn out.'

'Just the one time?'

'Yeah. Freaked me out.'

'There must be a fault. I can run diagnostics next time I'm there,' she says. 'Don't worry. There'll be a logical reason. You might be in some freaky twilight zone down there in Ghostville where the technology goes loopy.'

'You think?'

'It seemed fine when I was on site, unless it's been possessed.' She snickers.

'It'd better not be.' I know she's joking, but my arms prickle with cold goosebumps. We didn't sink everything into this place for it to be derailed by some ghostly presence.

'Weird, if you ask me,' she says.

'Those evil spirits are a bummer.' I try to make light of it.

'There isn't a cellar, is there? Or a locked room behind an old wardrobe?'

'Knock it off,' I smile. 'You'll give me nightmares.'

She laughs and claps her hands, looking even younger. The conversation's going the wrong way when I wanted a rational explanation. Does she think Anorak Man is a ghost?

'I'd be taking a crowbar to bed,' she says.

'Do crowbars work against ghosts?'

She grins and takes a gulp of what looks like green juice.

'Could it be a cabling issue? Kev said not, but I don't trust his word.'

'If one of the cables is being pinched or squeezed some-where in a wall, then it can cause a break in service. Have you got a mice problem? They can get inside the walls and nibble the wires.'

'It's possible, out here in the countryside.' But that doesn't explain Dora's growling or seeing Karl Winter on the CCTV.

'What if it's a person, not a ghost?' I ask.

'I'd be on red alert, but I'm paranoid anyway.'

'Are you?'

'Sure.' She smiles, as if paranoia is a good thing. 'Most IT people are because we know the harm it can cause.'

'Like what?'

'Hacking, for starters.' She sees my look and checks herself. 'Not this system, *obviously*. Joe wanted it super-secure, but it's a huge industry in Russia. Not that Russians are your problem if no one's demanding money. It makes my life harder. If some-one's determined to hack your data, they probably can. It gives the impression that my work is at fault, but I try really hard to keep clients' data safe.'

Her view is more worrying than Joe's, but at least she's honest.

'The audio's bothering me,' I say. 'It's not just the music, it's the growling I heard upstairs.' I'm not in the mood to tell her about the disturbance, not until I've found out more. I expect her to reassure me from a professional perspective.

She gives an exaggerated shudder. 'Have you googled to see if there's any history about the place? Like the woods out there. It might be haunted.'

My goosebumps are back and I rub my arms. 'I'm not sure I want to. I'm freaked out enough.' It's worrying if the tech expert thinks our home is possessed.

'No wonder, out there in the sticks. Sorry, I'm not helping.'

'From what you say, it's possible for someone to hack into the system and sabotage it.'

'It's really unlikely,' she says. 'Even if someone has it in for you, they'd need to be very skilled or to put their trust in someone else who's very skilled. Why would anyone do that?'

I stay silent. She doesn't need to know about Karl Winter's vendetta. Even after all this time, I don't talk about him willingly.

'What about your electrician?'

'*Kev?*'

'Yeah. I don't think much of him, I'm afraid. I overheard him calling me a dyke to Joe.'

'Oh no, I'm sorry. You shouldn't have to put up with that when you're working.'

'I shouldn't let it get to me.' She bites her lip, turns away and taps furiously at a second laptop to cover her upset.

'He resents you doing the installation, same as if you were a man.'

'But he wouldn't talk about a man like that.'

'No, you're right.' And I'm complicit in letting Joe use Kev's services, but at this rate, I'll ban every man from the house.

'The system's secure, so don't go freaking out on that account. I don't want to make you paranoid. Might be one of those weird unexplainable things. I'll check on the security this evening.'

I don't want to make you paranoid. God forbid that anyone would think me paranoid when I try so hard to cover it up. Joe secretly thinks I am, which I know from the way he looks at me. At least Nicole believes me, even if she can't resolve it. I want to ask her more, but Joe's coming down the garden path towards me.

'I have to go,' I say.

'Listen, if the sound goes weird again, record it on your phone for me.'

'Good idea. Thank you.'

We wave goodbye and she logs off as Joe opens the studio door.

'How's Dylan?' I smile at him.

'Glad it's half-term as of three thirty today. He's here for the day tomorrow.'

'I'll make his special pancakes.'

'Who were you talking to?' He motions to my phone.

'Nicole. I wanted her take on the smart hub.'

'Why didn't you speak to me? I know the smart hub inside out.'

'Yes, but—'

'Lauren, I'm in business with Nicole. She'll think it strange that you're asking her instead of me.'

'Okay, but I noticed something strange about the CCTV, so I ran it past her.'

He leans in the doorway and jams his hands into his pockets. 'What is it?'

'You know I said that man on the tour came back for his key, and I was suspicious of him?'

'Uh huh.'

'I checked back on the CCTV to the tour and it's not on there. Someone's wiped both his visits.'

'Are you sure?' He starts tapping and swiping on his phone.

I wait for him to check it out. He puts down his phone and rubs his face tiredly.

'What do you think?'

'Glitchy connection?' he suggests.

'You told Kev it wasn't glitchy.'

'I'm not giving Kev the satisfaction of saying *I told you so*. The CCTV might not be recording properly.'

'Funny how the man's not on there, but it recorded Nicole arriving and leaving in between times.'

'Did you wipe it by accident?'

I sag a little in the chair, feeling as tired as he looks. 'How would I even do that? I only know how to call it up on my phone.'

'What does Nicole think?'

'Glitchy connection, a break in the service, the undead.'

'The *undead*?'

'Let's not go there. She says to record any weird noises on my phone to play back to her.'

'Good idea. Don't worry; I'll check it out some more with her, see what we can work out.' Joe turns and walks back towards the house. He's saying the right things to pacify me but isn't taking it seriously.

I lock the studio and catch him up. 'That man broke off from the tour to fiddle with the hub. I didn't imagine him. He was here.'

'*What?* Who fiddled with the hub?' He turns towards me and looks as violated as I feel.

'The Anorak Man on the tour.'

'Why didn't you tell me before?'

'I was going to tell you, but you rushed off straight after, and then I didn't want you to think me paranoid about strange men, so I left it. Who were those people anyway? I'd expected them to be Alistair's clients.'

Joe goes through to the utility room, and I follow. He checks the control panel.

'Alistair's guys blogged about this place. Remember I showed you the blog post? A few people asked to view it, so they put an invite out to people wanting a look-around.'

'Seriously? A bunch of internet fanatics who nobody can vouch for? Was it wise to let them in the house?'

'It was fine.' He peers at the control panel. 'This looks okay. Did he touch it?'

'He either touched it or studied it really closely.'

'He was just interested, whoever he was.'

'That's exactly it! We don't know who he was. And they're IT experts, so for all we know they can hijack the system.'

I go and light the wood burner, needing to calm down. At least the firewood can't be controlled via an app, not yet anyway.

Joe comes in. 'Here.' He opens his laptop to the settings screen for the smart hub and taps at the keyboard. 'I'm disabling the sound system for the whole house.'

'Thank you.'

'I want you to feel safe. Okay?'

We're both over-tired. The simplest explanation is a system malfunction, which is hard to believe when it only malfunctions around me. We were doing so well, settling into our dream home in the country, but I can't settle here now, not with all the weirdness.

Nicole thinks it's far-fetched that someone would hack the system. I didn't tell her that my computer was hacked before, by Karl Winter. He didn't just set up the revenge porn site, he emailed my entire contacts list with a link to it.

What if . . .

Stop it, I tell myself. *The stalker's dead*. That's what Joe would say, and he's right.

CHAPTER THIRTEEN

Joe's gone to collect Dylan, and I take a run on the treadmill in the spare bedroom. My feet pound in a steady rhythm and I look through the window at the countryside. I should be out there with the fallen leaves underfoot and wood smoke in the distance. I used to feel safer indoors, but I'm not safe anywhere now. I ramp up the speed and run faster.

Joe wants to spend more time with Dylan to reinforce the rights and wrongs of internet use. We had no idea he'd hacked his school's system until Joe took a call from the head teacher back in the spring. Joe tried to convince her that Dylan didn't mean any harm and only wanted to satisfy his natural curiosity. We assumed that his technology obsession drove him look at how their IT system worked. In truth, none of us had a clue why he did it and Dylan never enlightened us.

By the time they're home, I've hit the shower, am dressed and towelling my hair dry.

'We're back,' Joe calls out.

'Hi.' I come to the top of the stairs and smile at Dylan who has Dora nestled in his arms. The two of them are inseparable when he's here. Dora gets the best of him. When she's not trotting alongside him, he carries her or she snuggles on his lap.

'Hey, Dylan.'

He avoids eye contact and gives an awkward half smile. He's always had a cute smile. Joe never expected me to love Dylan, but I do. It's an arm's length love, but I want the best for him.

'We're going to play Xbox games,' Joe says.

'Can I join you?'

We go upstairs. Joe's regime of no internet use without supervision is working, even though it's straining relations with Dylan. We're making more time for him, which I doubt he sees as a consolation. In Dylan's room, a black plastic bat with white fangs hangs upside down from the window. In the first flat we renovated, I painted a mural in his bedroom of him with a bunch of animals, which he loved. I wanted to paint something funky for him here, but when I asked what he'd like, he shook his head and looked away, so I took that as a no.

Joe and Dylan set up the bubble cylinder and light show, and fire up the Xbox. The two of them are so attuned to technology, it's like a part of them. Joe would have the smart home app embedded in his brain to play music just by thinking about it. He says people can be microchipped, the same as pets, removing the need to carry cash or cards. You can be scanned like a product at the till and the payment comes straight from your bank account, which sounds awful.

My heart rate increases as the battle starts. I'm not a natural at computer games, but I throw myself into the gritty battlefield scene. Joe and I differed in our opinions on gaming when Dylan was younger and I said they weren't helpful.

'I used to play them as a kid,' Joe had said. 'I'd spend hours blowing things up. It didn't make me a deviant.'

'But they're so mindless. How is it fun?'

'It's better than watching crap TV. You're working towards something.'

'Working towards killing people.'

'I like killing people.'

'Really?'

'Killing the bad guys. Gaming's escapism. You're part of the story. You can be something different. You can be the hero.'

He didn't convince me, but it animates Dylan and is a way to connect with him. He isn't a kid you can be hands-on with. Even when he was little, he would huddle in on himself if I came close. That's who he is, but I have an unvoiced hunch that Tara coaches him to shun me.

It's gloomy out, but the room has biodynamic lighting to mimic natural light and regulate the body clock. In the evening, the down-lights are programmed to turn sunset orange for a calming effect. Not that the Xbox is calming. After an hour, I escape the explosive sound effects of war games for the calm of the studio.

The horse portrait needs finishing touches, but I google Kev first. I saw his van on Mitchell's property the other day, tucked round the side instead of out the front, when he would usually park it in the most convenient place. Were they swapping grievances?

Kev's online presence amounts to a few mentions for his five-a-side football team, and a Facebook profile that I don't check because it'll be all beer and football. And because I've avoided social media since Karl Winter hacked into my online accounts.

Both Kev and Nicole are skilled enough to mess with the home hub. Joe chose Nicole on Alistair's recommendation. She wouldn't jeopardise her business, and how could she or Kev know about the stalker to use footage of him for the CCTV? We don't talk to other people about it. My identity was protected and Joe was never publicly identified as a person of interest. The police never arrested him, although the altercation was a contributing factor in Karl Winter downing enough alcohol to fall drunk into the river.

Joe wanted to forget it, and I'm pretty sure he hasn't told anyone. I haven't either, except Annette in our sessions. Brooke was on the email list that Karl Winter hacked to send the revenge porn link, and we've talked about what went on, although she doesn't know that Joe saw him the night he died. I didn't tell her because she can be negative about Joe, who she thinks can be a little controlling. She doesn't understand that he's just passionate about his ideas. They got on when they met before she returned to Australia, but I've noticed her animosity since. It's because she looks out for me and has a zero-tolerance approach to dealing with relationship crap. But then again she is single. As unkind as it sounds, I don't think she has any idea of how relationships work in reality.

As for the revenge porn, I still burn with humiliation at Karl Winter emailing the link to my contacts. Most people were kind, but I'd done some work for an older couple, the Lassiters, who saw me in town soon after. I waved to them from across the road and she nearly recoiled from me. She said something to her husband, who ducked his head and ushered her away. I reddened in shame as if they really had caught me out as a naked porn queen. The commission they'd promised me of their daughter's cats never materialised.

'Fuck 'em,' Joe said, but I cringe when it comes to mind.

I tap in Kev's company name and read a few mixed reviews of his professional services, the bad ones about his attitude, but one stands out from the rest. Mrs JW posted a one-star review last month:

Don't let this person inside your home. We made that mistake. He set up our internet-connected devices. He messed us around, did a terrible job and stormed out when we complained. Then we started hearing heavy metal music in the night. We tracked it down to one of the devices. We can only surmise that it was him. We threatened to tell the police and it stopped. I wish we had never let him in.

Kev wanted to install the smart home and he resented Nicole landing the contract. He's well-placed for an inside job and might somehow be in cahoots with Mitchell. Is he twisted enough? Yes, if he wants to discredit Nicole and make us regret choosing her. I know what Joe would say to that, since he rarely thinks the worst of anyone. I can see him in the kitchen making lunch, so I lock the studio and come indoors.

'Look—' I open the laptop on the kitchen counter where he's making Dylan's favourite lunch of cheese toasties. Dylan's sprawled on the tiled floor with Dora, and Joe leans down to peer at the review. My eyes are drawn to the last line:

I wish we had never let him in.

He looks at me, eyes wide. 'Wow, that's some recommendation. I'll ask him what happened.'

'Is he doing the same thing to me?'

'I doubt it. Maybe it's nothing to do with him. He's not that underhand.'

'Isn't he?'

'I haven't heard anything like that before.'

'It's recent. Maybe he did it to that woman and then decided to have a go with me.'

'Or the job turned sour. I heard he once had a customer who refused to pay, a shop owner, I think. Kev went in and disconnected everything he'd worked on.'

'That's fair enough, but hijacking someone's sound system is out of line.'

'I'll ask him,' Joe says. 'See how he reacts.'

'Why would he do it to me? Is there something I don't know about, other than him not getting the smart home job?'

'Lauren, I doubt he's done anything other than be his usual dickish self, but I'll definitely find out from him.'

There's no point in keeping on, so I push the laptop away and help with lunch.

'Any plans for Halloween, Dylan?' I ask when we're sitting round the table.

'No.'

'What shall we do to mark it?'

I used to carve a pumpkin with him every Halloween, but he lost interest when I bought one last year and I carved it alone.

'Can we watch *The Haunting of Hill House*?' His usually monotone voice has a hopeful lilt.

'Not if it's for adults only,' Joe says.

'It's a fifteen rating.'

'You're thirteen.'

'I've seen *Scream 4*.'

Joe sighs. 'Does your mum know you watch adult films?'

He hides behind his fringe and nibbles his toastie in silence. Joe and I have salad with ours, but Dylan says salad is boring, since he doesn't like dressings. Watching haunted house dramas will freak me out, so I'm relieved that Joe has quashed the request. After lunch, he asks Dylan to load the dishwasher.

'Wanna play Xbox,' he mutters.

'After you've loaded the dishwasher.'

'No.'

'Lauren and I made lunch, so you can help clear up.'

Dylan mutters something inaudible under his breath and shoves his plate across the table.

'Dylan—'

106

'Fuck's sake.' He stands up and goes to lumber out.

'Don't swear!' Joe raises his voice, his authoritarian side coming out.

'Mum swears.'

'Well, she shouldn't swear around you.'

'She doesn't swear *around* me; she swears *at* me.' He strops off upstairs.

Joe tuts and gets up.

'Thirteen's an awkward age,' I say. It's becoming a mantra between us.

'He has to learn to pitch in. Leave it all. He'll do it before he goes home.'

He follows Dylan upstairs. I leave them to lock horns and go to finish the portrait. It turns colder, so I light the little studio wood burner. We have a bigger one indoors, which we light on cold evenings.

The autumnal chill is upon us, and the wood burner fills the studio with cosy heat. By late afternoon, I've finished the portrait and glow with satisfaction. I love completing a painting. It's a big one, so I can charge more. Joe pokes his head in to say he's taking Dylan home. Dora snuffles around the garden and Dylan loiters on the patio, nursing a dark look in our direction.

'Is Dylan okay?'

'We had one of our chats.'

He tries turning every strop into a learning experience once Dylan's temper has subsided. Joe goes to get something from the garage and tells Dylan he'll see him out the front. Dora ambles over to see me and I crouch down to pet her.

'Are you taking her with you?' I call over to Dylan, still on the patio.

He looks daggers at me. I walk towards him to encourage Dora in his direction. She runs to him and he scoops her up to take along for the ride.

'See you next time,' I say.

He slides a filthy look at me and mutters what sounds like *fuck off*. I stop, momentarily shocked. He's never sworn at me before.

'Sorry?'

He buries his face in Dora, but I see the glint of his eyes through his fringe.

'Did you just swear at me?'

Joe comes back to round Dylan up. 'What? He swore at you?'

I shake my head at Joe to say *it's okay*, avoiding another meltdown.

'Dylan! Say sorry to Lauren.'

He darts past Joe towards the car.

'Leave it for now,' I say.

Joe goes after him. It's cosy back in the studio with the last log on the burner. I email Miranda Hanson to say her picture is finished and I'll drop it off next week. By the time I've caught up on emails, including one to let the next client know I'll start their painting on Monday, it's nearly dark. I tuck the laptop under my arm and lock the studio door behind me.

Joe's not back yet. Tara must be keeping him talking, since she often invites him in for a chat. I don't complain, even if I've been kept waiting in the car, not that Joe lingers when I'm there. She hasn't had an easy time of it. Her last relationship broke down after having their baby girl, leaving her a single parent struggling with Dylan and her younger child. I walk along the stepping-stone path to the cottage. A branch snaps as if someone's trod on it. I jump and glance around, but no one's here.

The wind rustles through the trees in a shushing noise. I stop ... it's wrong. The air is cold and still, not windy enough for fluttering leaves. An icy chill engulfs me. It's not the wind. *It's a voice*, a woman's voice shushing.

'Shuuusssh, shuuusssh ...' The ghostly voice comes from the trees.

Fear floods through me. I spin round, scanning the trees, caught in a supernatural game of hide and seek. What's going on?

'Shuuussssh.'

I run for my life. My urgent breaths sound like they're amplified. I don't care because it drowns out the sound of that terrible voice. I scramble inside and lock the door. Adrenaline pumps and I lock myself in the cloakroom. Sweat clings to me, along with pure terror. I stand with my head to the door, listening, swaying, light-headed with fear. I crouch down and pull my phone from my pocket. I'm shivering with cold or panic, I can't tell which.

Where are you?

I message Joe in a rush, still listening for any noise. I use the app to turn all the lights on indoors and out.

Still here, he texts. Talking about D. x

Come home.

Moments later, he calls me on speakerphone in the car. 'You okay?'

'No. When are you back?' I lick my dry lips.

'Fifteen minutes. What's wrong?'

'I heard someone outside. Come home, please.' My voice is low, urgent.

'Hang on, okay? I'm on my way.'

CHAPTER FOURTEEN

I look out of the bedroom window at the overcast morning. What happened yesterday still gives me the chills. Joe buttons his shirt behind me.

'I can't live here, Joe. It's freaking me out.'

He stops and wraps his arms around me. 'There's some weird shit going on. And we need to work out what it is.'

'How?'

'Let's go out there for a proper look, now it's daylight. See if we can find anything.'

I turn in his arms and he cups my face in his hands, his thumbs brushing my skin. 'And then we'll see what the doctor says tomorrow.'

This is how Dylan must feel, handled with exaggerated patience. Joe's talking like a sensible parent, pacifying me as if it's a bad dream he can soothe away.

'This whole place is possessed.'

He looks at me with sad eyes and doesn't answer. He put it to me last night that it was the wind in the trees, implying that I'd spooked myself over nothing. But I insisted that it wasn't windy. The otherworldly shushing voice makes me wonder if Nicole is right about the supernatural. The idea of a ghostly presence isn't exactly comforting, but it could explain the unexplainable. I think of Dylan wanting to watch *The Haunting of Hill House* and I shudder.

'We'll have to sell up and find somewhere closer to civilisation,' I say. 'We can do up another place.'

'I get what you're saying, but we can't afford to leave.' He rubs my shoulders. 'We didn't buy it to sell on. We did it for us. It's too niche to get back what we've sunk into it.'

'It's not about money, though. Renovating was never about making money, we were working towards our own place, but I can't settle here. Not now.'

'Saying it's not about money is fine if we actually had any. If we lose money on this place, we won't get funding for another home.'

'I nearly died of fright out there,' I say.

'We'll check the garden, then shall we take a drive out somewhere? Have a quiet day away from here.'

I rub my gritty eyes. 'Okay. I'll wake up in the shower.'

I go and stand under a hot jet of water to revive me. A day out might help, even if I know the strangeness will be waiting for me when we come back. I shut off the shower and reach for a towel. Joe taps on the door.

'Can I come in?'

'Sure.' I wrap my hair turban-style and brace myself for another pep talk.

He stands in the doorway, his face anxious, and a cold draught seeps in. 'Where'd you put the painting?'

'What painting?' I pull the bath towel tighter around me.

'The horse one you finished yesterday.'

'It's in the studio. On the easel.'

'It's not. The customers are here.'

'They're here?' Panic rises in my chest.

'They said you emailed yesterday, so they dropped by on the off-chance. They emailed, but you probably didn't see it.'

'It's on the easel. I'll go down.' Clutching the towel around me, I go to throw on some clothes.

'Hold on.' He reaches his arms out to stop me. 'It's not on the easel or in the studio. You stay here and I'll tell them you brought it in for some finishing touches or whatever.'

Joe goes back down and I pull on my jeans and a sweatshirt. It's best I don't see them with dripping-wet hair and no idea where their painting has gone. Car doors slam out the front. I go to the window as the Hansons drive off, and then I tear down to the studio. Joe follows me from the hall. It only takes a second to confirm it's not on the easel, and moments more to see it's nowhere in the studio.

'I thought you'd brought it inside but it's nowhere obvious.'

'I didn't bring it in. I left it here.' I clutch the sides of my face with both hands. Sweat forms on my top lip and along my hairline. 'Was the door locked?'

'No.'

113

'But I locked it. Someone's got in here.'

'Lauren, the state you were in when I came home ... you'd had an episode.'

'I locked it. I always lock it. Fuck, Joe, the sound effects were bad enough, but this is my livelihood.'

'Lauren—'

He steps forward to hold me, but I back off.

'No! You have to believe me.'

'What if you've put it somewhere else?'

'Joe! I didn't leave a giant canvas *somewhere else*. A piece of art isn't something I mislay like my car keys. I left it here in case it got smudged moving it. Someone's taken it, same as someone or something made those shushing noises out there. The two are connected. It's all connected.' My words tumble out in a frantic rush.

'Lauren, you're getting manic.'

I step back, bruised by his words. 'I am *not* manic.'

'There's a logical explanation.'

'No way did I put it somewhere else. That makes no sense. We need the money.'

'Yes, but ...'

'This fucking house is enough to drive anyone crazy.'

'The house isn't at fault and neither are you.' He's trying to defuse my argument but it's not helping.

'We have to sell up,' I say in a choked voice. 'I can't live here.'

'We'll sort it out.'

'Can we stay in the Airbnb until it's sold?'

He sighs. 'We'll see about moving in when the guests leave after half-term. And we'll talk to Dr Reeve tomorrow.'

We have to leave this creepy cottage with its malignant forces. Our friends' Airbnb flat is a lifeline while they're away travelling. We handle the bookings and clean it. They've let us stay there for a mate's rate when we've had no water or electricity. It's safe and secure, and I have to get away from here, to escape the awful trepidation roiling inside me. If we go somewhere safe, I'll sleep at night and breathe more easily without staying on red alert for what will happen next.

'I'll make it up to you.' Although I'm not sure how. I don't know what to do about the missing portrait. Someone stole it as a message to me, but take away my painting and it strikes at the heart of me.

I grab hold of Joe's hand. 'Let me show you where I heard the sound. We can work out where it came from.'

'Okay.' We lock the studio, even though the worst has already happened, and retrace our steps along the higgled path.

'Right.' I pause partway back to the cottage. 'It was about here, and I heard it up in the tree.'

'Was it dark?'

'Dusk, but I'd have seen if anyone was actually in the tree, although I didn't hang around. How can someone play a recording from up there?'

We stand with hands on hips and peer up at the high branches. I'm safe with Joe beside me, but still, my breath hitches and my pulse speeds as I relive the terror from yesterday and fight the urge to bolt back indoors.

Joe keeps looking up at the tree. 'Someone could climb up there and fix a device with some kind of remote-control playback.'

'I'll get the binoculars from the car.' I go inside for his car keys and grab the binoculars. Away from Joe, I prickle with fear, but he's only out the back. I take the binoculars through to the garden.

'Someone must have been watching me to time the voice for when I walked past.' I focus the binoculars on the higher branches.

'It's best not to speculate. You'll only stress yourself out. It's the same with your online research. I don't think it's helping.'

I can't see anything suspicious in the tree and pull back from the binoculars to look at him. 'I need to know what's happening.'

'If you look for scare stories, you'll find them and they'll feed into your stress.'

Joe goes inside and starts checking in cupboards, hunting around as if I've absent-mindedly put the painting somewhere. A part of me wants him to find it and spare me the soul-destroying need to start again, but at the same time I don't want to give him the satisfaction. He's looking for a rational answer to what he thinks is irrational hysteria. The whole thing is made worse by him thinking I've done something with it.

'Did you put it somewhere safe?'

'Somewhere safe? I told you, I left it to dry.' I cover my face with my hands. We've gone beyond the option of mislaying it. 'The voice scared me enough that I ran indoors and whoever it

116

was took the painting.' It sounded otherworldly, but Joe doesn't believe in ghosts and neither should I. Anyway, ghosts don't steal. 'What if someone knows about my mental health from the past and they're playing on it? So you'll think it's flared up and maybe I will too.'

'Who would do that?'

'Karl Winter.'

He looks at me, mouth agape. 'He's dead. You know that, don't you?'

'But what if he's not?'

'Why are you bringing him up?' he asks. 'I thought we'd put all that behind us.'

'He could have faked his death.'

He shakes his head slowly. 'It would be very hard for him to start again with a new identity.'

'He was devious. He might have laid low and now he's back.'

'Why would he start again now? He's been gone for what ... four years?'

'Five. Maybe he didn't have an opportunity. The smart home's left us vulnerable to this sort of thing. He hacked into my emails before. He's doing it again, isn't he? But this time it's worse.' I wrap my arms around myself.

'Sweetheart, let's not get carried away. We have to keep it real,' he says.

I narrow my eyes at him. 'I am keeping it real.'

'That's the thing with it. You perceive things differently. The voices, the distortion in your head, it seems real, but it's not. The mind's powerful. It can play tricks.'

'This isn't what I had before. I didn't hear things.'

'But it can manifest in different ways. It takes a while before you see it objectively. That's part of it, right? The paranoia makes you believe something's real when it's not.' His voice is soft and imploring, but I hate what he's saying.

He's painting me as someone suffering from delusions, but it only happened once. He wasn't even there, since we hadn't met back in my art school days. The doctors referred to it as an 'episode' that I had after smoking cannabis. It fuelled a terrible paranoia that my friends wanted to kill me, lasting long after the drugs should have worn off, but I haven't had it since. How dare he blame what's happening on that? He's never even witnessed it.

'It's not like before. That was a psychotic episode.' The upset wells in my chest and throat, thickening my voice with emotion. *Psychotic*. My fingertips latch onto the kitchen tabletop. I'm not that person. I'm not psychotic. I hate that word and what it represents ... violence ... madness ... the stigma that psychotic people can't be trusted and they struggle to know what's real. That's not me.

'I'm not psychotic.'

I can't bear to be labelled and misjudged as someone who could turn volatile. Even when I had the episode as a student, I never harmed anyone. My thinking went off-kilter, that's all. I'm not a scary person; I'm a *scared* person. I just want a normal life that's not defined by something that happened years ago. I try to remember what it was like the first – and only – time I had it. My thinking was all over the place and I wasn't rational, not like now.

118

'Paranoia's part of the condition,' Joe says, pulling out a dining chair for me to sit down. He sits in front of me, holding both my hands. 'You were anxious about being alone the other night and you thought people were breaking in.'

'But this is *different*.' It's even worse to have him explain my mental state to me.

He won't believe me if I tell him I saw Karl Winter on CCTV. Joe thinks he can save me from myself. Paranoia is a close friend of psychosis and I'm careful not to scare anyone. I told Joe that once and he said I was the least scary person he knew. The way he's been watching me lately tells a different story. There's a wariness in the way his gaze follows me, assessing my mental state.

CHAPTER FIFTEEN

I wake up in the night, breathless from a fevered dream and push back the duvet. In the dream, I saw myself as if removed from my body, watching the CCTV. I can't shake the feeling of being watched and I seek out Joe's sleeping body for reassurance. As a child, I was scared of the dark, scared of ghosts and faceless men taking me in the night. I would look out for black shapes moving in my bedroom. My fears surface in my dreams. Some fears you never outgrow and the older you get, the more you realise the harm people can do.

First thing in the morning, I log onto Airbnb and disable future bookings for the rental flat. Joe made the right noises about us staying there once the half-term guests leave, if I can last that long. It's low season after the school half-term holiday and the flat usually stands empty for six weeks. We'll pay for it, although I'm not sure how. It's already booked for Christmas, but I'll worry about that later.

'Shall we leave in ten minutes?' Joe says.

'I'll just smarten up.' I'd better present myself in the right way at the surgery, so that I come across as rational. I brush my hair, slick on lipstick and swap my grey sweatshirt for a white blouse and my favourite sky blue jacket, keeping on my dark jeans. A glance in the mirror confirms that I look like someone holding it together.

Joe drives us to the surgery. My skin crawls at the thought of the intruder listening in to my doctor's appointment, so I turn off my phone when we reach the waiting room. I don't know how easy it is to covertly listen to a conversation through a mobile. Joe would know, but I won't ask as he'll suggest I'm paranoid again.

We're called through to Dr Reeve's ground-floor office and go inside the boxy white room with standard issue NHS furniture. Joe and I sit alongside his desk.

'What can I do for you?' He's youngish with a mop of ginger hair and a scholarly look.

I open my mouth, but Joe jumps straight in. 'We wanted to talk to you about Lauren's mental health issues. She's having hallucinations, hearing things that no one else hears. And delusions in the form of irrational thoughts, like believing someone means her harm.' It's a textbook summary of a psychotic episode: hallucinations, delusions and irrational thoughts.

I stay composed until he finishes, even though I'm itching to contradict him. Dr Reeve listens carefully to Joe and then looks at me, earnestly. 'Lauren, how would you describe your mood recently?'

'It's been fine. We've moved into a new home, I was happy there until the sound system started playing up.'

'How does it play up?'

'It's a smart home, with multi-room audio and voice commands for the locks and lights. I've heard some odd sounds through the audio.'

'Do you think the smart home as you call it, is ...' he waves a speculative hand in the air, 'out to control you?'

'No. It makes me uneasy. I'm not into technology and I don't know how to work it properly.'

'Can you turn it off?' the doctor asks.

'We've disabled voice commands and the audio system,' Joe tells him.

'What about the painting that went missing?' I ask.

'There's probably a logical explanation. And the sound system isn't installed outside where you heard the voice.'

'I'd like it all disabled.'

'That sounds like the wisest action,' the doctor says, scrolling through my case notes on his desktop screen. 'If you find the features unsettling, the stress may have triggered a psychotic episode. How are you sleeping?'

'I have trouble going to sleep.' I don't tell him it feels like someone is watching me. 'I heard a playback in the bedroom of our dog growling—'

'It wasn't a playback,' Joe interrupts.

'And I lie awake.'

'Are you taking any recreational drugs?'

'No. Never. That's probably what triggered the psychotic episode, back when I was a student. I smoked cannabis at a music festival. It triggered hallucinations, like tripping on acid,

122

long after it should've worn off.' I'd wanted to embrace student life, idiot that I was. It had the opposite effect.

'Drugs can sometimes cause hallucinations and paranoia,' the doctor says.

I remember the awful fear and disorientation. 'I wouldn't leave my room because I overheard my housemates plotting to kill me. They talked about disposing of my body, or so I thought. When they got me help, I thought the mental health professionals were part of the conspiracy. I can see it for what it is now, but at the time it was a form of madness.'

He looks gravely at me the whole time I'm speaking.

'That was thirteen years ago and I haven't touched drugs since.'

'You don't need to take drugs to have the symptoms,' Joe says.

I take a breath and keep it reasonable. 'It was different last time. I was scared my friends were about to murder me. Anyone who didn't believe me was part of the conspiracy. This isn't the same. It's external. Someone is doing it to me.'

Dr Reeve nods sagely and we all fall silent as he takes my blood pressure. I stare at the window, its frosted glass guarding against the curiosity of passers-by. I've played into Joe's hands by saying someone's trying to cause me harm, since it backs up his view that I'm paranoid.

The doctor slides the cuff back off my arm. 'It's slightly raised, but that's to be expected.'

'Last time my head was a mess.' I try making the point more strongly. 'Everything was wrong. It had a manic quality that I was caught up in. This time it's not going on in my head. External things are happening.'

'It sounds like you're having a psychotic episode. Often with psychosis, your brain is trying to make sense of what's going wrong, so you rationalise it and believe it's real. Early treatment is the most effective way to bring it under control.'

I can tell by the careful way Joe is listening that he's storing it up to quote back to me later.

The doctor goes back to his screen. 'I'm going to prescribe medication that should settle it down.'

'Anti-psychotics?' I ask.

'Yes, to be on the safe side. It's a different type to the one you had before, and it can help you sleep better. The treatment is effective these days, so most people who experience psychotic episodes can have a fulfilling life. I'll arrange for the mental health nurse to get in touch.'

The swift diagnosis doesn't surprise me; he's not taking any risks based on what Joe said. We pick up the prescription in the pharmacy next door and return to the car. I clutch the paper bag of meds, hating all this getting the better of me, forcing me back on anti-psychotic medication that I don't need.

We're quiet on the way back. I can't bear to believe the psychosis has returned, meaning I can't control my brain or tell the difference between reality and what's in my freakish imagination. A call comes through and Tara's name flashes on Joe's dashboard screen. He taps a switch on the steering wheel to take the call.

'Tara, hi,' he says, all businesslike.

'Dylan's been upset since he was at yours—' she launches straight in, a harsh edge to her voice.

'Yeah, well, I told you about his swearing when he refused to load the dishwasher.'

'You didn't tell me that Lauren was having a go at him. She accused him of telling her to fuck off, when he did nothing of the kind. He might say *fuck* now and then but he doesn't go round telling adults to *fuck off*. Now he's upset and—'

'Hang on a minute . . .'

'She's not his mum, yeah? She can't go telling him off when he didn't swear at her in the first place.'

Joe tries placating her, but sod that.

'I'd watch her if I was you,' she snaps, talking over him.

'What does that mean, exactly?' The sharpness in my voice cuts through them both. I can almost feel her pull back in surprise. 'Tara, it's Lauren.'

She doesn't reply so I keep going. 'I can promise you I didn't have a go at Dylan. He swore at lunchtime. When I said goodbye to him, it sounded like he told me to *fuck off*, but I wasn't certain.'

'If you weren't certain you shouldn't have had a go at him. You may not realise it, *Lauren*, but he takes things like that badly. I'm his mum and it's me who has to deal with him.'

'This is ridiculous. Are you telling me you've never had a cross word with Dylan?'

'That's different. *I'm his mum*. After everything he puts up with at school, it's a bit off that he's getting grief from *you*.'

'Tara—' Joe tries to intervene.

'Tell your wife to watch herself. If she crosses my boy—'

Joe terminates the call mid-rant, cutting her off. He sighs, shaking his head. I clutch the car armrest and look at him, appalled, my heart pounding. How often does she rage about me like this?

'Ignore her,' he says.

'"Tell your wife to watch herself?" Is that some kind of threat?'

'She gets like that when she's rattled.'

'I've never had a go at Dylan.'

'You can't reason with her.'

'Joe, I can handle Dylan's meltdowns, but she can't threaten me over something I haven't even done.'

'She explodes sometimes, but she'll calm down.'

Another call comes through, from one of the landlords who outsources to Joe. It stops me from saying I won't take threats and accusations from Tara. Not that he'll stamp it out when he's scared she'll limit his contact with Dylan. I turn my phone back on and play a voicemail from Brooke, her bouncy Australian voice providing light relief.

'Hey, Lauren! Oh mate, I had to call when I read your email. That is utterly freaky. You must've been so scared. Do you have a gun to shoot the bastards? Call me back if you want to talk, otherwise email me. Look after yourself.' She blows a kiss down the phone and hangs up.

I snort at the gun comment and tell Joe. He nods half-heartedly, still bruised about the smart hub and riled by Tara. He puts up with too much from her, but I won't have her slagging me off. As for the hub, I'll give him time to accept the switch-off. We've pared it back in stages, first the voice commands and the disembodied home assistant voice that I never liked, and now he's disabled the sound system. The rest can still be controlled via the app. For as long as the smart hub stays on, it permeates everything like a crouching predator ready to do harm.

I tap out a quick reply to Brooke on my phone. Her ranch is so remote that she doesn't have reliable internet and sometimes goes to a café to email. She was 'on the cans' for our last Christmas catch-up over the phone and a bit drunk, which made for a raucous time. It's good of her to check in on me, but I won't call back because her lack of WiFi means racking up phone charges we can't afford.

'Joe?'

'Hmm?' He looks at the road ahead.

'I mean it about us disabling the smart hub until we leave next week. And Dr Reeve agrees.'

'Yeah. I'll get it sorted. We just need you back on an even keel. Now you've got the meds, they'll help you feel better.'

Joe acts as if the meds will solve everything, but I'm less sure. The pills will flatten me out, make me less fearful, but less *me*.

'Can I ask you something about Karl Winter?'

He looks at me.

'Who identified his body?'

'Um, his grandad.'

'Are you sure?'

'Yeah, I remember. I thought at the time the body could've

127

been some random drunk or a homeless person who no one reported missing.'

'Did they test the DNA? Say if the body was bloated from being underwater and couldn't be identified?'

'I expect they would if there wasn't a positive ID. But the police said his grandad identified the body. Why do you ask?'

'I don't want him coming back for me,' I say in a low voice.

'He's not coming back for you.'

There's no point telling him what I saw on the CCTV. It would convince him of the psychosis, since delusion is part of it – thinking someone is out to get me even though it's implausible. And it *is* implausible when the person is dead. I hate bringing it up, when Joe felt responsible for Karl Winter's death following their altercation, even though he was only protecting me.

Does someone mean me harm or am I the dangerous one, a danger to myself? Either something terrible is going on within me or it's being inflicted on me. I don't want either option. Joe's distant all the way home. Something has shifted between us, a gulf opening up, and I don't know how to bridge it. Trying to imagine life without him brings on a physical ache. If a door handle comes loose, he opens the toolbox and takes on an air of determination until he's put it right. Maybe he wants to fix me.

CHAPTER SIXTEEN

Joe had stayed with me since the weird noise in the garden, but now he's gone to the builder's merchant. I log on for my second session with Annette. She appears on the screen. Sunlight spills into the room, highlighting her silvery hair.

'I don't know what's worse,' I say after updating her, 'that I'm in danger, or that I'm supposedly hallucinating.'

'Both are worrying.'

We sit in silence for a few moments, hers companionable, mine awkward.

'It's good that you saw the doctor. Have you accessed mental health services since we last worked together?'

'No. I'm not psychotic.'

'I'm not saying you are,' she says in her mild voice. 'I recall that you had the psychotic episode as a student. How did that feel?'

I take a long breath. 'The paranoia took over. It had me

scared for my life. I felt cut off. I didn't trust anyone and had to protect myself.'

'Do you think that's had a lasting effect? Feeling cut off from others and needing to protect yourself?'

'I guess.'

Annette gives me a reassuring smile and nod. 'And that was when you were diagnosed with brief psychotic disorder?'

My jaw tightens. The rest of me tenses too. An episode can last for a month and might reoccur, but most people never have it again, so I want to be one of them.

'You say it's been thirteen years. Have you had an episode since?'

'No. Joe thought it had flared up when I was scared of seeing the stalker in crowded places. They were external factors, not screwy shit going on in my head, but I've always been scared it'll return.'

She nods.

'It's different now. It's external.'

'It's no wonder the stalking made you fearful. If you were on edge, perhaps Joe misread that.' Her benign gaze rests on me through the screen. 'At times like this, it's good to remind yourself how far you've come. You're in a stable relationship, you have a home, you run a business.'

'I guess so.'

'You're taking care of yourself by going to the doctor, and you're seeing the mental health nurse.'

'Is it good that I haven't taken the pills?'

'What's stopping you?'

I look out of the window. 'The official answer is that I want a second opinion from the mental health nurse.'

'And the real answer?'

'I want a break from the technology to see if the weirdness stops.'

She nods. 'You say Joe's never around when the weirdness happens?'

'No.'

She lets it sit there for a few moments.

'Joe's so invested in the smart home, he can't admit it's hackable. It's easier to say I'm paranoid.'

'What's happening to make him think you're paranoid?'

'The sound system only malfunctions when I'm alone. Someone wants to freak me out.' I should have told the doctor this, to avoid his rush to medicate me, but Joe kept it squarely on the paranoia instead of saying that someone's up to no good. Once the seed of paranoia is planted, it colours everything and whatever I say about feeling watched or under attack feeds into the diagnosis.

'Who would want to freak you out?' she asks.

'Karl Winter. I know he's supposed to be dead, but he hacked my computer before.'

'Okay, let's explore this. Let's say he really is dead, because that's logical, yes?'

'Yes.' It's a relief to talk through the options.

'Who else knows what Karl Winter did to you and the impact, and who has the inside information to manipulate the smart home?'

131

'Only Joe.'

'Only Joe,' she repeats.

Her tone unnerves me. 'What are you saying ... are you saying he's messing with his own tech? That doesn't make sense. He doesn't want to leave. He's desperate for us to keep living here.'

'Lauren, I'm hearing a lot about what Joe wants: Joe wants the smart home, he wants you on medication, he wants to keep living there. What do you want?'

I look out at the blood red roses just beyond the window. 'I want to feel safe and I don't here, so it's time to rein in the tech.' It helps to have a reality check from someone who's on my side. Joe says he's on my side, but he's so in love with the technology, I wonder what'll happen if I can't live with it.

We end the session with a talk on staying safe and looking after myself. Even if Annette didn't come out and say it, I know how it looks. But Joe wouldn't try to terrify me. He's under the spell of the smart hub, but that's just Joe. You can't share your life with someone and not know their true colours. Annette's never met him. She doesn't know how scared he is of me slipping backwards. I have to prove I'm not. I'll insist he turns off the home hub.

I go into the kitchen. Joe's laptop is on the table and I have an urge to turn off the smart home. I don't know how, but he says the system is user-friendly, so I'll test it out. Nicole changed the passcodes after her last visit and emailed them to us both, so there's nothing to stop me having a go. I tap in his password and his email screen appears. When I go to access the smart hub settings, the subject line of an unopened email catches my eye.

```
Loan repayment overdue.
```

What loan? I'm floored. We don't have any loans other than the mortgage, which is barely manageable as it is. It's from our usual lender, and not spam. Has Joe taken out a secret loan? And by the look of things, he can't afford it. Our finances are shared, so why didn't he tell me? It shocks me, when Joe and I are a solid unit. I try to absorb the blow that we aren't so solid after all.

CHAPTER SEVENTEEN

Brooke sends another email.

Hi Lauren,

How are you? Any updates on the strange goings-on?

Have you made a list of suspects? The old guy up the road is weird. He resents you interlopers and wants to scare you away. If it's him, stand your ground. What if he's a ghost? He could be haunting you. Check out the local graveyard. I bet he has a headstone.

She really does have a twisted mind. He'll be haunting the council offices too, since he complains to them about us.

Or what about the Sarky Sparky? He's a devious bastard. Didn't you call him out on his sexist bullshit? That's enough for some men to do the dirty and get their revenge.

Joe was going to have a word with Kev about that online review, but he hasn't mentioned it since.

How do they know about the stalker? There's no way they could have found that out, right? This is difficult to bring up and I don't want to offend you or cause any upset. So I'm just gonna say it . . . are you absolutely sure Joe has nothing to do with it?

Looking at it with a level head, Joe isn't capable of harm. He's too straightforward. He did the right thing by Tara, staying friendly with her for the sake of Dylan. He's not one to shirk family ties, and anyway, he loves me, dotes on me even. So yes, I'm sure.

Just then, Joe walks in. I close the email and face him in the kitchen.

'What's happened?' He assumes from my look that something else has gone wrong.

'Have you taken out a loan without telling me?'

He drops his keys on the counter. 'How did you find out?'

'Never mind that. What's it for?'

He rakes his hands through his hair. 'It's for the smart home business. Because of the initial outlay.'

'You said it would only take time early on, not money.'

He won't meet my eye. 'A solicitor advised on protecting the concept. It cost more than expected – you know how it is with legal fees – but it needs protecting so we don't lose out. If a competitor swoops in and steals the idea, we'll have nothing.'

'You could've told me.' I don't hide my accusatory tone.

'I don't want you to worry. Your business didn't need much upfront funding, but it's different with a high-tech concept. It's only until we're making money.'

'Until then, we're in deeper debt. How will we manage?' I call up our budgeting spreadsheet on the laptop.

'I'll reduce costs on the maintenance business. It means more work.'

'Can you handle it?'

'I've got broad shoulders. I've cut back maintenance payments for Dylan.'

That'll make us unpopular. 'Does Tara mind?'

'Of course she minds. I've cut it back to the statutory amount. But she knows it's temporary.'

I can imagine how that conversation went. Tara's always squeezing more out of Joe for trainers and school uniforms. She stayed in their house and Joe left with no home or money. She acts as if I've robbed her of the opportunity for a home like this. Her modest house on an estate isn't much different to the one I grew up on. Even if Dylan showed willing, she'd never agree to living on building sites, sometimes with no electricity or hot water and everything covered in dust. I do commissions alongside pitching in with the heavy grafting, not to mention the financial risk, when Tara just wants the end result.

'So you told her about our money troubles, but you didn't tell me?' This bothers me more than the actual loan.

He pulls out a dining chair and sits with his head in his hands, looking worn-out. 'I was trying to keep things stable.'

'By taking out a secret loan and not keeping up the repayments?'

'I wanted to protect you.'

'Protect me?'

'I'm trying to make things right for us.'

'I don't need protecting from the truth.' I sound terse and I don't care. 'Is there anything else you're keeping from me?'

'It's not like that. I had to give her enough notice because of Dylan, and I wanted a plan for repaying it before worrying you. I'm so sorry, Lauren. I should have told you.'

I look at his imploring face. The secret loan has rattled me, but he must feel bad about the maintenance payments, especially when he hates not being around all the time for Dylan.

'We'll go short if Dylan needs anything,' I say. I angle the laptop towards me and update our budget spreadsheet with the figures he gives me. 'We can make the overdue payment by delaying other bills in the short term. Now we've finished the house, we only need to spend on essentials. We'll deal with it together,' I say pointedly. 'Okay?'

'Okay.' He gets up, wraps his arms around my waist and nuzzles into my neck. 'What would I do without you?'

His phone buzzes and he pulls away. 'I'd better go. I only dropped in to see how you were. Thanks for understanding about Dylan.' He grabs his keys, still contrite after being caught out over the loan.

I stand in my makeshift studio at the front of the house and watch him drive away along the track. It's lower risk to paint here, near the front door where I can escape. Nicole says to record any weird sounds. I want evidence to prove I'm not imagining things, unless I'm so spooked I have to make a run for it. My keys and mobile are beside me.

I've emailed Miranda Hanson to apologise for their wasted journey. I said we had a break-in at the studio and the painting was taken. She replies:

I can't believe someone's taken our Freddie! Have you reported it to the police?

I lie and say yes but that it's not a high priority for them. I want to report it missing, but I've blown my credibility since Joe told that police officer I was paranoid. At least nothing strange has happened for three days, not since the ghostly noise when the picture disappeared.

The easel is set up with a stark blank canvas. If I needed any proof that this isn't all in my head, it's the missing painting. Joe still thinks I mislaid it and that it will show up. I've stopped arguing with him, but I *know* he's wrong. Before starting the painting, I turn to my laptop and look up a number from way back. Detective Sergeant Foster. I call the number, expecting her to have moved on, but she answers with a curt, 'DS Foster.'

'Hello, this is Lauren Geddes. We haven't spoken for a long time. You handled a case five years ago ... a man called Karl Winter drowned in the river on his way home from the pub.'

She pauses for a few seconds. 'Oh yes, it's coming back to me. Sorry, give me your name again.'

'Lauren Geddes. Karl Winter had been stalking me.' I pick up a stray paperclip on the desk and prise it open.

'Ah, Lauren, hello. Five years? Was it that long ago?'

'I think so.'

'What can I do for you?'

'It's a strange question, but do you know who identified his body?'

She pauses. 'It *is* a strange question after all this time.'

Dora makes whimpering sounds in her sleep and her paws quiver and jerk.

'It's just I thought I saw him, or someone who looked exactly like him. Do you know if his body was identified by anyone?'

'His grandad. I remember because he was estranged from his parents and grew up with his grandparents.'

'Could the body be identified? Or could it have been confused with someone else, say a homeless person who'd fallen in the river?'

'No, he was found early enough for identification to be straightforward.'

'Oh.' The paperclip slips and takes a chip out of my thumbnail. 'Did you do a DNA test?'

'It probably wasn't needed. I can't recall the finer points, but I seem to remember his wallet was in his pocket, so it was pretty clear cut.'

'Is his grandad still alive?'

'No. He had a massive heart attack not long after the inquest, and his wife died a few months later. She was in poor health and he was her carer.'

'Did Karl Winter have any brothers?' I'm clutching at straws, but he might have had a younger brother who looks like him and is out for revenge.

'None that I remember. Am I right in thinking the stalking went on for a long time?'

'Three years.'

'Stalkers often keep going until they're stopped.'

I don't ask if they keep going from beyond the grave.

'Listen,' she says. 'It's a fairly safe bet this person you saw isn't him. It's not unusual for someone in your situation to think they see their stalker, attacker, whoever. When you've had a trauma, your brain can stay on red alert so it's subconsciously on the lookout.'

'After five years?'

'It's possible, so this person you saw is probably someone who looks like him.'

I thank DS Foster and end the call. There's no time to dwell on it when I need to redo the horse painting. The money pressures push me to keep going. So long as I have a steady income from commissions, we'll hang on by our fingertips.

I face the blank canvas. Even after years as a professional artist, I start each painting with a sense of trepidation. What if I can't pull it off? What if the client hates it? I don't have the luxury of waiting for the muse to strike, so I lay out my paints, cloth and jam jar of water. The wasted effort makes me furious. No way am I leaving this in the studio overnight. It'll come into the bedroom with me.

I pick up my thicker brush to paint the base coat of the horse, washing in the shape that I'll add definition to with a finer brush for the clean, sinewy contours of his body. I check that I've mapped out the right perspective and then become absorbed in the watercolour scene. It turns out I don't need the right frame of mind because painting soothes and engrosses me.

I work on the portrait and push all the weirdness from my head until my fingers stiffen and I realise the room is suddenly freezing. I breathe out a chilly white plume and go to investigate before my muscles seize up. The boiler pressure is fine and the thermostat is set at a comfortable temperature on the app. Joe might have messed it up from turning off some of the settings. I'll ask him to take a look when he's home.

I need to move around to warm up, and I take Dora for our afternoon walk. We trudge up the nearest hill. Mist hangs over the field, and Chilwood Cottage looks otherworldly, the hazy light draining it of colour. It blends with the landscape, flint-fronted with its slate-grey roof, the garage in the style of an old barn conversion to suit the surroundings. The house looks traditional, but looks can be deceptive.

You'd never know from here that ours is a smart home. From this angle it's barely spoilt by signs of modern life and could be in a different century, nestled in the South Downs. The first time I saw it, I thought it would make an idyllic escape from everything bad in the world. Now, as I survey it from the top of the hill, it's not idyllic at all. The house is ghostly in the sullen landscape, with no sign of life and low-lying mist creating the illusion of it floating in the valley.

A light turns on in the house and the downstairs windows

look like two yellowed eyes. I jump, scanning from my vantage point for signs that the intruders have returned. Then I remember it's the automated hall light that comes on at dusk. Joe can't have disabled the light settings yet and my attempt to turn off the hub was derailed by the surprise of the loan email.

We walk past Mitchell's house. He comes across as lord of the manor. He's nowhere to be seen, but the hairs on the back of my neck stand up as if I'm being watched. On instinct, I turn towards his upstairs window. *Fuck.*

I recoil and stumble backwards, nearly losing my footing on the uneven track. A telescope is trained on our cottage, and a pair of binoculars rest on the windowsill. My gaze follows the trajectory of the telescope. It's pointed at the side window of our bedroom. I steady myself and stare in dismay.

Seriously? I didn't have him down as a peeping Tom. The urge to march up and bang on his front door is strong, but Dora's off the lead and speeding up now home is in sight. I quicken my pace to catch up, my indignation brewing strongly. His bin patrol the other day might have been an excuse to watch me from the hedgerow.

Back home, I kick off my wellies on the outside doormat and unlock the door. Joe's home and he wraps Dora in an old towel he's had warming on the under-floor heating. He sits with her cradled like a baby, rubbing her wet paws with the towel.

'Bloody Mitchell.' I shake off my jacket.

'What's he done now?'

'He's got a telescope trained on our bedroom window.'

'Really?' Joe looks amused.

'It's not funny. I know he's an old man rattling round on his own, but he's spying on us. He was loitering by the hedgerow the other day, and Nicole had a run-in with him when she came over.'

'He's only checking we're not building anything else to obscure his view.'

'We haven't obscured his view. The council approved the garage, and we didn't need permission for the studio.'

'The studio that he can barely see from his place.' Joe takes his binoculars that we'd left in the hall after checking for hidden devices in the tree, and he stands out the front for a better view of Mitchell's house.

He comes back in. 'I'll talk to him later. Find out what he's playing at.'

'That man who came back after the tour stopped and spoke to Mitchell when he left.'

'Oh yeah?'

'And did Kev mention that he's doing work for Mitchell?'

'No ... is he?'

'I saw his van parked there the other day.' Kev mostly works on developments and hates *changing light bulbs for old dears*.

'Mitchell must've been nosing around and bumped into Kev, asked him to check something out.'

'Did you ask him about that online review from the woman who said he messed with her sound system?'

'Oh yeah.' He scratches his head.

'And?'

'He was completely thrown by it. Said it's fake. He didn't

143

know who the woman was, but then he had a sneaky suspicion his ex-wife's behind it. He's going to contact the review site for it to be taken down.'

'So he's denying all knowledge? That's convenient.'

'It might be someone malicious having a go at him.'

'Or it might be someone genuine.' But I've no way of proving it since the reviewer only left her initials. Ex-wife or not, I'll keep a close eye on Kev.

'It turned ice-cold in here earlier. It's not the first time; there are pockets of cold air in the bedroom.'

'I'll take a look,' Joe says. 'Don't worry about Mitchell. You know he's an awkward bugger. I'll speak to him about the telescope.'

That night, I lie awake, my mind turning over Joe's loan and how everything's gone downhill. I'm trying to return to how we used to be, but it won't happen overnight, the same as our money problems won't be fixed anytime soon.

When I fall asleep, Karl Winter comes for me in my dreams. I'm frozen in fear at the bedroom window, looking down at him on the patio, but it's his CCTV image. He's staring straight at me, those piercing eyes and his haunted, hungry look. When Joe wakes me, I'm whimpering like Dora.

'He's back.' I'm caught in a strange place between reality and the dream.

'Who's back?' Joe strokes the tangle of hair from my face.

'Karl Winter.'

'Karl Winter's dead.'

But is he?

'Hey,' Joe says softly, 'do you remember when that man terrified you in the garden?'

'Batman?'

'Yeah.'

When we first moved here, I'd come home to a man sitting in the dark beside the garage and let out a scream so loud he'd jumped right out of his fold-up chair. 'It's okay, it's okay,' he'd said hastily, recovering his balance. 'I'm doing a bat survey.' The council wouldn't let us replace the asbestos-clad garage with an oak-framed one in case bats lived in there. We couldn't knock it down until they gave us the go-ahead.

Joe keeps stroking my hair. 'Can you believe we paid all that money for a man to sit in a deckchair looking for bats?'

'I can't believe it, no.' It's not the only thing I can't believe. Joe's doing his best to soothe me, but my nerves jangle from the nightmare. 'Do you think it's cursed?'

'What?'

'This house.'

'Jeez, Lauren.'

'Everything's gone wrong. All those problems with the sale, then hassles at every stage of the development and now this.'

'It's to be expected with an old property in the country. The problems with the sale weren't cursed. It was annoying land issues about who owned what, then probate and planning hassles and our cantankerous mate up the road objecting to everything.'

'Hm.'

'Have you started taking the tablets?'

'Not yet.'

'Start them tomorrow, then you'll sleep better. Nothing is cursed.'

Cursed or not, I need to find out for sure that Karl Winter is dead. Since seeing his image on CCTV, I suspect he's connected in some way.

CHAPTER EIGHTEEN

Joe's in the shower and I brush my hair in the bedroom. His phone lights up with a message from Tara. My eyes are drawn to mention of my name.

> Hey, babe, don't worry about Lauren – us women are batty at times!!! You can talk to me anytime. You and me have a bond and we can share stuff. I'm here for you if it gets too much. Xxxxxxx

I am so furious that for a moment I'm paralysed. Then I march downstairs and try to calm down, unsure of who I'm more annoyed with – Tara or Joe. I bet she enjoys undermining me, but Joe's the disloyal one. What's he playing at? I unload the dishwasher to distract myself, clanking pans.

'Everything okay?' Joe comes down and eyes me suspiciously.

'No, it bloody well isn't.'

He gives me a harried look.

'I saw the text that came through from Tara.'

'What text?' He drags his phone from his pocket and frowns at it.

'It flashed on the screen when you were in the shower.'

He scrolls on his phone. 'I haven't had any messages since last night.'

'It came through just now, when you'd left it beside the bed.'

'Look.' He stands beside me and shows me the screen. 'Did you delete it? The last one she sent was the other day about seeing Dylan.'

'I didn't touch it. If anyone deleted it, it's you.'

'Why would I delete it?'

'*Hey, babe,*' I say in a fake Tara voice, '*you can talk to me anytime about Lauren. We've got a bond and I'm here for you.*'

He looks strangely at me. 'Lauren, there isn't a text. Did you imagine it?'

'I don't imagine texts! I read it.'

'Okay. It's not there now though.'

'She called you *babe*.'

'Lauren . . .' His weary tone stokes my anger.

'Have you spoken to her about me?'

'No! Well, I don't know, maybe in passing I mentioned the house stuff. Don't you ever mention me to Brooke or anyone?'

I suppose so, and Brooke always takes my side. But it feels wrong for him to discuss me with his ex, especially after her outburst when Joe had her on speakerphone. Maybe Tara's just taking advantage of the situation and Joe deleted the message. I drop it since it won't achieve anything. At least he knows I won't tolerate her talking shit about me.

Brooke said ages ago that Joe's a Facebook friend of Tara's, but maybe he's checking what she posts about Dylan. Joe thinks Brooke is a troublemaker who's down on men in general. The animosity is mutual since she won't pass up an opportunity to criticise him.

He kisses me before leaving, a distracted, dutiful kiss. When he drives off, I open my laptop and look up the old reports of Karl Winter's death.

Local man drowns after heavy drinking session ... In his drunken state, Mr Winter plunged into the canal ... The unemployed 28-year-old had been undergoing treatment for mental health issues ... his body found face down with his head submerged ... post-mortem examination concluded that he died from drowning, with 'serious intoxication' as a contributing factor ... the coroner said, 'He was four times over the drink-drive limit.'

My head swims and I go onto the patio to breathe cold air. The media coverage doesn't say who identified his body. There's no mention of any family or friends who I might contact to see if they can shed any light on what's happening. Only his grandad went on the record to be interviewed, but he's no longer around. I catch sight of my shadowy reflection in the patio window pane. My face is a picture of dread and fear. I wanted to live here so much and now it feels wrong, as if I'll never settle here.

It's then that I catch a faint drift of music. The sound of a faraway choir seeps into my consciousness and I spin round to locate it. It's barely noticeable at first, just a murmur behind me when I come inside and lock the patio door. It's the sort of noise I would zone out before living here, the sound of life going on around us, music through a connecting wall or an open window. But we don't have neighbours that close anymore.

Joe can't have left music playing because I'd have heard it earlier, and he's disabled the multi-room audio. I strain to hear the sound of melancholy church music. It's vaguely funereal. A chill goes through me at the realisation that I've just looked up Karl Winter's death and can now hear funeral music. It might be coming from my laptop. I close the web browser and email in case I've inadvertently clicked on an advert with music, but the singing and organ playing keeps on from somewhere behind me. The hairs on the back of my neck stand to attention as I swivel towards the sound.

I check there isn't a car pulled up outside playing music, but nothing. I'm totally alone here. I stand at the foot of the stairs and strain to hear. It's coming from up there. I grab a sharp knife from the magnetic strip on the kitchen wall and go upstairs. On the landing, I pause, tilt my head. No, it's more distant. Maybe it is coming from downstairs after all.

There isn't a church near here, but there's Mitchell. Perhaps he's playing hymns in his garden. Admittedly it would be weird, but Mitchell is eccentric to say the least. That must be it and the wind is carrying strains of it to me. I go back downstairs, checking over my shoulder more than once to make sure no one's behind me. I open the front door and go to the low garden gate, but I can't hear it at all out here and there's no sign of Mitchell. It's not windy enough for noise to carry on a breeze. I sense a movement behind me and swing round to see the front door closing. I race to stop it, but it shuts in my face, locked fast.

'Bloody house, I fucking hate you!' I kick the front door and go to the living-room window to check if anyone's in there. But it's the smart tech that's shut the door. I stare at the hi-tech keypad beside the door, but I don't know the latest code. Joe doesn't tell me as he knows I won't bother to memorise it, not when he changes it so often. Nicole emailed the smart hub passcode to us both, but the door entry code is different and I don't know if I can access it through the app. I fish my phone from my pocket to call him.

He doesn't answer straight away and I feel exposed, standing out the front alone, but then he picks up. 'Hey, you okay?'

'I'm locked out. Are you due back soon?'

'Not yet, but I'll give you the code.'

I hesitate, not wanting to go back in there alone, but I suddenly feel ridiculous and Joe will think I'm being weird again.

'Are you still there?' he asks.

'Yes. I heard some music playing and I came out the front, but the door shut remotely.'

'The wind might have blown it shut.'

'It's not windy.'

'The sound system's turned off now, but it might be coming from somewhere else. Did you record it?'

Shit, I forgot, but it was so faint that it might not have picked

151

up anyway. 'No, but I want the door thing turned off so it doesn't lock me out again.'

'Do you want me to come back?'

I hear a slight strain in his voice, the tech coming between us again. 'No, just give me the code.'

Back inside, I waste no time in taking everything I need back out to the studio, which I unlock and step inside for the first time since the aftermath of the ghostly shushing in the garden. I lock myself and Dora in, my phone and car keys within easy reach. No strange music out here, but I can't shake the creeping sensation of the funereal choir after I'd looked up Karl Winter's death.

CHAPTER NINETEEN

I stand in the studio and phone Nicole. Joe doesn't want me contacting her, but she gives me straight answers.

'Hi, Nicole, it's Lauren. How are you?'

'Great thanks, Lauren. I'm with a client. Are you around in about an hour?'

'Yes, I'm working at home. We'll catch up later.'

I should be working on the horse painting, but my mind's buzzing. With Nicole busy, I delve deeper into smart home crime, expecting to read about hacking but instead I find a report called *When smart homes are used for domestic abuse*, about people exploiting the technology to control their partners. They'll lock the other person in, set the temperature uncomfortably low, spy on them. The woman won't know the passwords so even when the man's out, he's still controlling her.

One domestic abuse helpline took a call from a woman who feared she was going mad. She would set the thermostat

153

in her home, but it kept switching to a colder temperature. The doorbell rang when nobody was there. Sometimes, she came home to find the digital access code for the front door had changed without warning, locking her out.

Abusers use phone apps to control internet-enabled devices in the home and to spy on their victims. It's a disturbing form of power play in which victims are left scared and confused.

An expert on domestic abuse says:

A woman will seem crazy for claiming her smart home is being used against her. She can appear paranoid for saying the lights and music turn on and off without her touching the controls when she's alone. If you are in this situation, stay rational and reach out to the police.

When I 'reached out' to the police, Joe told the officer I was paranoid. I close down the search and turn to my canvas, pushing myself to finish the horse painting. Just when I'm calm enough to go back indoors after hearing the phantom choir, Nicole's powder blue Fiat sweeps into the drive. I go to the front door, coffee in hand.

'I'm heading over to see Alistair,' she says, getting out. 'You said you were at home, so I thought I'd drop in.'

'Oh, that's kind of you.'

She comes inside, laptop tucked under her arm, bottle of green juice in the other hand, which she prefers to hot drinks.

'Joe's not here. He's doing repairs at a rental property.'

'How are things going?'

'We've dialled down the tech,' I say as we go into the utility room.

'Is there still a problem?'

'I wanted to go back to basics for a while and turn off the hub.'

'Okay.' She doesn't seem annoyed that I've rejected the smart home.

'Joe's already disabled the sound system.'

She blinks at me in surprise. 'How did he do that?'

'On his laptop the other day, he changed the control panel settings.'

'You can't disable the sound system. It's built-in.'

'But I saw him turn it off.' Or that's what he said he was doing.

She looks confused. 'You can only stop it by shutting down the whole home hub.'

Now I'm confused. Did Joe not realise? He told the doctor that the audio was disabled, as if that supported his view about the psychosis. Nicole opens her laptop and her fingers patter away on the keyboard. Music wafts out.

'That's coming through your sound system, not my laptop. I just clicked on Joe's trial playlist and it worked.'

'Right … he was mistaken then.' I don't want her to think Joe misled me. I don't want to think it either. I trust him so much, it didn't occur to me that the church music came through the sound system, not when he said he'd disabled it.

'While I'm here, do you want to play the track that sounded warped, so I can check it out?'

'Sure.' I call up 'Every Breath You Take'. 'It was this one.'

We both listen to it play at the right speed. After Kev called it a 'stalker song' I wanted to delete it from my playlist. She's trying to work it out, deep contemplation on her face. I like her for not taking it personally, unlike Joe, who won't accept the system's faults.

'Where were you when it sounded warped?'

'The kitchen.'

We go and stand in the kitchen. It sounds fine. Of course it sounds fine.

'Have you heard any other weird sounds through the audio since Joe thought he'd turned it off?' she asks.

'I heard church music earlier, but it was distant and I couldn't work out where it came from.'

Her eyes widen in horror and she takes a step back. 'Oh my God, I've read about that.'

'What?'

'It's a thing with haunted houses. People sometimes hear monks chanting or people singing churchy songs, but they've no idea where it's coming from.'

'Joe never hears anything weird, so why's it only haunted when I'm around?'

'Poltergeist? They attach themselves to someone who's troubled. Not that I'm saying you're troubled.'

Talk of hauntings is enough to trouble me, especially now the nights are closing in and Joe often isn't back before dark. 'Let's say it's the audio. I don't suppose it can be amplified outside, say if we were in the garden?'

'How do you mean?'

156

'Say if the music sounds like it's coming from the garden.'

'Not sure I get what you mean, but the garden hasn't been wired up, so you'd need a speaker out there.'

I stop short of telling her about the ghostly shushing outside or the eerie cold spots in the house, because she'll only go on even more about hauntings. 'How would I shut off the sound system?'

'You just turn off the home hub.'

'Does that affect the WiFi?'

'No. It's connected to the WiFi router, but that works independently, so you can still go online.'

'Would we have CCTV?'

'Not unless you rewire the components that you want to keep separately. But it's easy to turn off the hub. Let me show you.' She turns towards the smart hub. 'Just press this green power button so the light goes off. It closes everything wired through the hub. The CCTV can be rewired separately.'

'Does it mess up the system when it goes back on again?'

'You might need to reset individual aspects. You can restart the app, but it won't do any harm. You're the boss of the smart hub. It's not the boss of you.'

Proving that it's not the boss of me, I reach forward and press the green button so it goes off.

She grins and takes a sip of her juice. 'Doesn't all that coffee keep you awake at night?'

'It's decaf.' Although I often lie awake at night. 'Thanks, Nicole, that's everything I need for now.'

'Enjoy your coffee.' She leaves to see Alistair. I think about men using smart devices as a form of control. *A woman will seem crazy for claiming her smart home is being used against her.* I remember what Joe said to the doctor, and a splinter of pain stabs in my chest.

CHAPTER TWENTY

By the time Joe comes home, I've finished painting for the day and have emailed Brooke in Australia to update her on the latest weirdness. I recount Tara's angry phone rant, but bat away the suggestion that Joe is involved, because she needs no encouragement to criticise him.

I stand at the hob, cooking prawn masala.

'Mmm, my favourite.' He comes up behind me.

'Me or the masala?' I crane my neck to kiss him.

'You, of course.'

'Nicole dropped by.'

He pulls away and goes to the fridge. 'Oh yeah?'

'Yeah. The sound system wasn't turned off.'

'I turned it off. I did it online.'

'She says you can't turn it off online.' I keep stirring.

'Really? That's not what I thought. I must've done something else. Bugger. I'll speak to her.'

'Like you were going to speak to her about how to do it? If you had, she'd have said it's not possible to shut off the sound without turning off the rest.'

'Well, there's no harm done because you haven't heard anything through the sound system since, even if it was *apparently* turned on.'

'It was *definitely* turned on. Nicole played music through it.'

'Okaaay.' He opens a bottle of white.

'And I heard music playing in here earlier.'

'I'll ask her how best to isolate the sound system.'

'No need. I've turned the hub off.'

'What?' He abandons the wine and goes to the utility room.

I reduce the heat under the bubbling pan and follow him. 'Since we agreed to disable it.'

'Okay, Lauren,' he says with sighing frustration.

'Why are you being like this? You agreed to turn it off.'

'It's like you don't trust me, going behind my back to Nicole.' He looks at me with a flicker of resentment. He can't take criticism. We all have our shortcomings and that's Joe's. The smart home is his creation and he takes it as a personal attack that I don't like it.

'I want the bloody thing disabled.'

'Well, now it is, so you've got what you wanted. How are you feeling? Have you started taking the tablets?'

'No.'

'Why not?' He cocks his head.

'I'll talk to the nurse first. Now we've eased off the technology, we'll see how it goes.'

'Please don't go messing around with the hub when I'm not here.'

'Nicole was here. She knew how to do it.'

'Why are you going direct to Nicole? We've already talked about this.' He stands with both hands on his head.

'She turned up on her way to see Alistair. I asked her about the sound because this is our home and I'm trying to understand it.'

'It's a finely balanced system. This is the prototype. We don't want to mess it up by turning it off.'

'Nicole says we won't mess it up.' I'm furious at his churlish response. I bet he never intended to turn it off, stringing me along so he could keep his tech toys. 'Thing is, Joe, you said we could turn it off. Everyone agrees that we should turn it off.'

'Everyone?'

'Everyone we've told about it going weird – Annette, Dr Reeve, even Nicole gets it.'

He gives a sad sigh. 'That's because they're trying to help you. You've got this issue with it so people are being nice.'

He comes towards me. I want to shove him away. He holds my shoulders and I stand firm, keeping my face level with his. 'Don't patronise me. You know what I'm going through. You could've switched it off.'

He steps back. 'I thought we'd turned off the audio—'

'I want us to be on the same side, but you're pushing against me.'

'Hey, we are on the same side.'

'Now you're humouring me. Sorry, Joe, but if you don't believe me, I can't stay here.'

He looks at me as if weighing his words. 'But what if we leave and the problems follow?'

'What do you mean?'

He doesn't reply but the meaning is clear. He thinks *I'm* the problem.

Or, a little voice in my head says, *you won't be rid of the problem while you're with Joe. Maybe he's the problem.*

I freeze. Where did that come from? Are Annette's questions and Brooke's aspersions rubbing off? Do I *actually* suspect Joe? He's always been my shelter from the storms of life, but is he trying to unhinge me? I remember at art school when the wall sprang up between me and my friends because they didn't believe me. What if the paranoia really is returning?

'Lauren?' Joe is looking intently at me. 'Did you hear what I said?'

'I can't take any more of this. I don't want to move out without you, but I will if that's what it takes.'

CHAPTER TWENTY-ONE

Dora and I walk along the edge of the woods, avoiding Mitchell's house, since his telescope will annoy me all over again. Away from the cottage, my head is clearer. Someone wants to get at me through the cottage. Moving into the flat is an expensive option, but we can put the cottage on Airbnb. If Mitchell thinks we're bad, he can have a bunch of holiday-makers instead, not that Joe would go for that.

I have to work out who's doing this and why. Joe is closed off to what's really happening, while I'm making a mental list of suspects. No one quite fits, and Joe doesn't fit at all, not when he wants us to stay here. It keeps coming back to Karl Winter and whether or not he's dead. The only possible link to him is Anorak Man, since he acted suspiciously right before I saw Karl on CCTV. Whatever Joe and the police say about no intruders coming to the house that night, Anorak Man could have been downstairs when Karl was skulking on the patio.

I walk through the side gate with Dora and come to an

abrupt stop. Mitchell's in my studio. It's unmistakably him, from his shock of grey hair and oversized thick-rimmed glasses that look like they've survived the seventies.

Something moves beside him. It's Joe, who'd been bent over, reaching for something on the floor. He straightens up and the two men talk. Why has Joe taken him in there? They step out onto the brick path I laid between the patio and the studio. Joe sees me and waves. I turn and march indoors with Dora.

Minutes later, he lets Mitchell out through the gate and comes into the kitchen.

'What's going on?' I stand with a hand on my hip.

'I saw him coming down the lane, so I confronted him about the telescope.'

'And?'

'And he's a stargazer.'

'Well, he's not going to say he watches me undress.'

'He's harmless, too much time on his hands. He sold his electronics business and doesn't do a lot now.'

'Why did you take him in the studio?'

'He wanted a look. I thought it would keep him on our side.'

'That's my private space, Joe. You can't just take people in there without asking.'

'We just had a quick look. He didn't touch anything.'

'It's one thing having men I don't know touring round our bedroom, and now you've let a man with a telescope pointed at us into my studio.'

'Come on, Lauren. The tour was a one-off. Alistair asked if we'd do it. You and I agreed it would be a good thing. And

164

it's better to keep a dialogue going with Mitchell. He loves the house.'

'Has he been in here?'

'I showed him round last week. I thought I told you.'

'You didn't tell me.' I try to keep my voice even. 'You know he makes me uncomfortable. Can you not respect my feelings?'

'I didn't know you felt this strongly.'

'Well, now you do. I mean ... do I have to spell everything out?'

He's tight-lipped and folds his arms, leaning against the dining table.

'I don't want Mitchell in here. Okay?'

He assesses me warily.

'And if I say someone gives me the creeps, I don't want them in our home.'

'Okay.'

'No one else is to go in the studio.' I'm getting louder and I don't care. 'No one goes upstairs unless they're here for work, with a specific reason to be there. He might have slipped a device in and bugged the place.'

'Lauren, seriously. He hasn't bugged the house. That's ridiculous.'

'Why is it ridiculous? You just said he has an electronics firm. He's watching us, so he might be listening in.'

'I was with them the whole time, Mitchell and the group last week.'

'That's not the case though, is it? That man from the tour broke away to study the hub. You'd never have noticed if I

165

hadn't told you. And someone got in the studio to take my painting. It's no wonder, with everyone you're inviting in.'

'Okay, Lauren. Okay.' He throws his hands in the air and stands at the patio door with his back to me.

I can't see what Joe is finding so incomprehensible. He took the lead in the cottage, and the trade-off was my own low-tech private workspace. We've spent years working on properties for other people, and now we have our own place, it's pushing us apart.

'I know you're still showing the place off,' I say to his back, 'but we've had loads of tradespeople in everywhere we've lived, and then strangers coming to view the properties and poke around. We can stop that now. It's not okay to invite someone I feel uneasy about into my studio.'

'You've made your point, Lauren.'

I go and stand out the front of the cottage to avoid the argument escalating. How can Joe be so naïve? There is definitely something off about Mitchell. We've done nothing to provoke him, but all that time he spends rattling round on his own might have warped his mind. I call the police non-emergency number and leave a message asking to speak to someone about an issue concerning my neighbour.

CHAPTER TWENTY-TWO

I stay in the front garden and check emails. Brooke has replied to my earlier message. I'm too riled for snippy comments aimed at Joe, but she might give me some clarity in her blunt way.

Hi, Lauren,

Oh Christ, it's all kicking off at your place. Shit got real if someone's stealing your paintings. What's going on? It reads like someone's trying to unhinge you, but why . . . have you guys sussed it out yet?

I know you take a dim view of me saying anything against Joe, but you're my friend and I want you to be okay. I can't stand by while bad things happen to you. You won't want to hear this and I don't like to bring it up, but sometimes men have affairs and that might be a motive to freak you out enough that you leave, especially if Joe's making out it's all in your head. There's nothing going on between him and the IT woman, is there?

My stomach churns at talk of Joe having an affair. Other men might have affairs, but Joe isn't the type. And I doubt he's Nicole's type. Neither of them are flirty people, and Nicole's focused on her work. She mentioned boys her own age on Tinder. I can't see them being interested in each other.

> Or what if his bitter ex wants him back? You heard her slagging you off, so she's got it in for you. You only have to see her on Facebook to know she's trouble. All that 'Aw hun, bless you!!!' Fuck off, mate, you're as hard as nails. Those pouty selfies, sticking her tits out in a tight outfit like she's seventeen. Am I being a bitch? I'll stop now because I'm being a bitch. Keep me posted. Xx

Brooke's really stepped up a level, progressing from the scattergun accusations of her previous email to aiming her blows on Joe and his supposed infidelities, but I can't bear to consider a sexual motive. I'd expected her to say *what a bloody cheek* about Tara's phone call. It's a bit of a leap to suggest she's angling to get Joe back, when I didn't even mention her text that supposedly disappeared. But she probably does want Joe back. Brooke mentioned a while back that she'd looked her up on Facebook. *Are you cyberstalking her?* I'd asked at the time.

I'm just a stickybeak, but it's interesting, no?

I wouldn't go near Tara even if I were on social media, but Brooke sent me a screenshot of her selfies. Brooke might be right about Tara trying to look younger. She's thirty-eight, the same age as Joe, and prides herself on looking good. She had

168

the same expression in all the shots, self-satisfied and challenging, accompanied by a comment that she wanted *a handsome reliable man. Any takers?!!!*

Even if she knows her best angles for taking a selfie, she's as clued-up on technology as I am. Until Dylan got into trouble for his hacking, she left him to his own devices on his laptop, so Joe polices him remotely, which Dylan despises.

Dylan and his hacking. That's the thing. Is all this some kind of weird game in Dylan's closed-off life, like *The Haunting of Hill House*? My suspicion has grown since he talked about watching scary dramas, because Dylan is capable of hijacking the smart controls.

When he hacked his school's mainframe, he reset the local admin account password to gain access to their records. It was easily traced to him. When things calmed down, he showed Joe how he did it. He didn't grasp that it was wrong, so we tried analogies like, 'If you saw a home with an open window, would you climb through it and nose around inside?' He said no but didn't really see a connection. So now we don't trust him online. Whether he would hack the smart home is another matter, and I can't bring it up with Joe. I don't say anything bad about Dylan. I just can't, not when he's part of our family.

'Is Dylan back tomorrow?' I say to Joe later, when we're clearing up in the kitchen.

'Yeah. We'll stay out of your way if you're working indoors.'

'That's okay. When you take him home and go inside to see Tara, does he sit with you both?'

'No, he slouches off upstairs.'

Brooke asked if anyone else was in the frame, but I didn't mention Dylan because it felt mean to accuse a child. Plus, I don't want to email something so personal which could be read by someone else. If our smart home can be hacked, so can my email.

I can't shake the idea from my mind. Yet Dylan doesn't know about Karl Winter. Unless ... unless ... did Joe tell Tara, confiding in her at one of Dylan's handovers? He might have overheard or Tara might be directing him. I try to fathom whether he could have set up the ghostly shushing voice.

'Humour me for a minute,' I say. 'Who do we know with hacking skills who could mess up the sound system?'

He stops and stares at me. 'You're not blaming Dylan?'

'He was here on Saturday. Could he have put a tiny remote speaker outside? He came in the garden with Dora. You were round there when it kicked off with the voice outside. If he did it remotely, he had time to go upstairs on his computer after he got home.'

'Fuck, Lauren, he's just a kid.'

'He's your son, and we love him. He's also a kid who's hacked his school's computer system. If it's him, I'd be relieved because it'd be Dylan mucking about and doing his own *Haunting of Hill House*.'

'And that's okay, is it?' He straightens up. 'Problem solved that my son's done something criminal? We can blame Dylan instead of your paranoid thinking. Can't you see what this is doing to you ... to us?'

I wince at the venom in his words. 'No, but listen to me. If he did it, it's not because he means me harm. It's a game, like the Xbox.'

'You want it to be Dylan? Is that it? Blame the easy target. Tara was right.'

'What? What do you mean?'

His eyes flash with anger. 'Most people would be thrilled to live here. You've got what you want. You've got your dream studio out there which you don't like using now. You've got me covering for you with your clients. And what good does it do when you won't even take the meds?'

'Joe, don't—'

'What's the point?' He storms off and slams the front door behind him.

I listen for the sound of his car swerving out of the drive, scattering gravel, but nothing. It's night-time and I don't want to be alone here, even though the friction between us is almost too much to bear, our differences too great. A light in the garage catches my eye. It's where he stays for the rest of the evening.

Joe hasn't spoken to me since our bust-up last night. I heard him in Dylan's room after I'd gone to bed, so he must have slept in there.

I wake up needing to clear the air, and tap on the door. He's not there. He's taken Dora with him, so I start work on the painting, determined to finish it and distract myself from the upset. I paint for longer than usual, enjoying the sense of

171

calm. I weigh up whether we could stay here if life went back to normal, but the house is tainted. Even if nothing strange happens again, I'll always be wary.

Joe's car sweeps into the drive and I stiffen. I hate it when we argue and then after, when we circle warily round each other. He comes in with Dora, who makes a happy beeline for me. I scoop her up, glad to busy myself with her rather than deal with whatever mood Joe might be in after last night.

He perches on the side of my desk and assesses the painting. 'It's looking good.'

'Thanks.'

He reaches over and takes my hand. 'You know I like fixing what's broken. I just want you to be okay again.'

'Am I broken?'

'You might need a bit of mending, that's all.'

'I'm not an electrical item.' I look at his hand covering mine and remind myself that this is what we do in difficult times: I tunnel to safety and Joe shines a light through.

'I don't mean it like that. I know what you're going through. I thought we were going through it together.'

'But you're more bothered about the smart home.'

'No.' He shakes his head. 'I'm trying to help, but it's as if you don't trust me.'

'I do trust you.'

I *do* trust him.

'I've been to check Dylan's devices. He went to his granny's and Tara let me search his room.'

'And?'

172

'Nothing. He's not a bad kid. He's capable of hacking the smart home, but he's not devious or malicious.'

'I know.'

'And how could he have taken the painting when he was back home by then?'

He's right. At least we're talking, but there's an edge between us and a defensiveness in his voice.

'I wasn't saying Dylan means me harm, Joe. I'm just trying to look at this from all angles.'

He nods vaguely. 'I'm going back there for a few hours. Tara's going out with her mum and Harper, so I can hang out with Dylan. You have some space for your painting, and I'll be back for the mental health nurse at four o'clock.'

'Why don't you bring Dylan here?'

'It's sorted with Tara.'

'What have you told her?'

'Nothing much.' He shrugs. 'Just harmless chat over a coffee.'

'I get that you talk to her about Dylan, but I don't like you discussing me ... us.'

He turns his head away as if I'm being unreasonable again.

'It feels weird,' I try to explain without sparking another argument. 'I don't like it.'

'There's a lot that's weird right now. Talking is how I make sense of it.' He gets up.

Why can't he talk to me? He must have suspected Dylan too if he's searched his bedroom. And Dylan has form as a hacker, so I'm not completely out of line.

CHAPTER TWENTY-THREE

I tell myself to rise above it with Tara. Joe's married to me, not her. Before dark, I walk across the field with Dora and my phone rings with a call back from a police officer who introduces herself and asks the reason for my call yesterday.

'Our nearest neighbour along the road had a telescope pointing at our bedroom window.' I walk towards home, my gaze fixed on Mitchell's house. 'My husband challenged him, and he said he was stargazing. Last week he was lurking behind our garden hedge, which I found a bit strange.'

'Is the hedge between your two properties?'

'No, his is further up the road.'

'Anything else?' she says.

'I'm a portrait painter. The other day a painting I'd just finished was stolen from my studio in the garden. And someone might be tampering with our CCTV outside, but they're doing it remotely. Our neighbour used to have an electronics business, so he might have the means to mess around with it. I've no evidence, but I wanted to ask you about him.'

'Does he have access to your house?'

'No, but my husband showed him around without my knowledge.'

'I suggest you change the locks.' She takes my address and Mitchell's details.

I can still see his house, but there's no sign of him. 'Does he have a criminal record?' I ask.

'We can only tell you that in very specific circumstances, say if you have a child who might be at risk or if you're in a relationship with someone with a record of violence. You can't check on a neighbour.'

'I've already checked on him online and there isn't anything suspicious.'

'That's not to say he hasn't committed a crime previously. Data privacy laws mean that anyone can apply for their details to be wiped from search engines. We can talk to him about the telescope and ask about the missing painting. If he has a relevant criminal record, we can take that into account, but we can't disclose the information to anyone who asks.'

'Okay. Is it possible for someone to take our CCTV footage and put an image of a man on it who's not really there?'

'Come again?'

'This sounds weird, but I saw an image on the CCTV of an intruder, but it's a man who died. I think someone did it to freak me out.'

'It can be done with "deep fake" technology. There's been

some fake TV footage of famous people posted online. And then there's deep fake pornography where celebrities look like they've been caught on sex footage, but it's not them.'

'How easily can it be done on CCTV?'

'If someone has access, it's possible to alter the playback and plant something on there. As for seeing the face of someone who's dead, you can get face-swapping apps. Anyone with reasonable IT skills can do it.'

She gives me a crime reference number. If Mitchell has a criminal record, the police might speak to him and stamp it out. And then there's Anorak Man, who spoke to Mitchell from his car, so they could have a connection, strange as that seems.

I need to check with Alistair to see if he's tracked down Anorak Man. I'm convinced his lost key was an excuse, so what would he have done to me if I'd been alone in the house with him? I call Alistair and it goes straight to voicemail.

'Alistair, hi, it's Lauren.' I clear my throat. 'Please can you come back to me about that man from the tour? I need to contact him ... it's important. Thanks.'

If Anorak Man or someone else can lead me to Karl Winter, then it will prove it's not paranoia or Joe that's responsible. Alistair emails a bit later to say no one has replied to his message about the lost key. It must have been a ruse by Anorak Man to get back in here, and he knows we're onto him.

Alistair can't give me any contact details, so I call up his website's blog post about the smart home tour. Four people left comments asking to come on the tour. Three gave their real names and one of them included a photo for his avatar. It's not him. I find the photo of the second named man on LinkedIn, and another has a JustGiving photo of him doing a charity triathlon. I rule out those three and am left with one, MirrorMan, who has no avatar photo. The username doesn't stand out when I google it. He's untraceable to someone with my limited skills.

Nicole emails to check all is okay. *Not really*, I go to reply, and then waver over telling her. She'll start on about haunted woodland and ghosts. She's only joking, but it's Halloween this week and I don't need it spooking me. I close down the emails.

Things are tense with Joe, but we can make things right by moving out on Sunday once the Airbnb guests vacate after their half-term booking. If Mitchell's behind any of this, leaving will play into his hands, but my sanity's more important than standing our ground.

CHAPTER TWENTY-FOUR

Joe delivered the replacement horse painting to the Hansons before it could disappear. I've started the next one of a soulful pair of cocker spaniels, expecting it to calm me, but I'm still churned-up when he returns from seeing Dylan.

'All set for the meeting?' He kisses me. 'I phoned Anja earlier with an update.'

'Anja?'

'The nurse. We need to make best use of her time.'

I know her name's Anja, but I don't like him priming her. Did he tip her off to my resistance to taking the meds? I won't start another argument, so I stay silent until she arrives.

I've tried to look the part with freshly washed hair, understated make-up and concealer blended around my eyes to cover the dark shadows. I've dressed in a white shirt, fitted black jeans and smart black boots, so I don't look too arty in case I'm written off as 'woo-woo'. When Anja arrives, I slightly envy her free-spirited chiffon scarf, bobbly cashmere cardy and flowing skirt over trainers.

'So, Lauren,' Anja says when we're settled round the kitchen table with a pot of tea. Her mild, calm way of talking is almost hypnotic. 'Why don't you start by telling me how you've been feeling these past few days?'

I tell her about the strange sounds that come through the audio and the nocturnal disturbance, and how that's unsettled me in our new home. She nods, and I feel a fraud for taking up her time. You hear about mental health trusts turning away people in dire need. This seems like overkill when others must need her more than me.

'And now it's ramped up,' Joe says. 'Lauren was nearly scared to death by a voice outside, even though the audio doesn't work outside. You can't hear it out there with the doors closed, and a painting she'd finished went missing.'

'Where do you think the painting is?' she asks me.

'I left it locked in the studio in the garden. Whoever's responsible for the weird shushing noise took the painting.'

'Who do you think is responsible?'

'I don't know.' I keep my answers as plain as possible.

'Laur-en,' Joe says in the chiding drawn out way he says *Dy-lan* before a pep talk. 'That's not exactly true. You thought it was a stalker who's dead, and then you thought it was our neighbour.'

Anja writes this down. I bite the inside of my cheek.

'In my defence,' I say, keeping it calm, 'the neighbour was lying in wait behind our garden hedge when I brought the bin in last week, and he has a telescope trained on our bedroom window. The person who installed the smart hub had a run-in with him last week and she said he gave her the creeps, so it's not just me. If he wanted to upset me, it's not impossible for him to get into my studio and take the painting.'

'Okay. Thank you for that.' She assesses me with a cool, objective gaze.

I glance at Joe. 'If you think I did something with the painting, that's not the case. It was a commission and we need the money.'

'You may have experienced a loss of functioning,' Anja says. 'Maybe you weren't coping with the demands of your work schedule, so something happened to the painting as a result.'

Really? Am I so far gone that I can't see it?

'It could have come on as a result of feeling stressed by the smart home and perhaps hearing voices from it.' She flaps one hand vaguely, probably as woolly with technology as I am. 'Even if it feels different to your last episode, hallucinations and delusions are symptoms. With the right treatment, there's no reason why you can't go back to normal within days or a few weeks.'

It's true that the smart home has unsettled me. Could it have triggered a strange reaction inside my head that I'm convinced is real?

'Are you feeling suicidal?' she asks.

'No.'

'You're slipping back to the bad times, though,' Joe says. 'I know you don't want to acknowledge it, but we can't let it happen.'

Anja pauses politely while I ignore Joe.

'Tell me more about the stalker,' she asks.

180

'He followed me and cyberstalked me. He faked revenge porn with my face on naked bodies. Then he hacked my emails to send a link to all my contacts.'

She looks appalled. 'That sounds awful. Were the police involved?'

'They couldn't prove it was him, even though he had a record of stalking and harassment. Joe was out one night and saw him in a bar. He warned the man off and he apparently walked home drunk and fell in the river. He drowned.'

Joe bristles beside me, but I'm showing Anja that bad stuff happens which isn't all in my head.

'I had nothing to do with it, *obviously*,' he says. 'The police cleared me. He fell in by accident, taking a leak in the canal.'

'How do you know?' she asks, tilting her head.

'Because the police said his flies were undone and ... anyway, CCTV showed me driving in the opposite direction, towards home. Lauren forgot to say that I was home with her when he left the bar.'

'I don't think anyone's accusing you,' she says with a watery smile, looking from him to me.

What's happening to us? Upset wells inside me. It's turned into an unspoken competition of who can convince Anja that they're to be believed. It's not a game I want to play. I look at him as if to say, *please don't*, but he looks away. If he can't be supportive, I don't want him here, discussing my mental health as if he's the expert.

'Lauren, before you moved here, when was your last psychotic episode?'

181

'When I was twenty. That was the only one.'

Joe sighs and folds his arms as if losing patience. It's not much, but Anja clocks it.

I flash him a look and keep talking to avoid him jumping in. 'I'd had a psychotic episode when I was a student. It was a one-off, drug-related, so when things got bad, I went back on the anti-psychotics as a precaution. But I've always had a vivid imagination. As a child I was scared of ghosts. Now I channel my imagination into my work as an artist. It doesn't make me psychotic.'

'You had some issues after the stalker died,' Joe says.

'It wasn't an episode,' I say to Anja. 'After he died, I didn't go out much. Joe said I shouldn't let it get the better of me, so I tried, I really did, but when I went to public places, I panicked at the thought of seeing him in a crowd.'

'The stalker?'

I nod and bite my lip. 'I was shaken up by it, that's all.' I reach for Joe's hand. He resists at first, his arms stiff, but then his hand softens and clasps mine.

'So you didn't actually think you saw him?'

'No.'

'I think you're playing it down,' Joe says.

'I never actually saw him. I'd sometimes see a random man who looked like him and I'd panic but then realise it wasn't him.' I say it as mildly as I can, and slide my hand from his. 'It probably seemed a bigger deal to Joe, but it wasn't psychosis. It's different to actually believing he was back and meaning me harm. The detective sergeant on the case said it's not uncommon when you've had a trauma to think you see the perpetrator.'

She nods more vigorously in agreement, rather than her previous *I'm listening so go on* kind of nod.

I have to present myself as rational, because that matters very much. Once you're in the system, they look for signs of someone who's a danger to herself or others. Joe wants to help, but he goes too far.

She tells me about meds and talking therapies. 'You have your support system here with Joe. That's important. Do you have anyone else who's aware of the situation and can help?'

'My friend, Brooke, but she's in Australia. We message a lot. And my CBT counsellor.'

'Good. CBT can help with your coping skills. Do you think it's helping?'

'She helps me see things rationally. She was the first person to suggest we turn off the home hub. Dr Reeve said to turn it off too.'

'Keep talking about it. That can help to rationalise it. I agree about turning off the hub, and start taking the meds, give them time to work.'

'Is it true that if you remove the stressor, you don't need the meds?' I ask.

'If you've removed the stressor – so the smart home – then great. Have you disconnected it?'

'Yes, but only just.'

Joe stiffens, but I don't elaborate.

'If possible, don't isolate yourself here, since that's where the

183

incidents all happen. Can you look at renting a shared space for artists?'

'I feel better now the home hub's been turned off, and we're moving out on Sunday, into a rental property. If it's an external issue, I'm reluctant to be drugged-up.'

Joe's staring at me but doesn't contradict me.

'Short-term medication is part of the treatment plan I'm going to suggest for you, based on the medication Dr Reeve has prescribed. We find it's very helpful and it can calm confusion, sometimes in a matter of hours, even in acute cases.'

'They made me lethargic before.'

'This is a different type, so you might find they don't affect you as much. The earlier the treatment, the better the outcome.'

Joe nods sagely.

'And because it's for brief psychotic disorder rather than an ongoing issue, you needn't be on them long-term. The medication should ease the symptoms or completely eliminate them. Okay?'

I haven't made my mind up yet, so I stay non-committal.

'Email me your new address and I'll check back in with you in one week. You have my number if the situation gets worse.'

We see Anja out and Joe shuts the door. 'What are you playing at?' he says.

'I'm not playing at anything, Joe. This is deadly serious.'

'Exactly. So why pretend everything's okay?'

'We need to talk—'

'How can we get you help if you pretend everything's okay?'

'It's not okay. It's a long way from okay. I admit that *we're* having problems. Maybe you're the one in denial.'

'What's that supposed to mean?' His eyes widen.

I don't know how we're so far apart on this. 'You keep rushing to defend the smart home at my expense.'

'Lauren, the house is freaking you out. I get that. I'm doing what I can, but I'm out of my depth. Can you please just take the tablets?'

'Why do you undermine me when we're around other people?'

'I'm not undermining you. The medical professionals are trying to help you. How can they if they don't know what's going on?'

'I'll be better once I'm away from here. I've taken the flat off Airbnb. We'll go there when the booking ends on Sunday.'

'What's all this about moving into the flat?'

I look at him, confused. 'We talked about it after the painting was stolen. I said I wanted us to go there when the half-term guests leave.'

'We can't afford the rent.'

'Hang on, I said I had to leave and you agreed that we could see about staying there. We can rent this place. I'll upload it as a rental tonight.'

'This is our home!' His face is a picture of dismay. 'We can't rent it out.'

'I can't live here. Not after what's happened.'

'Maybe it's nothing to do with the house.'

'You don't believe me.'

'I'm trying to help you,' he says with a sour note. He goes to the garage, slamming the door behind him.

Dora whimpers in the hall. She's trembling, so I pick her

up and hold her to my chest. 'Sorry, baby.' My neck and shoulders ache with the tension I've been carrying around. Joe's stalling and backtracking maddens me. We're stretched to breaking point.

I watch a YouTube tutorial on how to fit an internal lock. Turning off the home hub isn't ideal when it can be turned back on at the press of a button, so we'd better lock the utility-room door. My carpentry skills aren't great though, and Joe would have to replace the whole door if I bodged it.

The video finishes and an image flashes on the screen. It's me. *It's the revenge porn.* My face superimposed on a naked woman, tanned legs splayed, limbs oiled, propped on shiny black pillows. I recoil. The image disappears before I fully take it in, although it's imprinted on my memory from last time.

The screen goes black and a cursor blinks in the top corner. Three typed words appear on the screen as if someone has hijacked my laptop. Terror grips me.

I'm watching you . . .

CHAPTER TWENTY-FIVE

The screen goes blank again. The blood drains from my face. I press the spacebar, but the typed message is gone along with the porn image. It's not on YouTube or from an email or saved anywhere. Is it possible for someone to even plant it on my screen and remove it so fast? It looked real, from my fleeting glance. I try to get some traction on what's happening. Do I even tell Joe about the revenge porn reappearing? He'll say I should take the meds.

He comes back in when it's dark, his face etched with worry. I'm still shocked from the image and the chilling message, but the evidence has gone so I don't tell him. I leave the YouTube tutorial up, in case the image flashes back on the screen. Then he'll believe his own eyes, even if he won't believe me.

'What are you watching?' he asks.

I angle the laptop screen towards him and make a renewed effort to be reasonable. 'Can we have a lock on the utility room?'

'We don't need a lock.'

'I'd like one.'

Joe goes into the utility room and I follow. He crouches down to rummage in his toolbox, takes out a small roll of black insulation tape and positions a strip over the power switch.

'What good will that do?' I ask. 'Anyone can pull the tape off and turn it back on.'

'But we'll see if it's been tampered with.'

'Joe, you say you want to help me, but you're only paying lip service.'

'Come and sit down.' He takes my hand and we go to the sofa. 'I know you don't want to acknowledge your mental health issues, and I understand.'

'It's frustrating to keep defending myself.'

'You see it as defending yourself. It comes across as you *being* defensive.'

'But—'

'Listen for a minute.' He holds my hands in his. 'Can you at least consider the possibility that there's an issue with your mental health?'

'I'm having CBT, we've seen Anja and the doctor, I get that I'm not doing as well as I could be.'

'I love you and I want you to be okay.'

'But you'd rather stay here?'

His hands clasp mine a little tighter. 'You're way more important to me, but the voice outside—'

I pull away.

'Let me help you. Give the pills a chance. They'll get you

188

through this rough patch. It's not good for you, all this. Let me look after you.'

'By us moving out?'

'Okay. Once the guests have left the flat.'

A gloom has descended over us. We call an uneasy truce and Joe watches a Netflix documentary before he starts nodding off. I can't concentrate. And I can't take any more of this. Joe wakes up and says he'll get an early night.

'It's not even nine o' clock.'

'You stay up. I'm knackered.'

I'm not staying down here alone, so we go upstairs. We usually leave the lights on until we're in the bedroom and then turn them off via the app, but we can't do that now. Joe falls asleep instantly. I'm alert to every sound. The double-glazed windows are closed against the autumnal chill, but it's still a creaky old house. I drift towards sleep—

'Lauren,' a ghostly voice whispers through the dark.

I gasp and shoot upright in bed. *What the—?* I turn on the bedside lamp.

'What?' Joe wakes and reaches out to touch my back.

'That voice. Did you hear it?' I clutch at my racing heart and look at him, appalled. 'Someone said my name.'

'I didn't hear anything. Maybe you dreamt it?'

'No. Someone said my name.' I say it firmly because I didn't dream it.

'What did it sound like?'

'Lauren,' I say in a breathy whisper, my hand still on my fluttering chest.

'A woman or man?'

'I don't know. It was a whisper.' A ghostly whisper that freaked me out.

'Come here.' He eases me back to the pillow.

'It was like that shushing voice outside, but it said my name.'

My mind grapples with what just happened. Joe's falling back to sleep, but I want him to stay awake in case he hears the voice too.

'Can we go and check no one's turned the smart hub on?'

'No one's here except us. There aren't microphones so a voice won't come through the sound system anyway.' His voice is a murmur. 'Kev's back tomorrow. We'll ask him.'

What's going on? I've no explanation for a ghostly voice calling my name. Joe goes back to sleep. It's the first time he's been here to witness something strange happening, and he didn't hear it. Fear gives way to a creeping sense of doubt. What if my mind really is playing tricks? What if Joe's right that if I leave here, it'll follow me?

I lie awake, listening in the silence, holding Joe's hand for reassurance as he sleeps. I'm dimly aware of slow-moving shadows on the edge of my consciousness, but when I focus they're gone. The urge to escape is strong, unless the dark forces are a part of me. When I fall asleep, my night is disturbed by a murky fear of the stalker. The ghostly voice sends chills through me. When I wake to the sun rising, I realise I don't know what's real anymore.

CHAPTER TWENTY-SIX

It's not just Joe who thinks I should be back on the pills. Annette, Anja and Dr Reeve think I should be too. Perhaps everyone else is right. Everyone except Brooke, who would remind me in her blunt way that it's my mind and body subdued by the chemical kybosh of medication, not Joe's. But if I take the pills I'll stop seeing and hearing things and fearing everything. Right now, I want that more than anything.

When we get up in the morning, I'm still bleary-eyed from a restless sleep. 'I'm going to take the meds.'

'Really?' The spark of hope in Joe's eyes gives me hope too.

'Yes. Because if it is in my head, the meds will make it go away and I want that.'

'I do too.' He cups my face and we kiss; not much of a kiss, just a grazing of our lips, but a kiss all the same.

'We need to sort this out,' I say. 'I'll take the pills, so long as we deal with the external things.'

I kiss him again, a sweet little kiss to say we're still a couple and we can be good together. I expect him to downplay the external factors, but he sits facing me on the sofa and asks what we need to do.

'We'll move out temporarily on Sunday and stay in the Airbnb until things are stable. The home hub stays off until then and I'd like a lock on the utility-room door.'

Joe goes straight to it, finding a lock in his maintenance supplies in the garage. He's doing his best. I chat to him while he crouches by the door and fits the lock.

'Here.' Joe finishes off and hands me the keys. 'Try it out.'

The keys work and we take one each. 'No one else can get in here. Just us. Have you heard any strange voices since that one in the night?'

I shake my head, still keeping quiet about the porn image.

'The tablets will kick in soon enough,' he says.

The lock is a peace offering in return for me taking the pills. I go to the sink and waver over the packet of anti-psychotics, and then fill a glass with water and take a pill.

The day passes without incident and I go to bed early, my eyes heavy. Anja was right about the meds working within hours. It's already blotting out the fear and suppressing my hyper nervous system. Maybe it will keep things under control until life is stable again. The pills knocked me out swiftly last time, and better sleep is a bonus when night-times are the worst and I don't trust what I see and hear anymore.

The next morning, I wake up after an unbroken sleep, feeling the first sluggish effects of the medication. I slept well but can already feel the pills slowing me down, turning me docile. I fight against it and go to crack on with the painting. With a mug of coffee in my hand, I step inside the studio, gasp and drop the mug.

It's the missing painting.

The mug smashes on the brick floor, brown liquid spraying and pooling. Mouth agape, I stare at the original horse painting, propped in front of the wood burner.

'What's wrong?' Joe's voice comes from behind me. 'I opened the patio door and heard your mug smash.'

I turn to him and then look back at the painting.

'Oh,' he says, seeing it too. He steers me back from the puddle of coffee and broken china at my feet. Then he stands the canvas on the ramshackle worktop and grabs a cloth to mop up the spilt coffee.

'How did it get back in here?' he asks.

'No idea.' I keep staring at the picture as if it will reveal the secret. Only Joe and I have a key to the summerhouse. It can't be opened remotely through the smart features. 'I haven't seen it since it went missing. Someone's got in here.'

'Was it unlocked?' Joe looks up at me from where he's crouched beside a sodden cloth, building a neat pile of broken china.

'No, same as it was locked when it was taken. Someone has a way in.'

He rips a square of kitchen paper from the roll on the work-top to dry his hands. 'Did you lose the other painting too?'

'What painting?'

He nods to a much smaller work in progress beside the wood burner, which must have been propped behind the horse painting. He lifts up the cottage portrait that I'd intended to give him for Christmas.

'I'd forgotten about that one. They must've taken them both.'

'Interesting.' He holds it at arm's length to assess. 'It's a different style for you, more Gothic.'

I look at it from a few steps away. It's certainly darker in tone than I remember.

Joe swears under his breath.

'What?' I look from him to the painting.

'The bedroom window.'

Coming closer, I see a ghostly face has been painted in from Edvard Munch's *The Scream*, the shocked white skeletal face looking out in horror, the hands clasping it.

'Oh God. Who did that?' I back away. It's monstrous. Icy fear grips me. Did someone deface it here using my paints?

'Good job Dylan hasn't seen it.' He points at a crude addition of Dylan cross-legged on the lawn with a laptop. It's his thick, dark hair with an evil Joker-style smile, nothing like his sweet smile. The 'scream' person in the window looks down on Dylan.

'I didn't do it. I wouldn't paint that. It's sick.' I grip the wooden worktop with one hand, the other covering my mouth.

Joe casts me a hurt look, as if he doesn't believe me. 'You say that you sometimes paint in a trance state . . .'

'Joe! It was supposed to be a present for you. I'd never paint Dylan like that. Someone's defaced it. Remember how you looked all over the house for the horse portrait? It wasn't anywhere. I'd have needed to consciously hide them both and then bring them back. How is that logical, when I didn't want to redo it?'

Joe leaves the canvas on the worktop and walks back towards the house. 'Don't let Dylan see it.'

After he's gone, I pace around the garden, a mess of shock and upset. I perch on the edge of the garden bench and close my eyes, but I still see the hideous 'scream' face looking down on a ghoulish Dylan who's up to no good on his laptop.

I go back to the studio and wrap the broken mug bits in old newspaper left behind by the previous occupant, that I'd kept to use on the fire. Who's been in here when only Joe and I have a key? I force myself to look at the unfinished painting of Chilwood Cottage, the ominous sky, the tendrils encroaching. The painting feels alien, ruined, the face in the window too much to handle. But even before someone defiled it, it's strange to see the painting now. So much has changed, when I only started it a week or so ago. I wonder about my dark rendition, the foreboding creeping out even before any of this started happening.

Joe's right that it's darker than my usual style. Did I somehow go off the rails and paint Dylan and the face in the window? It's not plausible, but now I'm taking the meds I'll reserve judgement until they balance me out. In the meantime, I can't have my livelihood threatened, so I paint all day to prove that I still can.

CHAPTER TWENTY-SEVEN

Joe wakes me with a coffee the next morning, his cheeks flushed from the brisk outdoor air. 'Hi sleepy. You looked so peaceful, I wasn't sure whether to wake you.'

'What time is it?'

'Half nine.'

'What?' I push myself up in bed. I haven't slept this late in ages. It's the meds taking hold, the same as last time when they muffled the fear and sent me to sleep for twelve hours at a stretch.

'I've walked Dora and I'm off to see Dylan for the day. How's it going with the tablets?'

'I'm a bit woolly-headed.' The dulling effects of the pills are already slowing me down and blurring my thoughts. I should have got up earlier for a walk to clear my head.

'Take it easy. I'll be back by five.'

He kisses me, his face cold, and he leaves. My mouth is

dried-out so I lean back on the pillow and drink the coffee. Dora curls beside me and I stroke her absently.

'We'll get through this, Dora, and I'll wean myself off the tablets.'

It takes a monumental effort to haul myself up, but I make it into the shower to wash away the grogginess. When I start painting, it's obvious the fog of medication has descended, leaving me weighed down and stupefied, my energy drowned out. But painting gives me a focus, so I keep on as if I can paint my way out of this.

When the spaniels portrait is finished, I walk Dora before dusk, the landscape misted in fine rain. Joe's car pulls in just after five, when I'm clearing up for the day. He stays in the driving seat, talking on the phone. Halloween night is set to be a washout, not that we'll be visited by trick-or-treaters. No one will trudge half a mile along a pitch-black muddy track to reach us.

He comes inside. 'I have to go back.'

'Back where?'

'To Dylan. He was okay when I left, but Tara's just called.'

My heart plummets. 'What's wrong?'

'Kids have been throwing eggs at his bedroom window and someone shouted, *Dickhead Dylan.*'

'Oh, poor Dylan.'

'He's having a meltdown and Tara's trying to settle Harper. I tried calming him down on FaceTime but it's not enough. I'll go and sit with him for a while.'

'I'll come with you and wait in the car. Then I'll see if the kids come back.'

'That's sweet of you, but I'm not having you sitting in the car while I'm inside. You stay here. Tara can take over when Harper's asleep.'

Dylan's need is greater than mine. Anyway, the medication has evened me out, when a couple of days ago I'd have been twitchy at Joe leaving me here alone on Halloween night. I'll tolerate the brain-numbing effect of the pills for the sake of dialling down my fear factor.

Joe brought my car into the garage the other day to vacuum it out and I haven't driven it since. I'll keep my keys beside the internal door to the garage and can drive off if things turn weird. I won't even need to venture out in the rainy night on foot.

'I'll make a fish pie. Will you be back to eat?'

'I'll be back by eight. We'll eat then.' He kisses me on the forehead and leaves.

Dark clouds block out any trace of moonlight. I select a claw hammer from the toolbox as a makeshift weapon. Hammer in hand, I close all the curtains upstairs. Coming back down, a scratching noise grabs my attention, the sound of fingernails tapping on a window. I steel myself and follow the sound to my temporary studio at the front, where a dark shadow moves on the floor. Heart in mouth, I tighten my grip on the hammer and look at the window, terrified of seeing the ghoulish figure of Karl Winter, his repellent stare, fingers tapping on the windowpane.

Holding my breath, I realise it's the rose bush in front of the window, silhouetted by the garage light as it sways in the wind, one ragged branch scraping and tapping at the wet glass.

I breathe out and calm my racing heart. The pills don't suppress everything, but without them I'd be an unholy mess.

Cooking will keep me busy until Joe's back. I fiddle about with the manual switch for the smart glass blackout downstairs, and leave the hammer resting on the worktop while I peel potatoes. I set the robo-vac to buzz around upstairs, since Dora the scaredy cat is in the kitchen waiting to be fed. By seven thirty the pie is bubbling away in the oven when a message pings through from Joe.

> Dylan's still freaked out. Turns out he's being bullied online as well as having eggs and abuse thrown. Sorry, sweetheart, can you eat without me? My phone's nearly out of charge, so I won't text again. Remember to take your pill. I'll be back before bed. x

My heart twists for Dylan, mixed with a familiar surge of protectiveness. I take today's tablet with some water, grimacing at the bitter taste of the uncoated pill, and then watch a rom-com, anything to distract me. At ten, Dora nips out in the drizzle of the garden and I stand by the back door, clutching the hammer, which feels heavy in my hand. I try not to imagine Karl Winter hiding in the bushes.

Every rustle in the trees, every creature in the undergrowth is someone out to get me. Each sound is magnified, the garden alive with some malignant force. Tension ripples through me, but the meds flatten out the worst of it. Dora darts back in.

She takes the first few stairs and looks back to check I'm

following. I was going to wait up for Joe, but I'm tired. I leave the hall and landing lights on. The sensation of being watched is still there, despite the meds, since it's early days. I try to ignore it and when I'm ready for bed, I tuck my mobile under the pillow.

CHAPTER TWENTY-EIGHT

Dora wakes me. I must have sunk into a thick sleep, but now her rumbling growl goes right through me. The hairs on my arms stand on edge. The bed's shaking. *No*, Dora's shaking and butting up close to me. It's happening again. With a sickening sense of dread, I hear a voice downstairs. My breathing hitches. It's ice-cold in here. I place a steadying hand on Dora and sit up, grabbing the hammer beside the bed.

Wait . . . Joe's back. I can hear him downstairs, talking on his phone. I switch the bedside light on and shuffle to the landing, groggy.

'Joe?' I call out.

Silence. The lights go out. I catch my breath. Is there a power cut?

'Joe?'

I can't hear him now. I stand dead still, don't move a muscle, surrounded by silent menace. My eyes haven't adjusted to the claustrophobic dark, not even a glow of moonlight to help me see.

'Lauren.' Joe's whispered voice sounds unnervingly close. 'I'm going to kill you.'

I gasp and instinctively clutch my throat. My blood runs cold. *What ... where?* I can't make out the shape of him in the darkness. Can he see me? What's going on? Oh God ... somebody help me.

I fumble towards the banister, one shaky arm outstretched. Something rushes at me with a whirring sound. I scream. The robo-vac's been activated and butts into me. The shock of it sends me reeling backwards into the wall. Dora scuttles downstairs. My back's pressed against the wall. Someone's turned on the hub. Is it Joe, here in the darkness?

Blind with panic, I'm desperate to escape. My trembling fingers reach for the staircase handrail. I pick my way down the stairs, terrified someone will knock me headlong. Dora's already bolted through the dog flap; I heard her go barrelling through. I wish I had her instinct to pelt downstairs with no inhibitions, but fear engulfs me, like a nightmare where you have to escape the terror bearing down, except your legs don't work properly. Mine are shaking like crazy.

Then I hear it. The ethereal voice that I first heard outside. *Shush, shusssh, shuuusssh.* My stomach drops in pure fear and the blood drains from me. The house is possessed. I'm an easy target, every agonising moment of coming down the stairs in the dark, trying not to break my neck. My phone's under the pillow. I'd have grabbed it if I hadn't heard Joe ... can't go back ... fuck, but it's bad.

'Laur-en.'

It's the voice. The ghostly voice from the other night, in a sing-song whisper.

'Laaaaur-ren.'

It's taunting me, sounding so close. The hairs rise on the back of my neck and I can almost feel the breath on my skin. I force myself forward in heart-stopping fear. So dark. The house turns eerily silent, and I try to calm my panic but it's futile. The danger could come at me from any direction.

Then I hear an urgent whisper, too quiet to make out the words. There it is again, a little louder, the same woman's voice whispering.

'*Fear and guilt are sisters.*' It's loud enough to hear, not that I want to hear. Not that it makes sense.

Then the music starts. The opening bars from 'Every Breath You Take' morph into a slow-mo distorted headfuck of sounds. Dread twists inside me, matching the mood of the music. An image flashes in my head of the cottage painting, the branches like bony, grasping fingers, reaching out for me. I steal a glance over my shoulder and miss my footing. Stumbling down the last few stairs, I collapse in an awkward heap on the floor. Blood roars in my ears, my entire body trembling.

The music keeps on. Part of me wants to huddle in a ball. If I die here, curled helpless on the floor, will Joe still think I've imagined it, that I've scared myself to death? The darkness bears down on me, I can almost feel its weight. If I make it to the kitchen, I could grab a razor-sharp knife glinting in the dark from the magnetic strip on the wall, but it's further from the front door.

I have to get away. I shift onto my hands and knees. It's

freezing in here, but I'm slick with sweat. My clammy palms pressed to the floor, I push myself up and pain knifes through my right heel and ankle from falling down the last few stairs. Stars shoot in my vision from the searing agony. I hobble towards the door, trying not to put pressure on my injured heel.

Car key— I fumble round and grab it, clutch it like a tiny dagger. Thank God it was where I'd left it. I lurch to open the front door. It won't budge, locked remotely. I'm trapped, whimpering like Dora because I'm going to die in here. I yank at the door, frantic to escape and wheezing with fearful breaths. It's useless, the door's locked firm. There's a way to override it but I can't work it out in the dark.

'Lauren.' It's a sharper whisper, closer. Another wave of terror rips through me.

Don't look behind you.

But wait, my car's in the garage. I'd forgotten in my terror. I pivot and lurch towards the internal connecting door. It opens and I cry out with relief. The garage light activates from the door opening and I limp barefoot to my car, squinting from the harsh overhead light. A quick check confirms that no one is hiding in the back, and I throw myself in the driving seat. Safely inside, I lock the doors.

I'll get help and come back for Dora, who must be cowering in the garden. I start the engine and flick the switch for the garage door to open. I take a breath. Nothing happens. The door doesn't open. All my muscles tighten and I take a few gulpy deep breaths. Something's wrong. The air ... I try to inhale ... it feels like ... I splutter, try to get out but it's too late.

CHAPTER TWENTY-NINE

Last night, I dreamt the house tried to kill me. My eyes are still heavy from the meds and it's a monumental effort to push through the grogginess. My muscles ache and it's harder than ever to open my eyes. I must be coming down with something.

The terrible dream ended with me being gassed in the car. It seemed real, but I'm lying in bed so I must be okay. A sour, chemical taste coats my dry tongue and throat. My ribs are sore and it's painful to breathe, my mouth so parched it hurts. What's wrong with me? It's like a hangover but immeasurably worse.

I go to turn in bed, but it's not right. The sheet is stiff. Strange noises break through my consciousness. A voice echoes down a tunnel and pulses around my sore head. A clank of metal drops on a hard floor. The rhythmic whirr and squeak of rubber wheels trundle towards me. Where am I?

I force my eyes open and my vision blurs and swims. I'm in a side room in a hospital ward. I blink a few times, trying to work it out, squinting at the corridor through the large window alongside the bed. A woman wheels a trolley past. My mind connects the dots. It hits me with a deadening thud that the nightmare was real. I clutch the sheet and try to remember what happened after I went to the car, but it's a blank.

Just moving my eyes dizzies me. I try to sit up and pain sears through me. I wince and take it slowly, shuffling up in the bed. My forehead throbs and a shrill laugh from the corridor reverberates inside my skull. A flu-like achiness weighs down my limbs, and my arm shakes as I reach for the plastic water jug and beaker on the table. My throat feels as if I've been screaming, but I don't remember screaming.

I take a few sips of water to wash away the bitter taste coating the inside of my mouth, and slump back, exhausted from the effort. I'll replace the blue hospital gown with my own clothes when I find them. That way I can look like a normal person when the medical staff come, because I need them on my side.

At least the room has its own bathroom, since I don't have the strength to walk down the corridor. It takes ages to hoist myself up so I'm sitting on the side of the bed. I manage to stand, but my legs nearly give out and a wave of nausea hits me. I crumple back on the bed, one leg hanging off the edge.

I strain to make it up again. On my second attempt, I take a step towards the bathroom and my head spins. I buckle, about to pass out and I collapse back on the bed until the dizzy spell eases.

On my next try, I go the long way, holding the wall and shuffling like a frail, elderly person. A twinge of hurt in my ankle reminds me of stumbling downstairs, the awkward fall and sheer terror. The pain is less acute now and I can put pressure on my foot.

Fighting dizziness, I make it all the way and catch sight of myself in the bathroom mirror. My hair is wild, my skin ashen, eyes bloodshot. I splash water on my face and try to smooth my tangle of hair so I look like someone with a normal life. The dizzy spell worsens and there's a high-pitched ringing in my ears. I lean against the basin and wipe away tears.

I make it back to bed, and press the call button hanging over the metal slats of the headboard. A nurse comes in and picks up my notes hooked at the end of the bed. 'How are you feeling?' she asks in a heavy accent. Spanish, I think.

'My head hurts. What happened to me?'

'The doctor will see you. I'll check if I can give you something for your head.'

'Please can you call my husband? I'd like to know what happened.'

'Sure.'

I must have gone back to sleep as I'm dreaming again, but it makes no sense. I'm aware of a presence beside me and open my eyes. Joe's standing over me and I nearly cry with relief. I manage a woozy smile, and he bends to kiss me on the forehead.

'Dora?' I ask, fearing the worst.

'She was cowering in her basket. She's fine though. I nearly smuggled her in to see you, but I dropped her off at Chris and Ava's on the way here. I left her running around with their kids.'

'What happened?' I ask.

'I was hoping you'd tell me,' he says with a forlorn smile,

holding my hand. It's taken a toll on him too. There's a darkness in his eyes and a nervous look he only gets when stressed.

My throat's still sore, but I tell him about last night: going to bed with the lights on, waking up in the dark and hearing his voice.

'You actually heard me say that?' He looks at me in horror, one hand pressed over his mouth. 'It wasn't me. I was lying on Dylan's bed trying to settle him. I know I promised to come home, but I was knackered. I fell asleep beside him. I'm sorry.'

Thank God it wasn't him, because how could Joe say he wanted to kill me? That really was madness. Of course, it wasn't him, I know that. So why am I relieved to hear his explanation?

'I thought you were doing really well on the meds. They seemed to be working.'

I gasp and it brings on a coughing fit. When I stop, Joe hands me the beaker of water. 'Do you still not believe me?' I choke out the words. 'Someone tried to kill me.'

'I do believe you.' He's trying to reassure me but his eyes are troubled. 'It sounds like you were freaked-out in the night again and there must be a fault with your car that caused an exhaust leak.'

'Joe, stop this. Someone tried to kill me.' My brain's still trying to recover from the effects of last night, but I have to keep a grip on what's happening. He's towering over me. I drag myself upright and he adjusts the pillows for me to lean back on.

'You need to rest. The doctor said your brain was starved of oxygen from carbon monoxide in the car. You've been cognitively impaired, so you won't think clearly for a while.'

'It's not permanent though?'

'Too soon to say. The best you can do is rest.'

The poisoning from the car fumes must have seared my mouth and throat. There's a tightness behind my eyes and all over my skull.

The doctor comes and checks me over. I have to muster my concentration.

'What's wrong with me?' My vision's still blurred and I can't focus on her.

'You were brought in with carbon monoxide poisoning.' She listens through her stethoscope and doesn't look at me. 'Did you do this to yourself?'

'No. I was trapped in my car, and then I woke up here. Someone was trying to scare me at home, but it was dark and I couldn't see.'

'Okay.' She writes something on my chart and doesn't ask me to elaborate. 'We have to ask in case you're suicidal.'

'I'm not.'

Joe gives me a look.

I ignore him and try to present myself as a coherent person. 'Might there be lasting damage?' I hope Joe's got it wrong, the same as he's got it wrong about why I'm here.

'A lack of oxygen rendered you unconscious,' she says. 'We gave you a high dose of oxygen when you were brought in to increase your levels and to remove the carbon monoxide from your blood. It'll take you a while to feel better because your vital organs didn't have enough oxygen to function. It can cause damage, but it's too soon to say. We'll monitor you for signs of neurological and cardiological damage.'

'When will I get the all-clear?' Assuming I do.

'It'll take at least six weeks. There's sometimes a delayed deterioration.'

Before I can process this, two uniformed police officers walk this way along the corridor, a tall man and a stout woman with auburn hair in a bun. They go to the nurses' station and talk to someone who's out of my sightline. I'd like to ask for their help in unravelling what's going on, but I can't manage to get up, and they'll be busy, here on important business.

'How long do I need to stay here?'

'We'll discharge you tomorrow, if all goes well.'

The nurse comes to the door and signals for the doctor. She goes out to talk to the officers. Joe tops up my water and offers me the beaker, still looking at me with serious concern. If I had the energy, I'd be furious at him still doubting me, but I'm too befuddled.

The doctor goes striding down the corridor, her white coat flapping behind her, and the nurse opens the door to my room for the police officers to come in. Joe hasn't noticed them yet. When he turns and sees them, his hand grips mine harder. I put the water down before it spills.

'Joe Geddes?' the female officer says. 'Can you step outside, please?'

Joe releases my hand and goes outside without even looking at me. The male officer walks him along the corridor where I can't see them, and the woman pulls up a chair beside the bed. I'm less interested in her than in what Joe's telling the other one about my mental state.

'What's going on?' I ask.

'We need to speak to your husband. He'll be coming to the station to answer some questions, and I'd like to talk to you about what happened last night.'

I tell her everything I know, desperate for someone to take me seriously. She makes notes. I reach the part where I blacked out after locking myself in the car. She nods.

'We believe an attempt was made to kill you.'

I stare at her. 'Do you know who?'

'We'd like to talk to your husband.'

'Strange things have been happening at home, but Joe doesn't know any more than me.'

She purses her lips and looks down at her pad, and then her gaze lifts to meets mine. 'Your husband will be helping us with our enquiries.'

I lean back on the pillows. It's an effort to follow what she's saying. If I don't concentrate hard, my mind drifts off and I can't let my concentration slip away. 'What happened last night?'

'Someone deliberately blocked your car's exhaust. It sounds like that same person hijacked your smart home controls and trapped you in the garage.'

I press my palm to my forehead. At least they believe someone tried to kill me and it's not in my mind, but I'm floored that someone did this. It feels so much worse hearing it from somebody else.

'Do you know anyone who'd want to kill you?'

'No one.'

'What about your husband?'

CHAPTER THIRTY

The police officer is still with me when a nurse comes in and takes my blood pressure. I think of Joe's voice in the darkness, threatening to kill me. It's been an effort to take in what's happening. So easy to drift off, my head steeped in fog from the carbon monoxide poisoning. The three of us are silent while the cuff inflates and the monitor gives a reading.

'It's quite high,' she says, noting it down. Hers would be too.

When the nurse leaves, the officer carries on. 'My colleagues in CID will visit you. They'll be talking to your husband and you'll be kept informed. If there's an ongoing investigation, it's likely that he'll be told not to contact you.'

'But what if it's not him?' Even though he said he was going to kill me, his voice coming through the sound system – but I'm too shaken and confused to work it out.

'We want you to be safe, so if you feel in danger from anyone at all, press your emergency call button and tell whoever responds to call security.'

I try to push past the disorientation and nausea. The nurse comes back and asks if I want them to inform anyone I'm in hospital. It hits me that I only have Joe and the blow nearly undoes me.

'There isn't anyone except my husband.'

'The police think he did this to you.'

I nod.

'You need to rest and get well. Press your call button if you need us.'

I have an urge to phone Dale and Kim, since they're my only family other than Joe and Dylan. I miss them, but I can't call them out of the blue. If Dale still sees Joe as a capitalist pig, he'll view what's happened to us as karma. They can't still bear a grudge after all this time, so I'll give it another go with them when I'm feeling better.

I drift in and out of sleep until a tall woman in a grey suit comes to the door, carrying a black holdall. Her dark hair is a mass of tight ringlets. I've no idea what she wants until she introduces herself as Detective Constable Karen Jones. The nurse leaves and the DC angles a chair towards me. 'I know you've been through it all with my colleague, but I'd like a handle on what's been going on.'

I tell her everything, including about Karl Winter and seeing him on the CCTV. 'Do you think he's connected to it?' I ask.

She listens intently, sitting forward in the chair, but now she leans back and looks doubtful. 'I'll check with my colleagues. Your house is a crime scene, but I went in and picked out what you might need.' It's only when she lifts up the holdall, I realise it's Joe's. It makes me want to cry all over again.

'I've put some clothes in for hospital and for when you're discharged, and some of your toiletries. I hope that's okay.'

'Thank you.' It's a relief, since Joe didn't bring me anything. He probably didn't have a chance. 'What's happening to Joe?'

'He's been arrested on suspicion of attempted murder.'

'Why ... what makes you think he did it?'

We've found incriminating evidence on his devices.'

'What evidence?'

'I can't go into detail until we have the full picture, but his search history indicates that he meant you harm.'

'*What?* That's not true ... it can't be.' I know I had my doubts, fuelled by Annette and Brooke, but it never added up. I've heard of men doing terrible things to their wives, but Joe isn't like that. He has a conscience. He was worried for me, or did I misinterpret it? My leaden thought processes slow me down.

'What's so bad about his search history?'

Her expression gives nothing away. 'We've found some disturbing content that's been deleted from his devices.'

'Joe wouldn't try to kill me.' I should ask what disturbing content they've found, but I can't bear to hear it, not yet.

'We're still working out what went on. Your husband has some debts—'

'Hang on. Joe saved me. He came home and rescued me. No one else would've found me in the garage. If he wanted to kill me, he'd have left me in the car.'

'He didn't save you. Our officers had to go and wake him at

215

his ex-wife's house after you were admitted to hospital.' Her voice drips with disapproval.

'So how did I end up here?'

'Your smart home supplier had an alert about a malfunction. Someone attended an emergency call-out and found you.'

'Nicole?'

She shrugs. 'I don't know her name. My colleague spoke to her and she's been helpful.'

'Hang on. Joe can't be the only suspect. I phoned the police the other day to check on our neighbour who's been acting strangely.' I tell her about Mitchell.

'Does he have a key or any means to enter the house?'

'No, but Joe showed him around the other week.'

'He invited a man in who you find creepy?'

I nod and realise I've shredded a tissue into tiny pieces, now scattered on the bed sheet.

'My other half wouldn't do that to me.'

But Joe didn't realise. Or did he? I'm too shattered to know.

'And there was a tour of the smart home that our architect arranged. One man was a bit too interested in the home hub, and I didn't like the way he looked at me. Then he came back when I was alone and wanted to come inside.'

'Your husband agreed to the tour?' Her sceptical look implies that he invited strangers in to unsettle me.

'His architect arranged it, but Joe was keen to show the place off. Oh, and two paintings I was working on went missing from my locked studio. Then someone put them back having defaced one of them.'

'Who had a key to the studio?'

'Just Joe and me.'

'Where's the defaced painting now?'

'I left it locked in the studio.'

She writes it down. 'Can we take it as evidence? Just the one that's been tampered with.'

'Sure. I don't want it back.' Not now it's been ruined by the ghoulish addition of Dylan. I wish whoever did it would leave him out of all this.

'We'll keep your husband in for questioning, so he's not a danger to you in here. It's likely that when or if he's released it'll be a condition of his bail that he can't contact you. Where will you go when you're discharged?'

'I'm not going back to Chilwood.' I'd rather sleep in my car, although the police have probably taken it to look for evidence.

'Is there someone you can stay with?'

'We manage an Airbnb flat that's vacant. I'll stay there.'

'Change the locks as soon as you move in.'

My head swims and it's hard to take it all in. Her no-nonsense approach is helpful, but can I trust the police version of the facts?

'What about seeing the stalker on CCTV?' I say.

'It's possible someone used fake footage to scare you and then removed it.'

They're playing a clever game, trying to destabilise me and conceal every bit of evidence. I picture the revenge porn image flashing on the screen and Joe at his laptop, but my head's a mess and I can't reconcile the two.

'We're still investigating. We believe an attempt was made to kill you. We're taking it seriously, and you should too for your own safety.'

'Can I talk to him?'

'No. As I said, when or if he's released, it's likely he'll be told not to contact you directly or indirectly.'

I cover my sore eyes with the palms of my hands.

'It's for your own protection. Do you have any family or friends you can stay with?'

'I'll be okay in the flat.'

'Can you give me the address?'

I reel it off and she writes it in her notebook and then delves into her black leather bag. 'Here's your phone back. Your husband gave us the passcode for it. We needed to check it over.'

She stands up and hands me a business card. 'This is my number. And call 999 if you're in danger.'

When she leaves, I sink further into the pillows, still reeling from the revelations. Left alone in the hospital bed, I grapple with the enormity of life without Joe, unless they have it wrong. Of course they have it wrong.

A nurse wheels in a medicine trolley and asks if I want more paracetamol. My head still throbs, so she doles out two tablets into a tiny paper cup. So long as they aren't anti-psychotics, because I'm done with them. I knock back the pills and turn on my phone to a message from Ava saying they're looking after Dora. She's added a photo of her two kids hugging Dora. I phone her.

'Hi, Ava, it's Lauren.'

'Lauren! Are you still in hospital?'

'I'm staying in overnight. Please can you keep Dora for me?' I don't know what to say about Joe, when they're unlikely to know that he's been arrested.

'Have the police let Joe out yet?' she asks.

'They're keeping him in until they've checked out what's been happening. How do you know?'

'Chris sorted out a solicitor for him. Why's he been arrested?'

'Strange things went on in the house when I was alone. Like that night you dropped him back home when the police were there.'

'But Joe wouldn't harm you. It's totally out of the question. Do you really think he'd kill you?' She's exasperated, as if it's my fault.

'No, but they took him away. They won't let me talk to him.' My voice quavers as a sob builds in my chest. 'I've no idea what's happening. I don't have much charge left on my phone. You sure it's okay about Dora?'

'Sure. What do you need? I can bring anything in for you.'

'No. I'm fine. I just want it sorted out.' It's kind of her to offer, but she'll make a case for Joe as if I'm responsible for his arrest.

'Phone me and I'll pick you up when you're discharged.'

'Thanks.' I end the call, wary of saying too much, since she and Chris are Joe's closest friends. I have to start thinking straight. I'd hate to always have this groggy head, as if I'm permanently waking from a heavy sleep, with no idea what's true and what's not. All I want is to sink away to a deeper place where none of this hurts so much. Closing my eyes, I drift off to sleep.

CHAPTER THIRTY-ONE

'Knock, knock.'

I open my eyes to Nicole coming into the room.

She stops in her tracks. 'Oh, sorry. Were you asleep?'

I try to focus on her through my blurry vision.

'How are you feeling?' she asks.

I attempt to sit up, but my body doesn't comply so I flop back on the pillows. 'I hear you saved my life.'

She lays a box of chocolates on the table and perches on the edge of the bed. 'I wouldn't say that. It was lucky timing.'

'How come?'

'I was driving back from a friend's when I got an alert for a malfunction at your place. The whole thing had been bugging me. I don't like what I can't explain, so I put extra monitoring in place, hoping I could crack it. I did a detour to see it go wrong in action. I tried calling you and Joe. Then I found you slumped in your car.'

'It was brave of you to go in the garage.'

'I was scared for you, but the paramedics came quickly.'

The sheer terror of making it to the car floods back and I start shaking.

'Hey, easy.' Nicole passes me some water.

I take a careful sip. 'What was the malfunction?'

'It was a cyberattack. The police wouldn't let me touch anything, which is fair enough. They have to catch who did it.'

'Did they tell you they've arrested Joe.'

'Oh, Lauren. I'm so sorry. They asked a lot of questions about him. I did wonder what was going on when you kept asking my opinion on malfunctions. Do you think he did it?'

'I can't get my head round it. Who else has the capability?'

'I've no idea. I said the police should look at whether Joe upset any contractors or anything like that. You hear of people owed money on building sites who turn up in a rage and demolish the building work. Someone's ruining it for you so you can't live there.'

'Do you still think it was Kev?'

She looks doubtful. 'He's a dick, but surely he's not twisted enough to kill you. Would he risk it for missing out on a job? You've known him a while. If he's a psycho, you'd have noticed.'

I'd expected her to blame him, but she's right that it isn't Kev's style.

'Unless his issues go deeper than we realise,' she adds.

'What about our neighbour who had the electronics company?' I say.

'What's the point? He scares you two away and he'll get new neighbours who might cause even more grief.'

222

I take in what she's saying, but I'm too wrung-out to handle the sheer magnitude of it.

'Try to rest,' she says. 'You've been through a massive trauma. At least the police are taking it seriously.'

I nod and gulp, fighting away tears.

'Don't cry, you'll set me off.' Her voice is throaty and choked. 'If someone cries I can't help crying too.' She clears her throat and pulls herself up straighter, like a child trying to be grown up. 'Listen, I'm off to the US on business tomorrow. The police have my contact details if they need to check anything. I've lined up someone good for call-outs. His name's David and he's very reliable.'

'Thanks, but I'm not spending another night there.' I want her nearby, which is ridiculous. I miss having friends I can count on. Nicole saved me, but I'm going back to low-tech or preferably no tech, so I won't need her.

'I'm sorry for upsetting you,' Nicole says.

The nurse comes in and sees me mopping my eyes with a tissue. She holds the door open. 'Visiting time's over.'

Nicole gets up. 'Joe's always been a nice guy to me. You're both ... I don't know.' She shakes her head, trying to put it into words. 'You're a normal couple. I don't get why this would happen, but for what it's worth, I don't think he did it. Go with your instincts, because what if the police have it wrong?'

I nod and blow my nose.

'What do you need? I'll go to the shop downstairs.'

'Nothing. I'm fine.'

'Try and sleep.' She waves and walks away.

More worn-out than ever, I sleep until someone wakes me with a plastic tray of heated-up food. I've no appetite, but I eat it to build myself up. Then I shuffle to the bathroom and test if my stamina is any better since last time. It's not. I hold onto the wall, still not trusting myself to walk across the room unaided. At least I make it back without my legs giving way.

When I root through the holdall, I see the police officer has packed my phone charger, so I plug it in and send a message to Brooke, letting her know what's happened. I can't confront the enormity of whether or not Joe tried to kill me. I ache for him, needing him to curl up beside me and tell me it's going to be okay. The shock of his arrest won't leave me. What if he really did do it?

That night, a call bell rings out down the corridor, waking me. I yelp at the black shape of a man crouching in the dark corner of the room, watching me. The whites of his eyes are visible in the dim lighting. Fear shoots through my veins. I fumble for the light switch. Is it Karl Winter? Has he caught up with me?

When I flick on the light, the man is gone, replaced with the squat cupboard in the corner, Joe's holdall on top. The studs on the handle fixings shine but look nothing like eyes. It must have been some kind of waking nightmare. I try to calm my crazy heart and slow my urgent breaths.

Not real ... he wasn't there ... your mind's playing tricks. But in that moment, he lurked with menace, eyes burning into me. Joe's right that my imagination gets the better of me.

Something nags at me, a whispered phrase from the ghostly

224

dismembered voice. The cadence of the sing-song phrase floats around my consciousness, but the words stay just out of reach. I didn't know what it meant during the cyberattack and now nothing will bring it back. But it feels significant, and I try to remember it.

CHAPTER THIRTY-TWO

Another call bell goes off down the corridor. Their insistent shrill keeps waking me through the night. I want Joe to turn up and say it's been a huge mistake and the police have found whoever tried to kill me. A tear slides down my face to the pillow.

I'd been dreaming about the ghostly voice, its sing-song tone whispering around my head. The words drifted around my subconscious as I slept, the eerie phrase during the cyberattack.

In a flash, the words return to me. *Fear and guilt are sisters.* What does it mean?

It puzzles me. The lights are subdued and my mind is clearer. I reach for my phone and google *Fear and guilt are sisters*, the bright screen hurting my bleary eyes. It's from *The Haunting of Hill House.* I inhale sharply and picture Dylan asking to watch it.

It's morning in Australia. I check my emails and see a reply from Brooke. At least I can count on her to bolster me.

My God, Lauren, that's so awful I don't know what to say.
How are you? I wish I was nearby so I could look after you.

Have the police sussed it out? Was Joe in debt or was he
planning to run back to Tara? Please keep yourself safe. Can
someone put you up until you sell that bloody house and get
a little place of your own? I don't like to think of you alone
over there with everything that's going on.

I smart at the suggestion of Joe running back to Tara. I didn't
even tell her he did it, just that the police arrested him. Brooke's
words keep me awake for the rest of the night.

In the morning, I take a shower. Even simple tasks take a
huge effort. A sour taste lingers in my mouth, the sourness
reaching down my throat and settling in the pit of my stomach.
I force down a lukewarm cooked breakfast, and the police
constable who spoke to me yesterday returns. This time I have
questions for her.

'Has Joe been released?'

'No. We can keep him in for the full seventy-two hours that
we're allocated when a suspect's been arrested.'

'And then you'll let him go?'

'That depends. If we have enough evidence to charge him,
he'll appear in court.'

I can't even picture Joe in a courtroom dock.

'Don't worry; *if* he's released we'll let you know. Either
myself or a colleague will discuss the options with you.'

'What options?'

'How to stay safe.'

She thinks I'm scared of him. I should be scared of him, but I'm a mass of conflicted feelings.

'We've found surveillance equipment in the house. Did you know there were spy cams and microphones installed?'

I shake my head, no. 'Was there a hidden camera in the bedroom?'

'A camera and a microphone.'

I flinch.

'So the strange noises and the voice probably came through the microphone. They would have used the camera to see when you were there to get the timing right.'

My skin crawls at the thought of someone watching me in the bedroom.

'Did they record me?'

'We don't know.'

Images flash into my mind: the two of us in bed, me coming out of the shower, getting dressed; footage watched covertly and uploaded for anyone to see.

'Have you spoken to Nicole? She set the smart home up with Joe. She said last week there weren't any microphones, same as Joe did all along. He said it was impossible for the strange noises to come through the sound system.'

'Nothing's impossible if you're determined enough.'

I feel sick. The cooked breakfast has left my mouth oily and the congealed scrambled egg sits inside me like I've swallowed an entire egg box.

'My colleague's been speaking to Nicole. She went through the technical aspects with our IT guys and gave us access to everything. She's with a client in America until next week, but she's available if we need to check anything.'

'Surely we'd have seen the cameras and microphones? Joe's tech-savvy and I had concerns . . .'

'Our guys say they were tiny and sophisticated, but your tech-savvy husband could've found them if he'd looked.'

She doesn't have a high opinion of Joe. If I'd known what to look for, I could have found them too. 'What about Kev, the electrician?'

'At this stage we don't believe he was involved.'

'And Mitchell Unsworth, the neighbour I told you about yesterday?'

'He checks out.'

'What does that mean?'

'We've run checks against Nicole and the other two. Mitchell Unsworth seems to have some issues with you opening an art gallery in the garden.'

'What— what gallery? I'm not opening any gallery. What makes him think that?'

'From a letter you and your husband sent him prior to moving in, hence him keeping a close eye on the property.'

I look at her, confused. 'We didn't send him a letter. We've never wanted to open an art gallery.'

'He didn't see anything incriminating through his telescope. We don't have any reason to suspect the people you flagged up. Nicole is helping with the investigation. She'll be here to testify for the prosecution if it goes to trial. Do you have any suspicions of Joe having an affair?' she asks.

'Not really. It's just his ex, Tara. He feels guilty about not being under the same roof as Dylan. She plays on it. Maybe she wants him back.'

The officer nods as if this is a likely hypothesis.

'A friend suggested he was having an affair with Nicole, the IT person, but no.' I shake my head as if dispelling the thought. 'She's too young, and he's not her type.'

She raises a sceptical eyebrow.

'I know it happens,' I say, 'but she's not like that. I've seen them together, and Joe isn't interested. The friend who said it lives in Australia. She has nothing to base it on. He's shown no sign of wanting to leave me, but if he did, I'd expect him to go back to Tara, because that's his ready-made family.'

'Okay. I know this isn't easy for you, but it's important we cover it.'

And I want to know what they're thinking.

'Someone tampered with your car, so whoever did it had access to the garage. When did you last use the car?'

'Not for a few days. I was unsettled and then fuzzy from the meds, so I hadn't driven.'

'Who had access to the garage in that time?'

'Only Joe and me. He moved the car into the garage to vacuum it for me, but if someone hijacked the system, they could get in there.'

She pauses to write it down. 'If the house is set up to be controlled remotely, then whoever harmed you didn't need to be there. It was a cyberattack. We think someone entered the property prior to the incident to block the exhaust, but they could've hijacked the smart home from anywhere. What's happened to you is extreme, but if someone has the will to harm you in this way, the tools are there to do it. By tools, I mean the way your home is set up makes you vulnerable to a cyberattack.'

In which case, it could be anyone. A cyberattack sounds like the action of a Russian state agency, or a lone teenager up to no good in his bedroom.

'How do you get on with Joe's son?'

'Dylan? Why?'

'It seems he might be involved.'

It's all too much, that Dylan and Joe engineered it between them. I suspected Dylan of messing around with it but hate to think either of them wanted to kill me. 'Could he have done it and treated it like a game, without realising the harm?' I think of *fear and guilt are sisters* from *The Haunting of Hill House*. I can't bring myself to watch it for context or clues, not when I've been scared enough.

'We're still unravelling that.'

I bite the inside of my cheek. 'How was he involved?'

'He appears to have hacked into your smart home controls. He certainly has all the passcodes. But we have evidence that your husband was the one directing him. And given that the worst of it happened when he wasn't with you, the surveillance equipment was a way to check your location so he could scare you remotely.'

I lie back and take a painful breath. 'Do you know that for sure?'

'We've found certain evidence, including an invoice he'd been emailed for the surveillance equipment. He'd deleted it, but we retrieved it.'

I picture Joe in a stark interview room at the police station, denying it all, his arms folded in defiance. Is he saying *No comment*, or still implying it's my mental state? No, stop, don't think like that. As for Dylan, he won't cope with the police questioning and might come across as guilty even if he's not.

'I have a photo here of Karl Winter. We're aware of what happened before and we're looking at any possible link. Can I show you the photo?'

At last, a line of questioning that doesn't blame Joe. I crane forward to see it.

'Have you seen this photo before?' she asks.

I take the picture from her. It's Karl Winter, looking suspiciously at the camera as if caught unawares. 'It looks like the image from the CCTV. I only caught a fleeting glimpse, but it could be this one. Why do you ask?'

'We found this photo on your husband's laptop. He'd deleted it last week, but our IT experts retrieved it.'

I'm floored. Why would Joe do that? He'd acted surprised when I mentioned Karl Winter, yet he'd kept a photo of him. 'Do you know what he did with the photo?'

'No. We've no trace of him using software to doctor it. That's not to say he didn't.'

'When I saw Karl Winter on the CCTV, I thought he was still alive.'

'He's dead. We've been over the records and eliminated him.

If you saw his image on CCTV then it's because someone put it there to scare you.'

'He hacked my emails and superimposed my face on photos of women. This is his trademark. What if he's made it seem as if Joe's doing it all?'

She takes a long breath as if composing a suitable reply. 'I hear what you're saying, but we've confirmed that Karl Winter is dead. After what originally happened to you regarding him, it's no coincidence you're going through this. Someone is using it against you.'

'Who?'

'Someone knows your personal history and used it to make it look like you were going mad. Did your husband have any reason to be in possession of Karl Winter's photo?'

'No.'

'He stored the photo on his laptop and then deleted it, which suggests he was involved. It's only circumstantial evidence, but when it adds up like this, we have to look into it.'

'What about Dylan's computer? What did you find on that?'

'It appears that your husband was directing him to carry out some aspects of the cyberattack. Dylan could undertake some of the low-level activity from his bedroom when Joe was with you, such as playing a recording of someone saying your name when Joe was supposedly asleep beside you.'

'That's absurd. Joe wouldn't do that.' I can't believe Joe would encourage him to do anything criminal.

'Unfortunately, Dylan is an easy target. He trusts his dad, and he has the aptitude for hacking.'

'Has Joe said he did it?'

'He's not co-operating with our enquiries.' She purses her lips and her nostrils flare. 'If someone pulled this kind of stunt on my other half, I'd do everything possible to help the police catch whoever did it. But he's not helping us.'

How did it reach this point where I was so exposed to danger? I never wanted the smart home and now I'm ensnared in its web of deceit. Even if Joe is innocent, he brought the tech into our home and urged me to stick with it. It wasn't just the sound system that warped. Our marriage has too, buckling under the strain of him pushing me to the outer limits of sanity.

'Why would he do that to me?'

'We don't have a motive. He hasn't shared that with us.'

Do his money worries go deeper than I realise, or does he want Tara back? 'If I died, he could move Tara and the kids in without giving me a financial settlement. But he's not that mercenary. Was she in on it too?'

'We've no evidence of that. She's been pretty hostile, but she's looking out for her son.'

I'm hot and woozy, and drink some water.

'How is your money situation?'

'Not great, but it's temporary.' No point in hiding it when they must have trawled through the finances looking for a motive. 'You know what it's like when you move house and the costs are higher than expected.'

She nods and says nothing.

'I wanted to sell up, but Joe said we won't recover what we've put in. It doesn't make sense that he did this for money, not when I was bringing money in with my painting. When the portrait went missing, it set me back, but if I'd kept working, we'd have managed.'

'Unless it wasn't enough for him. Or he was motivated by a need to be with someone else, like his ex-wife.'

I rub my aching forehead with the heels of my hands.

'I know this is tough on you.'

It shatters my belief in Joe. It's not only the betrayal, it means losing my reliance on him when I can barely venture out alone in public. Being with Joe made sense, but now nothing makes sense.

CHAPTER THIRTY-THREE

The doctor discharges me in the afternoon. I'm torn between wanting the safety of the hospital ward and craving uninterrupted sleep without call bells going off or someone clanking in with a trolley. Ava comes to collect me.

'Chris is home with the kids,' she says. 'He's doing lasagne and says I have to bring you back.'

'Thank you, but I've no appetite, and moving to the flat will wear me out. Is it still okay to collect some things from the house?'

'Sure.' When we leave the hospital, the exit doors slide open and an icy wind snatches my breath. I'm shivering within seconds after being on the hot ward.

'Here, have my scarf.' Despite my protests, she stops to wrap her huge woollen scarf round me. Her kindness is warming all on its own.

Dora's in the car, wagging and whimpering in delight. I bury my face in her smooth fur. The drive to Chilwood is a blur.

When we draw up at the cottage, it's so picturesque, I can barely reconcile its exterior with the horror that's consuming me.

'I can get what you want,' Ava says.

'No, let's go in.' I clutch the door key that the police returned. Going inside, I flashback to the terror of stumbling downstairs, convinced my killer was bearing down, ready to finish me off.

'Stay with me,' I say, looking up the staircase.

But no one's here. The police will have taken the microphones and cameras as evidence. We gather up what I need, including my painting materials, and I load the toolkit in her car boot.

'Why are you taking that?'

'Some things need fixing at the flat.' I nearly collapse back in the passenger seat, out of breath.

We drive to the flat, ten miles away. Ava talks about all the rain we've had, and then she pauses. 'Do you think someone's set Joe up?'

'Who would do that?' I'm still wading through brain-fog and the truth lies beyond reach. I try to force myself to be alert but can't fight the dull haze, my body steeped in drugs and sadness. The best I can do is piece together the facts.

'I've no idea, but Joe's a good guy. He adores you.'

When did life turn crazy? It was fine until Karl Winter barged in, and it hasn't been the same since.

'The police think it's to do with money,' I say, 'or another woman, or both.'

'Bullshit. What other woman?'

'Tara.'

'He'd never leave you for Tara! All she does is give him grief. He'd have nothing to do with her if it weren't for Dylan.'

'Have you spoken to Joe?' I ask.

'He's only allowed contact with his solicitor, but they'll have to let him go soon.'

We pull up at the flat and Ava turns to me, her hands still on the steering wheel. 'Do you really think Joe is behind this?'

'I don't want to think it, no.' It's the most honest answer. We bring everything up to the flat, which is in a good enough state after the half-term booking.

'I'll change the bedding.' She goes into the bedroom. 'You look ready to crash out.'

Ava's brought groceries along with Dora's bowls and bed. I unpack them in the kitchen area opposite the small living-room space. The rest can wait.

'Have a lie-down.' She shoves the bed linen into the washing machine.

'Thanks, but I'm fine now. You've been brilliant.'

It's a relief to be safely contained in a small space that's more secure than Chilwood Cottage despite Joe's cutting-edge security features. There's WiFi and a smart TV but no other tech. The living area is only big enough for a compact sofa, armchair and coffee table, with a small dining table and two chairs in the corner.

'Sure you don't want me to stay?'

'No, you've been great. I wouldn't have managed without you.'

She hugs me. 'Call me if you need anything. We'll be round like a shot.'

When she's gone, I gather what's left of my energy and venture out to the hardware shop. It's pouring with rain and a reluctant Dora grudgingly lags behind me. There aren't many people out, but I scan for dangers from under the hood of my rain jacket. My fingers are numbed from the cold and wet, but my gloves are back at Chilwood.

We reach the cramped, old-fashioned hardware store and the man behind the counter sells me a new Yale lock. I've gone from unwavering trust in Joe to changing the locks, but the police said to do it. Though I hate to admit it, I feel safer knowing he can't get in. I don't expect Joe to murder me in my sleep, but I've lost the ability to trust my judgement, so how can I trust anything?

On the way back, I buy a cheap pay-as-you-go-phone with a new SIM and new number. I'll give the number to the detective constable, but not yet because I can hardly function. I return to the flat, unplug the TV and drape a blanket over it. I picture Joe and Dylan monitoring me, filming my every move in the bedroom, watching my reaction to the ghostly voices.

Mustering my last remaining energy, I start changing the lock on the door. I'm just fixing the key plate in place when I hear heavy footsteps on the communal stairs and I lean forward to see who it is. A uniformed police officer comes into sight. He says DC Jones asked him to check on security and surveillance.

'Oh, okay.' I step back from the door to let him in, trying to remember if she'd told me, but my memory stays fuzzy. The doctor said that carbon monoxide poisoning can cause memory loss and difficulty concentrating.

He stands on the small, gloomy landing. 'Don't let anyone in who you don't know, and always check the ID of everyone who says they're here on business.'

'Sure.'

He stays put and the penny drops.

'Can I see your ID then?'

He opens a black card holder with his photo ID on one side and the police crest on the other. I nod seriously at it to prove I'm not a total airhead.

'Good that you're changing the locks,' he says and comes inside to check around.

I carry on, since my wobbly legs won't keep me upright much longer. He confirms that the place is secure and there are no hidden devices, then tells me to call 999 if I'm in any danger. By the time I've finished, the door shuts smoothly and the lock works, even if it's not straight.

I crash onto the bed, still fully dressed. A movement in the corner of the room catches my eye, a dark shadow that disappears when I focus on it. It's understandable in an old house with dark corners, but I'm still seeing things in a new-build flat with fresh magnolia walls. Too tired to keep my eyes open, exhaustion hits and all I can do is sleep.

CHAPTER THIRTY-FOUR

Dora's barking at the doorbell. I emerge from a deep sleep, assuming it's the middle of the night, but then I see the glow of daylight around the edge of the curtains. Woozy still, I'd rather stay under the duvet, but now Dora's up she'll want to go out. The shakiness from yesterday is replaced with a leaden feeling in my limbs. I drag myself to the hall and check the security chain's on before opening the door to Ava.

'Hey, sorry, did I wake you?' Her smile is warm, uncertain. She's holding a paper bag from the bakery and I catch a mouth-watering waft of sweet pastry. 'I tried calling but I think your phone's turned off. Are you okay?'

A determined little Dora squeezes through the gap and does a happy dance around her feet. She crouches down to pet her while I unhitch the security chain.

'It's good to see you. I'm not too steady on my feet. I don't suppose you could walk Dora round the block while I wake up?'

'Sure. We'll chat when I come back.'

By the time she returns, I've attempted to wake up and have pulled on some clothes.

'How are you feeling?' she asks, coming through to the kitchen and filling the kettle.

'I don't know which way is up.'

She buzzes around the tiny space, reaching in a cupboard for plates and sliding the pastries onto them. With all the energy sucked from me, I like her taking charge.

'No wonder when you've had a nasty shock. Let's get some carbs down you.'

We sit on the sofa with coffee and *pain au chocolat*.

'Joe's been released,' she says. 'Chris picked him up.'

'Oh.'

'So that's a blessing.'

I shred a piece of the pastry and nibble politely.

'The police reckon they have all this evidence, but Joe says it's been planted on his devices and then deleted. He never even saw any of it.'

'Have they charged him?' I lean back, one hand holding the padded armrest.

'No, but he's been told to stay away from you while they're investigating. He was worried about you when I said I couldn't get you on the phone, so I thought I'd come and see how you are.'

'Thanks.'

'He's back at the cottage. He said he can take Dora while you recover.'

I push the pastry away. My mouth's too dry and my stomach's

242

twisting. I picture Chilwood and our lovely walks with Dora. All the work we put in, and all for nothing.

'He swears blind he's not having an affair. He said you saw a strange text from Tara, but it wasn't from her. Whoever sent it could use something called SMS cloning to make it appear to be from her, and then they wiped it.'

I've never heard of SMS cloning. 'The police said they thought Dylan was in on it too.'

'Ridiculous, isn't it? I've known Dylan since he was a baby and he wouldn't hurt you. Joe would rather they came after him than Dylan, but whoever set this up has made Dylan a suspect.'

'How is he?'

'Dylan? He was questioned but he clammed up. Now he's completely withdrawn. Tara was with him the whole time, and they had to take it slow because of his special needs. It does my head in that someone wants to cause all that harm, hurting you and implicating Dylan.' She takes an anguished sip of coffee.

Even if Dylan did do something stupid, there was no malice or ulterior motive. He's not like that.

'The police don't get that you've been hacked and someone's planted incriminating stuff,' she says.

Ava's keen to defend Joe, but he didn't believe someone wanted to harm me, even as I lay in hospital. He refused to accept that I was being watched or that the voices were external.

'Joe's solicitor is working on it. He says the police can't make the evidence stick, not when it's a cyberattack.'

I turn my head away and sigh. Ava's trying to help, but her insistence that it's all a stitch-up is wearing. I want to go back to bed. However long I've slept for, it's not enough.

'He's devastated, but he's okay, working hard to catch up and make some money. Shall I take Dora so you can rest?'

Dora's my only comfort, but she's better off with Joe and she naps in his car when he's working. Ava helps me gather up her things.

She kisses me goodbye and I bury my face in Dora's warm body. When I lock the door behind them, I'm relieved she's gone even though she means well with her damage-limitation pitch for Joe. I need him more than ever, but I'm safer here until the police can prove whether or not he was involved. In my heart, I don't believe he is, but I have to take on board what they're telling me.

I open my laptop and change the password. When the officer returned it, she said nothing on there would allow someone to monitor it remotely. I didn't reply to Brooke's email and she's sent another one.

Are you okay? Ignore me if I came on too strong. I'm just fuming that you're going through this shit. You're my friend and I want you to be okay, and I can't stand by when bad things are happening to you. Let me know how you are. Is Joe still locked up?

I reply to say that Joe is out. I type,

The thing is, the police said to stay away from him, and I'm not sure I trust him. It's probably because I'm not thinking straight.

My brain's still slow to work things out. I need a reality check and can't share my views with Ava, but Brooke will put me straight. The day goes in a haze until I fall into another exhausted sleep.

'Lauren ... Lauren ... shuuushhh.'

It's the ghostly voice. I shout myself awake and push back the duvet in a sweat. Where am I? I turn on the bedside lamp, convinced that I can still hear the whispered voice. Someone's here. They've come for me in the night.

The room is empty. Holding my breath, I strain to hear, but there's no sound, not when I concentrate. Everything sounds off and a bit eerie in my head since I woke up in hospital. I'm shaking from the fevered dream, from the voice in my head. No one else is here, but the whispering comes to me sometimes, and then it stops when I try tuning in. I tell myself it's okay. If only that were true. I go to the window, fingertips touching the bedroom wall to steady myself.

The streetlights illuminate the rain-slicked road. The voice that woke me sounded as real as it did at Chilwood, but the police officer checked here for hidden devices. It was only a dream, but I'm so far gone, I can't tell what's real. I daren't breathe a word to anyone in case they think I'm mad. Annette's words come back to me, that the mind plays tricks.

CHAPTER THIRTY-FIVE

After my freaky dream last night, I fall asleep in the armchair and wake up with a stiff neck and a sense of dread. Nothing feels right because nothing is right. Tiredness seeps into everything as early morning light filters through the curtains. At least I don't have to walk Dora and worry about who's watching and waiting in the shadows.

I need a new email address, so I set up a Gmail account and don't tell anyone just yet. I'll limit who knows the address to narrow the field of suspects if someone uses it to undermine me. My email hasn't been hijacked, but I'm hyper-aware of electronic monitoring.

The doorbell rings just after nine and I open the door a crack.

'It's only me, Lauren,' the detective constable says. She holds up my car key. 'We've brought your car back. My colleague parked it along the road. Can I come in for a chat?'

She comes in and I go to fill the kettle.

'The car's safe to drive now. We've finished taking

forensic evidence. I phoned to see how you are. Is your phone turned off?'

'Oh sorry. I got a new one. I haven't given the number to anyone until I know who to trust.'

'Wise move. How are you getting on?'

'I'm trying to build up my strength.'

'Take your time. I'd left a message to say Joe was being released yesterday.'

'Do you still think he's involved?' My voice wavers, not ready for more bad news. The kettle boils and I clutch a mug in each hand.

'Let's make a brew first.' She takes over with brisk efficiency, telling me she likes her teabag left in. 'Gets better as it goes on.'

She plonks herself in the armchair and I sit at one end of the sofa.

'Joe's still a prime suspect,' she says, 'but there are issues with the evidence tying him directly to the attempted murder.'

'So it might not be him?'

'It's too early to say. It's an active investigation, but we don't have any new leads. We have reason to believe Joe is responsible, but the evidence could have been planted as part of a cyber campaign against you both. For now, it's a condition of Joe's bail that he doesn't contact you directly or indirectly.'

'What if he doesn't comply?'

'He'll go to prison on remand.'

'Even if he didn't try to kill me?'

'At this stage, we believe it's most likely he did. In cases like this where the suspect is known to the victim, it's important for there to be no contact. The suspect might threaten the victim or plead with them to not co-operate with the investigation, in the hope that no charges can be brought.'

'Oh.'

'It can put you in a vulnerable position.' She blows on her tea and looks at me the way Annette did when she waited for it to sink in that Joe might be to blame. It still doesn't ring true, but I keep an open mind.

'We need you to let us know if he has any contact.'

'But someone else could have set him up.'

'That's one line of enquiry but not our main one.'

'Why not?'

'If it was a cyberattack, it's very sophisticated. It would take a high degree of skill and resources, plus the risk of imprisonment. It's extreme and rare, especially against someone like you, who appears to lead a normal life. Whoever did it will probably be known to you and they'll have an axe to grind. Is there anyone else you can think of? Any business deals gone sour or estranged family members?'

'There's my brother in California and his wife. We had a falling-out when Joe and I got married. They cut off contact.'

'Why did you fall out?'

'Joe tried to encourage Dale to buy a property to do up and it somehow escalated to Dale calling him a capitalist pig.'

'Right.' She looks concerned. 'How are your brother's IT skills?'

'Average, I guess. His wife worked for an IT company, but as far as I know they're still in America. They'd have had to be here to block the exhaust and install the monitoring equipment. Apart from them, there's only Kev, the electrician, Mitchell, our neighbour and Nicole, who set up the smart home.'

'None of them are known to the police. We'll talk to Nicole again when she's back from her business trip. She's adamant that she wasn't aware of the cameras and microphones at any stage. She's been very helpful.'

Frustration creeps over me at the lack of progress, while I'm stuck in limbo.

'This sort of calculated criminal behaviour tends to build up over time, but there's no element of that here. Unless they're very young.'

'Like Joe's son?'

She nods.

'Is it possible he acted alone? The spooky voices, setting the robo-vac on me – he might have seen it as a Halloween prank.' Dylan mucking around with a real life *Haunting of Hill House* is a possibility. But there must be another explanation for the blocked exhaust.

'Dylan might be capable of setting up a cyberattack, but it's unlikely he had the means and the opportunity to do it all on his own. We've looked at all the evidence and Joe is the only person with a motive and the means.'

I stare at my untouched mug of tea, cooling on the table.

'Someone tampered with your car and installed monitoring equipment in the house that your electrician and IT expert say they knew nothing about. Again, Joe is best placed to do all that.'

I rub my eyes and gather my thoughts. My head's still fuzzy and I can't remember if I mentioned Anorak Man. 'Did I tell you about the strange man who came on the smart home tour?'

'We spoke to your architect about the tour. He gave us a list of the attendees. There are no criminal links.'

'Did you speak to all of them? One man studied the home hub and then came back on a pretext to get inside the house.'

'We spoke to everyone on the list that the architect gave us. What's the man's name?' She takes out her notebook and flips it open.

'I don't know, but Alistair will have his details. The CCTV was wiped the two times he came to the house. Don't you think that's suspicious?'

'I'll take it back to the team. We can question that person again. You said that other footage was wiped. Joe had access to the playback, so he could have deleted it to make you paranoid or so you'd suspect other people.'

I look down at my hands, tightly clasped in my lap. 'Was there really a disturbance at Tara's house on Halloween night?'

'There appeared to be something going on. His ex-wife made a call to us. It's a busy evening for uniformed officers, but someone went over and saw evidence of eggs thrown at the bedroom window. We assume it was targeted because there weren't similar reports in that area. It's not uncommon for Halloween. Do you think your husband set it up so he could be out of the house?'

'Or someone else did so he wouldn't be around. But he fell

250

asleep on Dylan's bed, which an outside attacker couldn't have predicted. He could've sorted it sooner and come home.'

'Or he fabricated it and had witnesses to say he was there all night,' she said. 'He was best placed to block the exhaust.'

'Or a mystery person gained access to the garage when they saw I'd gone to bed, same as they stole the paintings from the studio. The rest could be done remotely, so either someone did all the IT stuff and had an accomplice come to the house, or they acted alone.'

She takes her empty mug to the sink and then turns back to me, her expression grave. 'Until we have more to go on, don't have any contact with your husband. Are you okay here on your own?'

I don't have much choice, so I say a tight yes and see her out. On the doorstep, she tells me to lock the door behind her.

Biting my lip, I call up Tara's number in my contacts. Joe gave me it ages ago in case of emergencies, but I've never contacted her. I send a message to say I hope Dylan's okay and to say hi to him from me. I go online and see Brooke has replied.

Oh Lauren, it's so hard to know what to say, so I'll say what's on my mind. Point taken that I'm not there so I don't know, but it's all so dramatic. I've known you for years and you have such a quiet life. Why the hell would anyone try to kill you?

I did wonder about a financial motive – do you mind me talking like this? And why are the police so interested in Joe? If they're saying it's him, you have to listen. And until you

know what's behind it, trust no one! Hunker down in your
little bunker and get yourself BETTER and STRONG!

    Brooke xxx

    P.S. You can always come and stay here.

She means well, but the police might be missing something. I write a list of everyone who had the chance to fit surveillance equipment and tamper with my car, but it leaves me none the wiser.

DC Jones said there were no coincidences. I thought I saw Karl Winter on the CCTV, so whoever's doing this knows about him. He had mental health issues and died, and someone wants me to go the same way.

When I think of a cybercriminal, I picture a faceless young man tapping away in a darkened room, hunched over his keyboard, the screen filled with unintelligible code. I still can't picture Joe doing that. Is it Anorak Man? Whoever is behind it has a secret portal inside our home and marriage, and I don't think he's going to stop.

CHAPTER THIRTY-SIX

Dear Lauren,

The police came to see me about your terrible incident.
How are you, my dear? I'm so sorry that you've been under
attack. I've tried phoning because Deb and I wanted to
send flowers, but we don't have your temporary address.
Do let me know if there's anything we can do. We would
like to help.

Best wishes for a speedy recovery,
Alistair

I reply to thank him and then I have a go at my latest commission of an adorable ragdoll kitten. My hand trembles a little from the after-effects of the carbon monoxide poisoning, so I give it a hazy look to suit the softness of the kitten.

I'd like to contact Nicole, but she's arranged cover, so I won't bother her. I could talk to Alistair instead about Anorak

Man. If the police think Joe is guilty, they might not look into it, so if they don't, I will. Alistair said he can't give me any contact details because of data protection laws, but maybe there's a way.

I take my keys and find my car along the road, scanning for danger along the way. Behind the wheel, I'm transported back to the last time I sat here, terrified to death. I turn the key in the ignition, fighting the urge to go back inside and lock out the danger.

I drive to Alistair's home office and park by a dense laurel hedge on the road where he works in a converted outbuilding beside his thatched house. His Range Rover is in the car port below the upstairs office. I crunch over the gravel drive, looking up at the office through the big triangle-shaped window that reaches the top point of the roof. No sign of Alistair, but I go up the stairs that lead to the office space with an architect's table and desk.

His Mac is blank-screened on the desk. I catch my breath. What if I have a quick look? A frisson of danger ripples through me as I press the spacebar and the password screen comes up. I'll never guess it, so I scan around for another option. If he's not here, I might find the details and he'll never know. That's better than have him refuse me again.

A filing cabinet in pale wood stands beside the desk. Heart in mouth, I slide open the top drawer. It looks like client files, arranged alphabetically. Our 'Geddes' file is in the second drawer. Is the tour admin in there? My heart races. I rifle through—

'What are you doing?' Alistair's voice is loud and shocked from the top of the stairs.

I spin round and drop the file, scattering plans and scraps of notes.

He looks aghast. 'Lauren! What on earth?'

I crouch down and pick up the papers, my face flushing hot.

'What is this?' His voice is clipped with annoyance.

I'm too flustered to speak and so hot I could pass out.

Alistair comes towards me and shoves the drawer shut with an angry clunk. 'You can't go through the filing. It's confidential.'

'Sorry.' I shuffle the papers into a messy pile.

'You tried the computer, didn't you? The screen's lit up.'

I stand, queasy from the adrenaline rush, and lean unsteadily against the filing cabinet. His anger makes the whole situation worse. It's a side of him I've never seen before.

'Sit down.' He motions to the couch against the wall and snatches the messy bundle of paperwork from me.

I sit and try to marshal my thoughts.

'Well?' Alistair stands over me, fists on hips.

I take a breath. 'Remember I asked you about that man who did the smart home tour? He came back afterwards, but he was wiped from the CCTV. If he's a techie, he could've wiped it himself. He could've tried to kill me.'

'Why on earth would he try to kill you?'

'I don't know.'

I wonder what conclusions he's drawn from the police questioning him. Does he know they've arrested Joe?

'I didn't mean to go through your private things. When you

255

weren't here, I thought if I could just see the list of attendees then it wouldn't put you in an awkward position.'

'I didn't print the list off. It was done on email. I can't even place the chap.'

'That's the thing: he's unexceptional. He blended in.'

'Very strange, especially about the CCTV.' His bushy eyebrows knit in confusion.

'Are there cameras that might have picked him up when he came here before the tour? A dashcam on your car?'

'Lord, no. Deb hates that sort of thing, and we've never needed it. Very quiet out here, as we thought it was where you are.'

I lean forward and rest my chin on my fingertips. 'I don't know what to do.'

He stands over me, deep in contemplation. Then he goes to his Mac, taps on the keyboard, clicks an email folder and opens a message. 'Let's just say you came here and this screen was open, but I'd been called away. This is what you could find for yourself.'

I come towards the screen as if magnetised. He steps back and I peer at the message listing the attendees, sent by Alistair to his business partner. My heart thuds. I've already discounted three of them. I grab the pad and pen on the desk and scribble down the details of the remaining ones.

Alistair takes the pen from me. 'From how you described the man, it's not these two.' He crosses two names off the list. 'Too old to fit the profile. And this one had a ginger beard.'

It leaves one name only: Seb Alexander. I circle it and put

256

the pen down. Alistair looks at the name and shakes his head, nonplussed.

'Thank you, Alistair. I'm very grateful.'

He hands me the sheet of paper and pats me on the arm.

Back in the car, the paper is crumpled in my hand. I'm clammy and unsteady, but I have a contact email and phone number for Seb Alexander. Whether he'll talk to me is another matter.

CHAPTER THIRTY-SEVEN

I take Seb Alexander's name, email address and mobile number to run through online searches. There's a Seb Alexander on LinkedIn who works in IT development for a Basingstoke company. It could be him, but he has no profile photo. His online footprint is nearly as minimal as mine, but I expect he has various usernames, like MirrorMan, which he used on Alistair's blog. I call his number. After several rings it cuts off. I slump back on the sofa, listless.

Something stirs in the back of my mind from the day I woke up in hospital. A haze hangs over my short-term memory, but now and then a random snippet comes back to me. How did I forget? I take my keys and go back out. My drive takes me to the South Downs, to Chilwood Cottage, but that's not where I'm going. I want to see the letter that DC Jones said we sent Mitchell about opening an art gallery in the garden.

If he received a letter, it suggests that someone other than Joe is screwing with us. Joe had no reason to antagonise our neighbour, but is someone playing a long game? That someone might be Anorak Man, otherwise known as Seb Alexander, who I saw talking to Mitchell.

Fighting brain fog, I drive carefully, unsure of what awaits me other than a gruff response. On the approach to Chilwood Cottage, I'm overwhelmed with sadness that it's no longer our home. I swallow my upset that Joe and Dora are inside without me, and I pull up on the verge outside Mitchell's house. Before I make it to the front door, he opens it and glares at me.

'You,' he says.

'Hello.' I doubt he'll ask me in, which is fine because I don't want to go in. We'll stand with the statues of dismembered women.

He stares in contempt.

'The police said you received a letter about an art gallery.'

'That's right.'

'When was that?' I ask, keeping my voice neutral.

'Sometime before you moved in.'

'We didn't send it. We'd no intention of opening an art gallery, or inviting the public round. I wanted a quiet life here.'

His gaze drifts over my head.

'Do you still have the letter?'

'I burnt it on the fire. I was going to send it to the planning department. I phoned them and they said there's no need because you won't get permission since this is a national park and you're only allowed residential use.'

'Did you notice a postmark?'

'No.'

259

'Was it handwritten?'

He stands stooped in the doorway, one hand pressed against the wall, his long fingers splayed. 'No. Typed on a word processor. A scrawl for a signature. Then you moved in and built your art building at the back.'

'It's just a quiet place to paint. A summerhouse. Someone was being malicious in sending the letter. I only found out when the police told me.'

'All the people coming and going. That girl giving me filthy looks.'

'What girl?'

'The rude girl with white hair.'

I sigh. Nicole. She'd said he'd given her a death stare and now she's somehow to blame. 'What did the letter say?'

'That you would move in and build a whopping great art gallery with parking.'

'I'm sorry you had that worry. We only wanted to settle here for a quiet life. Is there anything else?'

'Such as?' He looks beadily at me.

'Has anyone approached you about us?'

'Apart from the police, you mean?'

'Do you remember a man leaving the house the other week? He drove past here and stopped to speak to you.'

'Vaguely.' He's mulling it over, looking past me.

'What did he say to you?'

'Idle chit-chat. He asked how it was going with my new neighbours.'

'Oh.' I don't ask how he replied. Anorak Man was digging

for information or maybe he wanted to suss out whether our nearest neighbour would notice the attack on me. But why draw attention to himself?

'Are you better now?'

Mitchell's question catches me unawares. I don't expect him to show that kind of interest. 'I'm getting better, thank you. There might be neurological damage from the carbon monoxide poisoning, but I won't know for a while.'

'Let's hope not. You have to hang on to the old grey matter.' He taps the side of his head.

'Yes.' I smile.

'Do you think the person who sent the letter is the same person who tried to gas you?'

'I do, yes.'

'They were trying to get rid of you even before you moved in.'

'That's how it seems. Do you have any idea? Maybe someone with a connection to Chilwood who didn't want new people moving in?'

'No idea at all. It's very strange and troubling. There's never been any of that around here. I wonder what's going to happen next.'

'It's targeted at me, and I've moved out, so you don't have to worry about your safety.'

'Indeed. But don't be parted from your husband.'

'Sorry?'

'I barely spent a night apart from my wife. Married for over fifty years, until Parkinson's took her. It's a cruel disease.'

261

'Oh, I'm sorry for your loss.' If he'd shown this chink in his armour sooner, I would have been more neighbourly. 'Joe's still living in the cottage. If you need anything, just ask him.'

'And as for you, you must look after yourself,' he says.

'Thank you.' I smile and go to walk away.

He waits in the doorway until I'm back in the car. I raise a hand in farewell to Mitchell and drive away. The letter explains his hostility and the way he watched us, and I'm sorry for mis-judging him.

The rear-view mirror frames a view of Chilwood that's more melancholy than ever, reminiscent of my creepy painting with the dark skies and atmosphere of dread. It has no appeal for me, but I ache for Joe and Dora.

If I asked the police about the letter, they would say Joe sent it to alienate me from our only neighbour and isolate me even more. For me, it confirms that someone was determined to screw up my life for some time, and I'm on a mission to find out who's behind it.

CHAPTER THIRTY-EIGHT

Back at the flat, I need to find out more about Anorak Man. He's still Anorak Man to me, despite the new information from Alistair. I try his number again. It rings a few times and a man answers.

'Hello?'

'Oh, hi.' My mind freezes in panic at having to talk to him. 'Um ... is that Seb?'

'Yeah, who's that?'

'It's Lauren Geddes. You came on the smart home tour of our house the other week.'

'Oh, hi. How's it going?' He sounds cautiously friendly.

'We've had some strange incidents at home. Can we meet up with you? Since you're interested in the smart home, we wanted to run a couple of things past you.'

'Run what past me?' It's definitely him. I recognise his voice and can picture his intense stare and semi-amused look from when he spoke to me.

'We wanted to ask your viewpoint. Since you're into the set-up.'

'Yeah, well, okay. I guess so.' He sounds hesitant but intrigued enough to agree.

I could question him over the phone, but seeing him face to face might offer up more clues. I gave him the impression that Joe will come too, so he won't turn up expecting to overpower me. He doesn't live far away, and we arrange to meet in a rural café near him.

I hang up and instantly regret it. What am I doing? I don't go to cafés to meet strange men. Before the attempt on my life, I'd never have contemplated it. Scared the paranoia would flare up, I dealt with it by controlling my surroundings, but the urge to know who's doing this burns strong. I look up the café, which has parking right outside and tell myself it's daylight and safe enough.

I set off, guided by the sat nav, wondering if my attacker could hack into it. A shiver runs through me at the thought of Anorak Man following my progress online, but if my car was checked by the police, they would have found a tracking device. I hate all this surveillance.

I turn off the M27 and drive along a rural road to reach what looks like a Victorian warehouse converted into a café and craft shops. I park and walk to the entrance door. Is he watching me? The back of my neck tingles and I tell myself to stay calm. The entrance is dark from coming inside after bright sunlight, and my eyes adjust to the gloom.

'Hello there.'

264

I look up and see him looming at the top of a metal staircase. 'Café's up here.'

I go to reply but the words stick in my throat. I hesitate and then take the stairs. He looks perfectly respectable in a pale blue cotton shirt that's open at the neck, with fitted dark trousers and shiny black shoes. When I draw level with him, he holds out his hand for me to shake. He's not that tall, the same height as Joe, with coal black eyes and receding dark hair.

'Good to see you again,' he says, not seeming slighted that I didn't let him search for his key the last time we met.

We order coffees and sit at a corner table. The café's industrial style suits the building, with concrete floors and metal pendant lights.

'Nice place,' I say. 'I've never been here before.'

'It's my office.' He smiles. 'I have most of my meetings here. The coffee's good. I've a flat along the road, in a similar building to this. It used to be a mental hospital.'

'What work do you do?'

'IT.' He doesn't elaborate.

I nod in response. We're not exactly bonding, so I mirror his relaxed body language, sitting forward, hands resting on the table. 'Thank you for meeting me.'

'No worries. How's Joe? I thought he'd come too.' He has the same strangely amused look from last time as if keeping a private joke.

'He couldn't make it. He sends his regards.'

A young waitress brings us cappuccinos in earthenware cups.

A drink might ease my dry throat. At least he didn't order them and bring them over, otherwise I'd be checking for a bitter hint of something he might have slipped in mine.

'How can I help?' He tips a sachet of brown sugar into his coffee and stirs it.

'There's been a cyberattack on the house.'

'The police phoned me. It must've been scary.' He looks intently at me, as if he's thinking beyond what we're actually talking about. Something unsettles me about him, the same as when he came to the house.

'Yes, it was scary. What did they want to know?'

'Routine stuff – how I came to be on the tour, if I knew you, had I noticed anything strange. Afraid I couldn't be much use. How are you feeling now?' His voice oozes concern and my skin crawls.

'Fine.' I look at the table. 'Seeing as you're an IT expert, is there anything you think could be behind it?'

He exhales deeply. 'Oh, Lauren, I wish I knew. What's your thinking on who did it? Is it a competitor trying to sabotage you and Joe?'

I didn't consider that, but surely a business wouldn't go to that much trouble. 'It's more likely to be an individual, but we've no idea who. We don't have enemies.'

'I'm sure you don't.' Another knowing look and a trace of a smile.

'How did you come to be on the tour?'

'A friend said about it. He knew I was into smart homes and you're fairly local, so it seemed a good fit. I was interested to come and have a look, especially as you've more room than I have . . .' a smile dances on his lips, 'to play around with.'

'How did your friend know about it?'

'He saw the social media posts that your architect put out.'

'Did he come with you?'

'I came alone.' He raises an eyebrow in a suggestive way. What's he playing at?

'Do you know Karl Winter?'

'No. Who's he?'

'What's the name of the friend who recommended the tour?'

'Dino. I say he's a friend, but he's someone I met in a forum.'

'What sort of forum?'

'One for smart homes. I don't know anything about him really.'

If it's someone online, Dino could be anyone. We're not getting anywhere. I push my coffee away and stand up. 'Okay. Thanks for your time.'

I go to the counter and take out my purse. He follows and I wave away his offer to pay. He walks out with me, reaching forward to open the door to the stairs for me.

'There is one thing,' he says at the top of the staircase. 'You say you don't have any enemies . . .'

'Go on.'

'It's just this guy, Dino.' He scratches his head and looks shifty. 'He told me that you and Joe are swingers.'

'What?!' I clutch the metal stair handrail.

He reaches out a hand in a conciliatory gesture. 'Which is fine. I'm totally cool with it. It's just, well, you know . . .'

I can hardly believe what he's saying.

'Those sorts of things might attract weirdos.'

'Are you seriously telling me that the tour of our home was touted as some kind of entry-level swingers' party?'

'No, you misunderstand. I *am* interested in the tech. I met Dino on a smart home forum. He mentioned the swinging in passing. Anything goes with me. It's only now we're talking about it that the whole thing sounds suspect.'

'We are *not* swingers.' I stare defiantly at him. 'Who is this Dino?'

'I don't know. Like I say, we got friendly on a forum, chatted about where we lived. He said he knew a couple doing a smart home tour round this way. Sent me the link to your architect's blog. He said the woman was hot – sorry.' He raises his palms in apology. 'He mentioned you were a couple of swingers. I was curious. Not that I expected to turn up to a swinging party. I've never tried it myself, but I'm open-minded.'

Fuck's sake. I wish Joe were here, but he'd have grabbed Anorak Man by the throat by now and pinned him to the wall. 'This Dino,' I say. 'Is he contactable?'

'No, that's the thing. He disappeared. I tried to message him after the tour, but he's gone without a trace. All his entries on the forum disappeared. We used to DM but it was encrypted.'

'Encrypted?'

'Like the dark web.'

I know nothing about the dark web, other than it sounds like a lawless and dangerous underworld. 'Why encrypted?'

'Because a lot of techies don't like their stuff being out there for anyone to see. They have the know-how, so that's what they do. I'm not bothered, so long as no one's ripping off my credit card. But Dino's gone. Untraceable as far as I'm concerned.'

'Did you tell the police?'

'No, it's an awkward subject to bring up, and I didn't think it had any bearing. Like I said, it's only through us talking just now that it seems a bit off.'

'Why did Dino want you to come on the tour if he disappeared straight after?'

'No idea.'

'Did he ask you to do anything at the house?' I say. 'Like take photos or tamper with the hub?'

'No! God, no. It's your home. I'd never do anything like that.'

'What about your key?' I keep on. 'That wasn't for real. You didn't drop a key.'

He holds his palms up again. 'Busted.'

'Sorry?'

'I thought if I came back when it was just the two of you, we might get chatting and you'd invite me to one of your parties.' He shrugs. 'Y'know, just so I could experience it.'

I'm prickling with heat and indignation. It all makes sense, the way he undressed me with his eyes, those salacious looks that creeped me out.

'This Dino person,' I say, gripping the handrail harder. 'Did he show you any photos of me?'

'No. Nothing like that. Look, I feel terrible now. Should I tell the police about him? Will that help?'

'Please.'

'Sure. No problem.'

I give him a small nod and then turn towards the stairs, not wanting to shake his hand. I walk fast to get away from him and lock myself in my car, breathless. What would Joe think of all this? He'd have laughed off the swinging if it weren't for the revenge porn and what's happened since.

But this Dino person ... fuck ... what's his motive? It sounds exactly the kind of stunt Karl Winter would have pulled. Sending random men to the house by telling them we're swingers isn't that different to emailing a porn image to my contacts. So far, only one random man has materialised, but are there more? And Dino's deleted his online account so doesn't want to be found. My nausea from the cyberattack has resurfaced, so I drive carefully home.

I don't trust Anorak Man. He's conveniently blamed all this on a mystery person who's disappeared. Maybe Dino doesn't exist and this is some fiction of Anorak Man's. He clearly spends time on dodgy internet sites and might have seen the revenge porn from way back. There must be a solution.

CHAPTER THIRTY-NINE

The dizzy spells keep knocking me off-balance, but when Ava calls to ask if I want anything, I say Dora. Then I email Nicole who might know how to track down Dino from the smart home web forum.

> Hi, Nicole, hope it's going well in the US. Have you had any more thoughts on the cyberattack?

I tell her about Dino, and press *send*.

My skin feels as if it's crawling with insects since talking to Anorak Man yesterday. The thought of him scoping us out for sex parties is revolting. He offered to tell the police, but I'll speak to them too, since the Dino he spoke about is a new lead. I call DC Jones.

'Lauren, how are you?'

'I'm okay thanks. I found something out from Seb Alexander, who came on the smart home tour.' My voice shakes a little.

'Go on.'

'Someone called Dino befriended him in an online forum for smart home enthusiasts. Dino told him about our tour and said we were swingers, which we're not. That was probably Seb's motivation. He admitted coming back on a pretext, hoping to befriend us so we'd invite him to a swinging party.'

'Okay. That's pretty weird about the swinging, but it's feasible this person called Dino is a cybercriminal who's targeted you with a planned campaign.'

'It's the same pattern as last time, someone spreading salacious lies to humiliate me. The only person who's done that is Karl Winter.'

'Karl Winter is dead. But if it's connected, someone else is continuing the campaign against you.'

'Is it someone who knew him?'

'Or someone who knows what happened and is using it to intimidate you.'

A headache pulses in my temples and forehead. 'Where does it leave me if you can't say who did it?'

'We're still investigating. Until we know more, you can't have contact with Joe. He's had conditions imposed so he's not a threat to you or others.'

'I want this resolved.'

'I understand, but if Joe makes contact with you, he'll be taken into custody. I know it's a big deal, Lauren, but if he comes near you, call 999.'

The doorbell rings. 'Okay,' I say to DC Jones. 'I have to go.'

Ava and Chris are at the door and my heart lifts at Dora

prancing around my feet. I crouch down to stroke her, damp from the rain.

Chris holds two bags of shopping and Ava has Dora's stuff.

'How're you feeling?' she asks as they come inside.

'It's an effort to get my head into gear.'

'We've brought you some healthy food to build you up. Dora's missed you. Joe says she keeps walking from room to room and wanting to check the studio.'

I scoop Dora up and nuzzle her floppy ears. 'That's kind of you.' I'm not eating much on my own. Food doesn't fill the hollowed-out heartache that's plagued me since I left the hospital.

'We went to see Dylan,' Chris says. 'Since Joe's not allowed contact with him.'

Joe will hate the separation from Dylan. I feel bad for them both. 'How is he?'

'It's been awful for him. He's off school. He's gone back to staring into space and rocking back and forth. He hasn't done that for ages.'

My shoulders sag. 'Poor Dylan. We need to sort this out.'

Tara's blanking me. She's read my WhatsApp message but hasn't replied.

Ava hands me a bunch of yellow roses. 'These are from Joe.' I don't know what to make of the gesture, since sending flowers would be frowned upon by the police, so I lay them beside the sink.

'Put the kettle on, Chris.' She ushers me to the armchair where I sit with Dora. 'We can't stay long. We've left our two playing Xbox games with Joe in the sensory room.'

Chris's lanky frame seems larger in the small space. 'Why's that blanket over the telly?'

'Someone might be watching me through it.'

'It's unplugged.'

I shrug and busy myself with Dora.

'Let's uncover it, shall we? It's company for you.' He whips the blanket off the TV, talking like he's visiting a lonely old relative. 'You'll go mad here on your own with no one to talk to.'

'Chris.' Ava shoots him a warning look.

'Oh, sorry, ha! Not mad, as such, but you know what I mean.' He probably does think me mad. Anyway, he's wasting his time. I can't concentrate on television when my tormentor is still on the loose.

Ava unpacks food. 'I've made you beetroot soup. It's good for improving your stamina. Something to do with increasing blood flow. I figured it would help you recuperate.'

Chris boils the kettle and clinks about with mugs. 'Joe's worried about you, here on your own. Whoever means you harm, it's not him.'

'How have the police left it?' I ask.

'Seems like they've literally left it. They've hit a brick wall. Joe's solicitor is keeping him updated. They need to get the bail lifted.' He spoons instant coffee granules into mugs and talks as if it's a formality. 'Come on, Lauren, you know Joe's not capable of attempted murder.'

'I don't know what to believe anymore.'

He tuts and we stare at each other across the room. I won't be pushed into agreeing that Joe's blameless.

'You're tired,' Ava says soothingly, piling food in the nearly empty fridge. 'You need lots of rest.'

'Joe was looking for his toolbox,' Chris says.

'I needed it to change the lock. It's in the hall cupboard.' It's strange to pass everyday requests through a third party. Would the police regard this as contact by proxy?

Chris goes to the door and runs a finger over my uneven workmanship. Joe would do the same.

'The police said to change it, since anyone could have rented the flat and copied the key.'

'Sure,' he says with a tone of dismissal. He'll tell Joe I've changed the lock and bodged it.

By the time they've finished their coffee, I'm about to be pulled under by another wave of exhaustion.

'I need to sleep.' I rub my face. After sleeping badly for so long, I could lie on the kitchen floor and nod off with no trouble.

They stand up to leave. Ava takes an envelope from her handbag. 'This is from Joe.'

I stare at the envelope she holds out, unsure if I should take it.

'Don't let the police know he's written to you.' Chris says, already opening the door.

'So you do know it's against the rules?'

'I don't think the rules apply in this case, do you?' he says over his shoulder.

'But Joe could be locked up for having contact with me.'

'Only if he's making threats towards you. Otherwise it's fine, but don't let the police know as they're looking for any excuse to have a go at him.'

Including attempted murder. It stays unsaid on my lips. Ava kisses me goodbye. I close the door behind them and tear open the letter.

CHAPTER FORTY

Dear Lauren,

How are you? I hope you're recovering after the terrible time you've had. I wish I'd been there to bring you home from hospital and look after you. I asked Dora to give you a kiss from me.

I've spent a lot of time thinking about what happened. More than anything, I want you to know that I'm sorry for not believing you. I didn't support you enough when you needed me most. Please understand that I'm not involved in any of the bad stuff and neither is Dylan. No way would I ever harm you, but I was wrong to think your paranoia had returned.

After stepping back from things, I can see I was so caught up in making the smart home business a success and creating our dream home that tunnel vision set in. Life was so intense and I didn't think things through properly, what with working all hours to pay off the loan. You've been dragged through hell and I was too wrapped up in everything else, but it's all for nothing if we're not together.

It kills me to think of how scared and alone you must have felt. I'm so sorry for that. If I could turn back the clock and do things differently, I would do in a heartbeat. When the police catch who did this, my bail conditions will be lifted and I'd really like us to find our way back to how we were before it all turned crazy.

I've no idea who put the cameras and microphones in the house. I wish I did. What I do know is that someone wanted to tip you over the edge. You could be right that it's someone who knows about Karl Winter. I wish the police would stop wasting time on blaming me and find whoever's done this. My solicitor is working on things this end. He says they can't make the evidence stick, not when it's all circumstantial.

You make me happy and I would never lie to you. When all this is sorted, I want us to be back together so I can look after you, properly this time, and help you feel better. I know I messed up, but do you think we can find the good times again? So much is out of my control, and it's too soon to expect you to forgive me, but I want more than anything for us to be back together and I'll spend the rest of my days trying to make it up to you.

All my love,

Joe xxx

Reading his words, I hear his voice in my head, soft and imploring, but his risk-taking stabs at me when the police banned us from having contact. And even if he's cleared of wrongdoing, I'll never live at Chilwood Cottage again.

Ava had put the roses in a vase. I can't help loving Joe. It's him and me against the world, and now he's wrenched from me. We've come so far together and he's taught me so much and not just how to bash down a wall and plumb a bathroom. He showed me how to snowboard and how to caramelise a *crème brûlée* with a builder's blowtorch. He's patient and kind when he's showing me something, and he's the best dad to Dylan without them actually sleeping under the same roof. We're meant to be together, sharing a bed so I can wake up with him next to me. Is someone trying to split us up in a jealous vendetta?

The doorbell goes again and I open the door to DC Jones. 'Hi, Lauren, can I come in?'

I realise I've left Joe's letter open on the coffee table. She comes inside and I close the door, resisting the urge to bolt past her and snatch it up.

'Is there any update?' I follow her in and discreetly lift the letter and envelope, sliding them in the nearest drawer.

'I was going to phone, but I thought I'd drop in and check how you are. Are you okay here?'

My hands are shaking, perhaps with the anticipation of why she's here. 'I'm fine. What were you going to phone about?'

'We've spoken to Seb Alexander.' She sits in the armchair and I sink onto the sofa opposite. 'He checks out, but we can't trace the person he calls Dino.'

'Can your IT people find him? If you find out who it is, it puts Joe in the clear.'

'What makes you say that, Lauren?'

'Because this person called Dino is trying to stitch me up.'

'But Dino could be Joe.'

They're determined to pin it on Joe. I look out at the grey sky above the rooftops.

'He could've posed as Dino online and manipulated Seb,' she goes on. 'Everything leads back to Joe.'

But Joe wouldn't do that. He wouldn't. I look at the closed drawer holding his letter. 'Is he your only suspect?'

'He's the main suspect, yes. The investigation is still open and it's important you don't have any contact with him.'

I wrap my arms around myself and nod slowly, but I don't really believe it.

'Is there someone you can stay with, so you're not alone?'

'No. No one else has a key for this place, so I'm safe.'

'Don't let anyone in who you don't trust. Take a photo of anyone you don't know who comes to the door.'

'Okay.'

'I don't want to scare you, though. You know that Joe was best placed to carry out the cyberattack?'

'I know … it's just … I can't bear to think of him doing that to me.' My voice chokes with upset. 'I just want things back to how they were.'

'Sometimes what we want and what we need are two different things,' she says in a mild way.

I know she's only looking at the facts, and the facts don't look good.

'We'll keep you posted.' She leaves and I lock the door behind her.

A stab of pain in my side catches me off-guard. I double

over, clutching for the wall, the door handle, anything to steady myself. I stay bent over until the pain is blunt enough for me to crumple onto the floor and sit with my head resting on my knees. It must be stress.

Eventually, I get up and take out the letter from Joe again. He's included a photo of Dora stretched out on a sunny patch of grass in front of the cottage. It reminds me of the estate agent's property brochure; the cottage a picture of idyllic rural charm, the photos taken on a sunny day with the deep red roses in full bloom outside. The brochure described the picturesque and unspoilt South Downs location.

We fell for the charms of Chilwood and saw through the years of neglect to the potential we could bring out. Shame we couldn't see the danger looming. The cottage isn't to blame though. If Karl Winter is the link, it started long before we found it. Opening our home to the online world only allowed someone to use it against us.

My heart tightens at our carefully nurtured hopes and plans. Look where that's got us, now Joe and I are forced apart. It's no use fighting back the tears. My eyes well and a fat tear trickles down my face. It's the end of our life in the country, and maybe the end of us. Hot tears of frustration course down my face. I sob into my sweatshirt sleeves, letting the fabric soak up my tears. This must be what heartbreak feels like, the heavy weight pressing on my chest and tightening my breath. My nose is bunged-up and I go to the bathroom for some tissues to swab my tears.

A quick look at the app tells me the lights are on in the

kitchen at the cottage, so Joe is probably there. Even the things that annoy me about him aren't so bad now, like the way he sets his iPhone to snooze for an hour before we need to wake up. It buzzes every ten minutes because he prefers waking up slowly. He can't even lie in bed without tech being part of his life. Whatever Joe says, I have to get used to living without him if the police keep telling me to keep my distance.

I need to talk to someone who's on my side. I can't afford any more sessions with Annette, but I can email Brooke. I tap a message out to update her on Joe and then I curl up in bed in a fug of despair. Rain hammers on the window. It's late afternoon and dark already. Now it's November, the long dismal nights suit my mood. I check my messages an hour later and Brooke has replied.

Sorry, Lauren, but you need a reality check. Don't take this the wrong way, but I'm all out of patience where Joe's concerned. You think he's a top bloke even though it comes across that he's manipulating you. Have the police talked to you about that? I've tried being understanding because you love him, but shit got real with the attempt on your life. Take off your blinkers. Your life is in danger. If the police say he tried to kill you, then you have to believe it. B x

What the—? Where did that come from? She says *don't take this wrong way*, as if there's a right way to say my husband contrived to murder me. She must have been drinking. Some friend she is to kick me when I'm down.

Drunk or not, she sounds exasperated. My face burns. Am I so far gone that I can't see the obvious? I delete the email and a tightening fist of pain in my stomach nearly floors me. It wells up in my throat in a big knot of a sob, catching me unaware, and I have to stop and breathe and tell myself it'll go away soon.

I haven't told anyone that I sometimes wake to the sound of whispering, and I still see ghostly dark shapes in my peripheral vision that disappear when I focus on them. It's my overactive imagination tormenting me. Even this basic new-build flat has taken on an ominous, creepy air. Joe might be right about the problem following me.

The room darkens as if the end of the world is coming. The sky through the rain-streaked window is a threatening inky-grey, ready for a downpour. Dora watches me from her bed. If it weren't for her I might knock back all the pills at once and blot out the piercing hurt. Defeat presses on me, a crushing weight on my chest. My life is trashed. What a relief to leave all this behind and not have to contemplate an empty future of hiding from harm.

CHAPTER FORTY-ONE

The rain has moved on by morning. Since the carbon monoxide poisoning, it feels like I'm nursing a queasy hangover, even though I haven't had a drink all week. My responses are slower, but a walk with Dora in the chilly November air clears my head enough for a plan to take shape.

I bundle her in the car to go somewhere I have no desire to visit – Tara's house. She'll find it harder to blank me in person. I blast myself with cold air on the half-hour drive in an attempt to stay alert. When I pull up outside, Dora perks up at the prospect of seeing Dylan. The doorbell doesn't work so I knock on the window of the white uPVC door. Dylan's shape comes lumbering towards me through the obscured glass, and he opens the door.

'Hi, Dylan, how are you?'

''Kay.' He picks up Dora and cuddles her, hanging his head.

'I'm sorry about what happened with the police.'

'Yeah.' He hides behind his thick dark fringe and looks at Dora.

'Who is it, Dyl?' Tara shouts from upstairs.

He doesn't answer.

'Could you ask your mum if I can have a word?'

He turns and goes upstairs, still carrying Dora. I wait on the doorstep. Tara comes downstairs in skinny jeans and a pink snug-fitting jumper with a sparkly star on the front, tweaking her head of artfully messy hair.

'What's this about?' She looks curious and hostile all at once, unsure of how to handle me without Joe as the buffer. He keeps us completely separate. I've never spoken to her before, never stepped inside her home. The closest I've come is waiting outside in the car.

'Hi, Tara. Can I talk to you? It's about Joe.'

Her highlights catch the sun and her vivid pink nails are salon-perfect. She looks nearly as polished as the Facebook screenshots that Brooke sent me. I try not to think of Brooke since her spiky email last night, but she'd get a kick out of this.

Tara purses her lips, stands back and tilts her head towards the lounge by way of an invitation inside. 'It's a bit messy.'

We go inside and I pick my way around the plastic toys strewn on the floor. She sits on the long corner couch, her arms folded and I join her at a polite distance.

'Where's Harper?'

'Nursery. I pick her up in an hour,' she says, her voice brusque.

'Chris and Ava came to see me. They said Joe's not allowed to see Dylan.'

She rolls her eyes. 'They came here too, like a couple of good Samaritans, Chris looking down his nose at me.'

I smile, picturing Chris doing just that. 'I'm not sure he's that keen on me either. The police think Joe's behind the cyber-attack, and I want to find a way to prove them wrong.'

'How you gonna do that?' She unfolds her arms.

'He was here when it happened. Do you think he could've masterminded it?'

'Not a chance,' she says with a firm head shake. 'I'm telling you, no way could he have done it with Dylan in such a state. We couldn't do anything with him, I had Harper hanging off me, upset 'cos Dyl's freaking out. I took Harper off to try and calm her down for bed. Joe was with Dyl in the next bedroom. I could hear him talking to Dyl the whole time. The walls are paper-thin.'

'But Joe fell asleep.'

'Yeah, but that's Joe. He'll sleep anywhere. I went in when Harper finally went off. Joe was still talking and Dyl had calmed down. I made him his favourite milkshake and when I took it up, they were asleep on the bed. Dylan exhausted himself and he must've calmed down and Joe relaxed a bit, then he was out for the count. I said all that to the police.'

'Did you wake Joe up?'

'No.' She stands up, gathers some of the toys and dumps them in a big empty plastic box. 'I was knackered so I went to bed. Harper doesn't sleep through. She woke me later and Joe was still asleep in the same spot.'

'He thinks someone set him up. Someone online called Dino is up to something, but I don't know his real identity.'

She closes her eyes. 'What a shitstorm.'

I nod in agreement.

'What if they put him in prison?' She stands by the toy box and gnaws on the tip of her little finger. It would be a disaster for them as well as us. 'How will I survive if he's not earning?' She looks at me as if I have the answer.

'If Joe's not guilty, we have to prove it.'

'Harper's dad's a deadbeat, so I'll be at the foodbank,' she keeps on. 'Will you sell the house?'

'I want to, even though we'll lose money. That's if anyone even wants it.'

She purses her lips and shrugs.

'Did Dylan have any idea who was harassing him on Halloween night?'

'It was just kids.'

'Is he being bullied at school again?'

'Something going on, but this was kids mucking about because they could hide behind Halloween masks.'

'It had a bearing on what happened.'

'How?' she asks.

'Whoever tried to kill me targeted Dylan. They wanted Joe here calming him down.'

The other option is hard to take – that Joe masterminded it. If he did, Tara could be in on it, so I won't take her at face value.

'Can I talk to Dylan, to ask him something?'

'Ask him what?' She picks up a discarded Peppa Pig toy dressed as a glowing pink fairy.

'I want to know if he's aware of anything going on. If the police think he was dragged in, he might know something.'

'The bastards. Dyl could hardly function after they'd given him the third degree.' She scoops up the other toys more fiercely.

'I'm sorry for what he's going through. If I can have a word with him, it might throw some light on what's happening.'

She stands at the window with her back to me, arms folded.

'You can be there too, of course.'

'I need to go shopping. It's easier without madam in tow.'

'Does he know what went on with the cyberattack?'

'Yes, but he hasn't talked about it. I doubt you'll get anything out of him.' She turns back to face me, arms still folded, one foot tapping.

'Let me give you my new number,' I say. 'In case you need me for . . . whatever. I'm careful about who has it, so please don't give it to anyone else. That includes Joe, since the police say I can't have contact with him.'

She fishes a sparkly phone from her jeans pocket and I ping her a text.

'Yeah, got it.' Then she goes to the hallway. 'Dyl? Lauren wants to see you.'

He opens his bedroom door and stands motionless. I go to the foot of the stairs. 'Hey, Dylan, how are you?'

''Kay.'

'Go on up,' she says. 'Just going to the shops, Dyl.'

I climb the stairs. 'Is this okay, Dylan? Can we have a chat?'

He turns and goes back into his room, leaving the door open, which I take as an invitation to follow him in. Dora is curled on the single bed in the corner of the darkened room. He flops out with one arm around her. I resist the urge to open the curtains and let some light in.

A desk and chair are wedged alongside a wardrobe with a wonky door. Cables from his gaming gadgets tangle down into a scuffed white extension lead. It's all flimsy, cheap furniture that looks tired even in the dim light. We'll buy him some new furniture when we can afford it. I sit at the end of the bed and lean against the wall, the same as Joe does at home when he chats to Dylan.

'I'm sorry for all the stuff that's gone on with the police,' I say.

''Kay.' He lies back looking at the ceiling.

'Did they tell you about the cyberattack on me?'

'Yup.'

'Crazy, isn't it?'

'Yup.'

'What do you think's behind it?'

'Dunno.'

'I just thought with your IT skills, you could help.'

He blinks at the ceiling.

'I'm trying to understand what happened. You're clever with technology. Could someone with no access to us hijack the smart home and then come inside, plant hidden cameras, mess around with the CCTV?'

'Yup.'

'How would you hack into someone's smart home?'

'Send a synchronisation command from the web interface.'

'Okay.' That means nothing to me.

'You get the serial number of the hub and send it a custom configuration file.'

I keep my voice casual. 'Is the serial number printed on the hub?'

'Maybe.'

'Is it printed on our hub?'

'Yup.'

My heart beats faster. 'So what happens with the, um, configuration file?'

'You extract the login. It's easy,' he says in his monotone voice. 'The password's harder. It's encrypted, but you can break it.'

Wow. Okay. 'I'm struggling with this, Dylan, so it's useful to have your take on it.' I say it kindly, since I'm not blaming him.

He keeps looking the ceiling, but he's listening.

'Do you know who might have done that to me?'

'Nope.'

'Is there anything you can think of that might help me?'

'Nope.'

I won't push it any further. 'Okay, thanks for that. I'll head off with Dora now. Are you all right here on your own? I can wait till your mum comes home.'

'I'm okay.'

I extract Dora from him and drive home, unsettled by his knowledge. No wonder the police were so interested in him. If Tara's telling the truth about Halloween night, then Joe can't be guilty. He would have been focused on Dylan the whole time. Joe's never been a multi-tasker. He does one job at a time and does it well. No way could he handle Dylan's meltdown alongside a cyberattack. And he falls asleep as soon as he lies down.

Tara made it sound entirely plausible, but the police think otherwise. Talking to her has been something of a breakthrough. I didn't expect us to be roughly on the same side after years of her seeing me as the other woman.

When I park the car, the phone pings with a message from Tara.

Thanks for upsetting Dylan. He's in a right state.

I call her straight back but it goes to voicemail. 'Tara, I got your message. I'm sorry about Dylan. I asked his advice on how someone might hack into the smart home. I wasn't blaming him for anything. He seemed his usual self when I left.'

Silence. I don't expect a reply. Back at the flat, I can't settle. Dylan seemed willing to talk, but I pushed it too far by asking how to hack into the hub. My mistake for trying to work things out and making it worse. I've always tried to be the understanding one, stepping back from conflict and letting Joe wade in. I keep checking for an update from Tara. I won't message her again as she'll have her hands full if Dylan's upset.

A couple of hours later, another text comes through from her.

Dylan says he did everything. His dad knew nothing about it. Can't talk. We're at the police station.

What? Dylan did everything? Was he pretending to be Dino? Did he block my exhaust and play the recording of Joe saying he wanted to kill me? I call DC Jones and leave a voicemail for her to call me back. My head swims and I recall Dylan's calm words about taking the serial number of the hub and sending a configuration file to extract the login.

Anyone with a smart home isn't that smart. I can hack a smart hub so fast it's embarrassing. You don't even need access to their WiFi. The serial number is the master key. If a cyberattacker knows the serial number of the hub, they can send it a custom configuration file and find the login just like that. The password is encrypted, but I can break it.

When I wasn't round at theirs, I watched them through the cameras and used listening devices to keep tabs on them. For someone with my skill, their whole life is open to me. I know more about IT than them, and more about security. They have a nice place with all the tech, but they're not so clever. I know the secrets they hide. Those suckers don't deserve a megabit of sympathy.

CHAPTER FORTY-TWO

After two hours, DC Jones still hasn't returned my call. I'd wanted Joe's bail conditions to be dropped, but not if it means trouble for Dylan. I can't believe he wanted me dead. DC Jones is probably all over it, which is why she hasn't called back. I try to paint but it's no use.

At last, my mobile rings with a call from DC Jones. 'Hi, Lauren, I'm calling with an update.'

'Is it about Dylan?'

'Yes. We've been talking to him, but it's a slow process, as I'm sure you can imagine.'

'And?'

'It appears he orchestrated the cyberattack. He says he kept it secret and Joe had no part in it.'

'What'll happen now?'

'We need more time to question him. I just wanted you to know at this stage.'

'What if he's only saying it because he's upset about his dad being locked up?'

'We found a secret laptop that he kept hidden. It backs up what he says.'

I cover my mouth with my hand. Joe speculated about Dylan having a hidden device and I'd refused to believe it.

'Do you know if Dylan is Dino, the man Seb Alexander met on a forum?' I say it without thinking, but Dylan isn't sophisticated enough to hoodwink Anorak Man.

'We're working on it. Now we have his devices, we're going over his internet use for a clearer picture of what went on.'

'If he did carry out the cyberattack, he was treating it as a game. I doubt he blocked my exhaust.'

'We don't know enough at this stage. He gets upset and won't co-operate when we talk about you being hurt.'

'He's not locked in a police cell, is he?'

'Don't worry, we're mindful of his needs.'

'Does this put Joe in the clear?'

'Joe has to stay on bail at least until we've investigated what Dylan tells us. That's all I can say at this point. I'll keep you updated.'

She ends the call. If Dylan did it all and posed as Dino, then I'm safe from the nameless, faceless harm. We knew about his hacking skills all along, even if Joe hated me suggesting it. Dylan could have picked up about Karl Winter from Joe and Tara, or even by listening in remotely to Joe and me talking. In Dylan's world, this could all be an elaborate computer game with Karl Winter as the bad guy avatar and Dino as his alter ego.

But he wouldn't block my exhaust, since what motive could he have for wanting me dead? Unless he thought Joe would get back with Tara in my absence. It would only take a careless comment for Dylan to latch onto the idea. Have the violent video games warped his mind so he acted out a dangerous game in real life?

I open the bottle of wine that Chris and Ava brought over and pour a large glass. It's our favourite Chablis, so Joe must have slipped it in with the groceries. What will he make of all this? The police will keep him in the dark until they've investigated further, which he'll hate. The wine makes me nostalgic and I long to hear his voice, despite the police warning me off. Joe's not in the clear, yet Tara's explanation of him falling asleep on Halloween night is more credible than him engineering a cyber-attack from Dylan's bedroom.

He'll be gutted that Dylan hid devices from him and carried on the illegal activity. Given the divisions between us, it might send Joe back into Tara's arms. I shouldn't think like that, but it's a downward spiral. I pour a second glass of wine for its relaxing effect to take hold, but it only darkens my mood.

I remember through the fug of alcohol that Nicole never replied to my email asking for her take on Dino. Isn't she back now? Maybe the police are talking to her, and I should be too. I knock back the wine and fire off another email asking for an urgent catch up. Then I push the laptop away, unsteady from drinking the wine too fast. It's gone to my head, intensifying the woozy after-effects of the carbon monoxide poisoning. It might be better if I lie down, so I stretch out on the sofa. I reach over to shut the laptop lid and vaguely register that the email to Nicole has bounced back undelivered.

Scamming people is like a drug. Some people are addicted to booze or pills, but risk-taking gives the best dopamine hit. I'm an adrenaline junkie, but I don't skydive from a plane at four thousand metres. Scamming is my drug of choice.

I accessed Joe and Lauren's private conversations, looking for anything incriminating, monitoring them for weak spots. I didn't make money from going after them, but it gave the ultimate pay-off in seeing them suffer. The key was to find their weak spot, the place it would hurt most to hit.

So obviously I chose the kid.

CHAPTER FORTY-THREE

I fell asleep on the sofa last night from drinking all that wine. Dora nudges me awake, impatient to go out. We shamble to the nearby green and I check emails on my phone, including the undelivered message to Nicole.

Her email might be down, so I look up her website to contact her through that. Her site doesn't come up, but I find another one in the search engine with a nearly identical name. The website doesn't look right. It's a more dated and generic version of Nicole's. It could be an old one from before she specialised in smart homes, although it's not her style. We walk back to the flat and I open the laptop to pull up her website on the larger screen.

I click on the 'contact' page. It's not so slick, just a web contact form and a postal address in Norwich. I vaguely remember her saying she's from Norwich. I fill in my contact details and in the message box type:

> Hi, Nicole, hope it went well in the US. Have you had
> any thoughts on the cyberattack? We're still drawing a
> blank here.

Minutes later, an email comes through from Nicole Cummings, different to her usual email address.

> You must have the wrong Nicole. I don't know anything
> about a cyberattack.

I fire back a reply:

> I'm looking for Nicole Cummings from Norwich who
> specialises in smart home technology. Her website looks
> similar to yours, but it's for smart homes.

The response is immediate:

> Sorry. Not me.

I search her website for a contact number. There isn't one, so I dash off another email.

> Please can I phone you?

She sends her mobile number and I call her. A woman answers with a hello.

'Hi, are you Nicole Cummings?'

'I am.' A baby squeals and babbles in the background.

I give her a brief appraisal of what's happened and say that the other Nicole was based in Surrey.

'It's definitely not me.' She sounds mystified and nothing like Nicole. 'I've never been to Surrey, let alone done business there. I only work part-time for a few local businesses.'

But if she's Nicole Cummings from Norwich, who was the Nicole who set up our smart home?

'That's strange,' I say. 'Your details are almost exactly the same.'

'Coincidence?'

There's a pause while I process what she's saying. Could it really be a coincidence? Same name, same place, similar website?

'Yes,' I say eventually. 'You're probably right, thanks.'

Nicole can't be part of this, not when she rescued me. How can the person giving me cybersecurity tips and goofing around with talk of ghosts have stolen someone else's identity? I want Joe's take on it, since he knows her best, but I call DC Jones instead. It's her voicemail again, so I leave a breathless message for her to call.

Alone in the quiet flat, it starts adding up – the conveniently timed trip abroad, the email no longer working. Did Nicole mean us harm all along? It makes no sense when I'd be dead without her, but none of this made sense from the start when the smart home only malfunctioned for me.

No matter how much I like Nicole, she was well-placed to carry out the cyberattack. I try DC Jones again and still get her voicemail, so I call the switchboard and insist on talking to whoever's running the investigation. The receptionist puts me through to a detective sergeant with a gravelly voice. I tell him about Nicole and he says he'll alert the detective constable to the new information, and the team will look straight into it.

I phone Alistair and tell him about my conversation with the other Nicole.

'This is awful,' he says, sounding as thrown by the revelation as I am.

'How well do you know Nicole?' I ask him.

'I only met her once before Joe linked up with her. I was impressed with her skills, especially considering her low costs. I thought she'd be charging big money in a year or two, so we should get in while she was starting out and her fees were reasonable. If only I'd known. You put everything into creating that beautiful cottage and now it's all tainted.'

The cottage is the least of my worries.

'I was pleased when Joe said he was going into business with her,' Alistair says. 'It seemed like a good fit for his business sense and her IT skills. What does Joe say about it?'

'The police won't let me talk to him.'

'Even now, in light of this?'

'I'm waiting to hear back from the detective on the case. Why do you think she's done this?'

'Gosh, I've no idea.'

'How did she get away with posing as someone else? Surely she'd have needed formal ID for setting up the business?'

'I remember Joe saying it wasn't a limited company, so there weren't any formalities,' Alistair says, 'and Nicole was laid-back about the contractual side.'

Because she knew she wouldn't stick around long enough. I doodle angry criss-cross patterns on the back of an envelope, the pen digging in. 'So he wouldn't have needed to register her National Insurance number or any other ID?'

'Probably not. If they're both self-employed, there needn't be much bureaucracy until they're actually making money.'

'How did you meet her?'

'She pitched her business to me, hoping I'd recommend her to clients, and then she met Joe by coincidence.'

I remember Joe saying he met her by chance at a smart home fair. He'd stopped for a coffee and Nicole asked if she could share the table while she charged her laptop. She asked about his interest in smart homes and told him she'd just set up as a specialist, after working in software development.

'It wasn't a coincidence,' I say. 'She scoped him out. If she hacked his emails, she could've known about you and that he planned on going to the IT fair.'

'It's all rather mind-boggling. Joe said she came up with the perfect solution without him having to explain much, as if she'd anticipated his needs. Which she did, if she'd hacked him.'

'Why go to that trouble? Do you think she's working for someone with a grudge against Joe?'

'Hmm . . .' He pauses in contemplation. 'No, she must be the one driving it.'

'Why?'

'How difficult would it be to find someone with her specific skill set who's prepared to put herself on the line like that?' I picture Alistair shaking his head, trying to work it out.

'I can't believe anyone would go to those lengths because of us,' I say.

'It's quite something, the way she's ripped off someone else's identity and fooled us all. That takes calculated effort. If she's behind it, she duped everyone.'

'But why? She's a sweet person. She gave me tips for staying safe online. Someone must have threatened or blackmailed her so she had no choice.'

'Only one person can tell us that and she's gone AWOL.'

'What if she's in danger? I'll have to speak to the police.'

'Hmm.' He sounds doubtful. 'While you're speaking to them, make sure they put Joe in the clear.'

My phone buzzes and DC Jones's name flashes up on the screen. I hurriedly finish off with Alistair and answer the incoming call.

'Lauren, thanks for the update. We've done some initial investigation and spoken to the real Nicole Cummings.'

'That was quick.'

'It appears the fake Nicole purchased her flights to the US in Nicole Cummings's name. She didn't show up for the outbound flight, which suggests she bought the flights simply to show us the details and keep us off her back.'

'So she's still in the country?'

'Or she has a different identity. Her phone's no longer in use, and her website and email are offline.'

'But she's the one who saved me.'

'She might have had second thoughts about killing you, but we can't really say at this stage.'

'Can you track her down?'

'We're checking on who owns her flat. We'll see if she's left any incriminating evidence or some kind of trail that will lead us to her.'

Now the lie of Nicole is exposed, I feel just as unsafe with her on the loose. 'If she tried to kill me, I'm still in danger. She's still out there.'

'It sounds as if she's gone to ground. Call 999 if you see her or if you're in any danger.'

'What about Joe?'

'What about Joe?' she asks.

'Now he's in the clear. It's Nicole, not him and Dylan.'

'Lauren, you know we talked about whether you thought Joe was having an affair?'

'Yes.' My chest tightens in nervous anticipation.

'I know this is difficult for you, but one line of enquiry is that Joe had an affair with Nicole, and this is her revenge because he didn't leave you. Either that, or the two of them acted together to destabilise you.'

'But ... that's crazy.'

'We found evidence of,' she pauses, 'let's call it a flirtation.'

'What evidence?'

'From his phone. They both denied it straight after the cyberattack, which is to be expected. When we questioned Nicole a second time, she said the emails were sent to her from Joe, but not reciprocated. She said she was embarrassed and blanked them, and that Joe didn't act upon them. She told us she was gay and showed us photos of her girlfriend on her phone.'

'She talked about dating men on Tinder to me.'

'Well, we're still investigating. I'll update you once we know more.'

I hate them having dirt on Joe. I can't bear to ask for the specifics because I've had enough sexual humiliation from the revenge porn, swinging parties and Joe's apparent affair. If I hadn't finished the wine last night, I'd hit the bottle again. But I've no inclination to go out for booze. And what if Nicole, or whoever she is, is out there? She might be looking for more ways to screw with me. God knows what's provoked her into all this twisted shit. She's gone to massive lengths to take on another woman's identity and create an entire business just to fuck with us. And I can't get my head round Joe sending her suggestive emails. What was he playing at?

It was easy to get Dylan onside. Never underestimate how much a kid of that age wants to feel understood, especially a little misfit like Dylan. Lauren thinks he's so savvy with the tech, but he's as naïve as her. It took me no time at all to track him down and figure out the basics from his sad social media posts, like his love of horror movies. Or that he has no friends.

When I targeted Dylan, I told him that aspies like us can't get regular jobs, so we need good IT skills to be in demand. Dylan hacked into his school's mainframe as the entry-level test. I had him believe we could go into business when he turned sixteen. As if. I don't hang around with actual aspies.

Joe had to pay and I intended to cause him maximum damage. I wanted to find him in a compromising situation and post it online. Lauren's the sort who wouldn't come back from that kind of hurt. But there was nothing. Joe Geddes is squeaky clean.

CHAPTER FORTY-FOUR

Since DS Jones planted the seed of an affair between Joe and Nicole, I've been caught in a fight between head and heart, not believing it, but Joe could have blinded me to the truth. I sit at the table with my head in my hands, overwhelmed with sadness for what we've lost. I miss the warmth in his voice, the togetherness. When did it start going wrong? Was it before the house turned creepy or after?

I picture him in a tender clinch with Nicole, kissing her the way he kisses me, one hand on the side of my neck, stroking my hair, cupping my face, holding me close. The shard of pain returns, digging in my side. I double over, clutching at the table edge. I push away the mental image of them together and take shallow breaths until the pain eases off.

I don't know why Nicole would try to kill me unless she wanted to be with Joe. That's stupid, though. Nicole isn't a *Fatal Attraction femme fatale*. She's sweet and normal, or at least that's what she had us believe. Maybe he flirted and she reciprocated, but he pulled back. Even so, it's an impressive line in revenge. And that doesn't explain how she met him. It's too much of a coincidence that she'd met Alistair and then bumped into Joe at a huge event. If Nicole is the person who wrote to Mitchell, then she planned it way back.

My mind replays the times we met, her fresh face, the cheery diligence, changing the passwords so I'd be in control. Someone else must be behind it, someone who made her a financial offer she couldn't refuse. If she's not Dino, then Dino might be paying her, but then she had an attack of conscience and rescued me before escaping. Whoever's behind it must have a pretty big motive.

It's early evening and the police haven't come back to update me. Once more, I'm blanketed by sleep. The next thing I know, Dora's nudging me. It's nearly six in the morning and I've slept for twelve hours in the chair. By the time I've woken up properly, DC Jones calls to say she's coming over.

The risks were high but the rewards were higher. I knew their next renovation would be their 'forever home' and the smart home became my way in. What if I played a twisted game? It would be hard to prove, less criminal than my other plans and I could still ruin their lives. They had to pay. But I had to be clever about how far to push it so the police wouldn't be interested in a neurotic couple who haven't suffered any quantifiable loss.

Scamming Joe and Lauren involved certain intricacies. I hacked that geek ahead of the smart home tour and saw he'd visited swinging websites. Tragic bastard didn't even have a girlfriend to swap, but inadequate people need hope. I figured his intense look would unsettle Lauren. You need an evil mind for this, and it's good to have a laugh along the way.

I learned about the technology and once I'd got inside the house, I owned them. They made it easy: dippy Lauren acting like a clueless idiot, and Joe so giddy about the smart home that he checked his brain out at the door. I kept them under surveillance, violating their rights. Ha ha, I'm joking. Those bastards don't have any rights.

CHAPTER FORTY-FIVE

'Have you found anything out?' I ask when DC Jones turns up.

'It's very strange. We visited the woman we all thought was Nicole at her flat after the cyberattack. It was a short-term rental set up in the real Nicole's name. She doesn't have a financial motive because she didn't defraud you. We're looking at some kind of revenge, but she didn't want to kill you.'

'No?'

'Because she rescued you.'

'But—'

'She's a dangerous person who wanted to scare you and possibly set Joe up.'

'So she didn't have an affair with him?'

'They might have had an affair that ended badly.'

'Do you have proof?'

'That's how it looks.'

'Was Joe involved?'

She holds the mug of tea I gave her. 'That's where it gets

difficult. The incriminating evidence against Joe could have been planted by Nicole, as we'll refer to her for now. That's unless they were in league to murder you until Nicole got cold feet and rescued you.'

I should ask what evidence they have, but I can't bear any more details of Joe's supposed affair.

'Sometimes people do stupid things,' she says. 'They don't always think. He might have been infatuated with her, or he might have been set up. Unfortunately, we don't know which it is.'

He never showed signs of infatuation, but I don't say it because she'll only give me another of her sceptical looks.

'Where does Dylan come into it?'

'His DNA is all over the house, obviously, but there's hardly any on your car.'

I exhale. That must mean he didn't try to kill me. Again, I don't say it in case she finds some way to make him guilty, the same as she has with Joe.

'Are you still questioning him?'

'He's home now.'

And traumatised, no doubt, but at least he's home.

'He says someone called Salty put him up to it,' she says.

'Salty?'

'Have you heard of anyone called Salty? It's someone he only knows online.'

'No. Is Salty another Dino?'

'They might be the same person. It could be Nicole, or Joe or both of them.'

Or someone else, I'm not discounting the idea that Nicole was acting under duress.

'This is a long shot, but you said that you and Joe fell out with your brother in America. Nicole's flights to the US weren't used, but she might have taken a different flight there. Is there any way she could be in league with him?'

'I've no idea. I did think there was something familiar about her. When I told her about the man having a sneaky look at the smart hub, she looked hacked-off. It was the only time her mask slipped and I thought I recognised her from the past, but I couldn't put my finger on it.'

'Could she have met your brother before he went to the US?'

'I doubt it. He moved there ten years ago, so she'd have been a schoolgirl.'

She asks for Dale and Kim's details and I give her their full names, ages and look up the last address I had for them.

'Can you find out if she's Salty and Dino or if it's someone else?'

'I'll update you tomorrow. There's only so much we can do when she's probably abroad with a different identity.'

'What about CCTV? Surely someone will know her. She had that distinctive white pixie haircut.'

'No one has a photo because she's erased herself from all CCTV.'

'Don't you have her on CCTV from the police station?'

'She didn't come to the station. She wasn't a suspect. We interviewed her at her home. She only needed to wear a convincing wig when she left the country and we'd never pick her up on camera. We have forensic evidence from your car that will be kept on record. If she reoffends and we get hold of her, we can charge her.'

'That sounds weak. She's capable of murder. Isn't she a danger to society?'

She looks gravely at me. 'She's not a known criminal. It looks like this was a personal attack against you, setting up Joe. Yes, she's a danger, but she's covered her tracks. We don't have the resources for an international manhunt when she's not a financial scammer or a murderer.'

'But she nearly killed me.'

'She didn't want to kill you. She wanted to scare you.'

'The carbon monoxide poisoning could've gone either way, but I've no idea why she'd want me dead. She stopped short so you wouldn't go after her. If anything, that makes her more dangerous.' I look out of the window.

'The case is still open. We can have a breakthrough any time. She's meticulous, but she might have made a mistake and incriminated herself. We're in touch with international law enforcement and the National Crime Agency.'

'What do they do?'

'They investigate cybercrimes.'

'And?'

'They've drawn a blank.' She picks up her mug and drinks half the tea in one go as if sinking a pint.

I can't believe Nicole is above the law.

'Our cybercrime colleagues say it's not the actions of an amateur. It's not something we see even at the highest level of criminal activity. Crimes aren't usually planned this well, not without a big financial motive. Yes, she's dangerous. Nobody's disputing that. But we believe she was driven by a personal vendetta.'

'Are you even looking for her?'

'Yes, but she's skilled and she has the resources to pull off an impressive scam. This probably isn't her first crime. I suspect her financial resources came from previous scams. We haven't found any trademarks to link this crime to any others, but she's young and has got away with it so far, or else other crimes she's committed haven't been of this exact nature.' She drains her tea and puts the mug in the sink.

'Could you still track her down?'

'Definitely. She's a risk-taker. Risk-takers tend to get caught eventually.' She adopts a softer tone. 'What she did to you was terrible. I'm just saying don't expect a swift conclusion.'

I see DC Jones out, frustrated by her polite stonewalling. I have to work out Nicole's motive; the fake Nicole, that is. She must hate us, risking so much to exact revenge. She might have disappeared, but she can still cause havoc remotely. Or is she nearby, watching for another opportunity? A plan forms in my mind. It's risky and Joe won't like it, but he's not here and I have to take action before she comes back for another go at me.

I wanted to get under her skin. Her art's important to her, so I targeted that. I was there when they fitted the summerhouse door, which had three keys and I took one. She must have thought it only came with two keys. Doing harm in the physical world is riskier than online, but it cast doubt over the smart home, so her fucker of a husband could cling to his precious toy until I ramped it up to breaking point.

I left nothing to chance. Anyone on site could make their own tea and coffee from Lauren and Joe's supplies in the makeshift kitchen. An arty sign by Lauren next to the kettle said, HELP YOURSELF, MILK IN THE FRIDGE. The dope even added a smiley face. None of the tradesmen touched the decaf coffee, but I saw Lauren having it so I switched it to full-strength coffee. She never made the connection between caffeine and her fitful, jittery nights, and why would she?

Towards the end, I hijacked the email of her Aussie friend to fuck with her even more and max out her suspicions about Joe. And I had a go at the old git down the road. Little touches helped, like recording the yappy dog and playing it outside his house at night, so he'd hate on them even more. Like I say, twisted mind.

CHAPTER FORTY-SIX

Ava calls to say that she and Chris have visited Joe. 'He's trying to stay positive, but it's tough on him.'

'Did he talk about Nicole?'

'Yes, he's gutted. Unbelievable, isn't it? That she'd cause all that trouble, and for what?'

'Hmm.'

'He absolutely insists that they didn't have an affair. He only wants to be with you,' she says in her earnest way. 'Not Tara or that bitch Nicole, whoever she is.'

'Can he think of anything else that might help? There must be something we can go on.'

'He says he's gone over every conversation, every email. There's no clue to her agenda, but he's trying to work it out. Then the two of you can be together again.'

Someone must know who she is. The police will only find a DNA match if she commits another crime. What if that never happens? I can't hunt her down alone, so I turn to the person who views me with resentment: Tara. I take the direct approach and drive back over to knock on their door, Dora quivering expectantly at my feet.

'Who the hell's that?' A harassed-sounding Tara comes through and opens the door. 'What are you doing here?' She glares at me. Harper does clumsy pirouettes behind her in a pink tutu.

'Hi, Tara.' This already feels like a mistake.

'"Ora!' Harper exclaims. Dora heads upstairs in search of Dylan, and Harper follows, both of them on all fours.

'Is that okay?' I point at Dora lolloping up the stairs.

'Yeah. They're always on at me to get a dog, but we can't afford one.'

'How's Dylan?'

'He's in his room. Recovering after what those bastards put him through.'

'I don't think he meant me any harm.'

'"Course he didn't. He's not like that. He was mucking about, but it got serious, with … well …' She motions towards me.

'I've had an idea. I want your opinion.'

She eyes me with suspicion but opens the door wider. 'It's a bit messy,' she says in a repeat of last time.

We go and sit on the couch, littered with dolls.

'What's Dylan actually confessed to?'

She flops back and picks up a Barbie with matted hair. She smooths the tangled locks. 'We're trying to unravel it. Someone's conned him into doing stuff. It doesn't amount to much, but Dylan's freaked out about what happened to you and gave the impression he's responsible for everything.'

317

'Who conned him?'

'Someone befriended him in a chat room.'

'Salty?'

'Yeah, this Salty, he groomed Dylan.'

'Was Dino ever mentioned?'

'No. He only knew Salty. It's been going on all year. He showed Dyl how to use the dark web. That's how he hacked into the school's IT. Salty helped him and treated it like a game.'

They really have been playing a long game. It wasn't just the letter to Mitchell before we'd moved in, he or she groomed Dylan.

'This Salty sent him a laptop, and arranged for him to pick it up from a delivery point and sneak it home when I wouldn't notice. The evil sod pushed him to find a hiding place where we wouldn't look, so Dylan dismantled the base of his wardrobe and made a secret compartment. Dyl's never even met him; it was all done online.'

'Does Joe know?'

'He does now. He feels shit that he wasn't there for Dyl during the police interviews, and that some bastard set him up.'

Harper bursts in. '*Peppa Pig*!' She points at the blank TV screen.

Tara jabs at the remote control and puts an episode on. Harper squats down inches from the big screen and watches with rapt attention.

'It's the only thing that shuts her up,' she mutters. 'Anyway, Dyl said he did everything, that it was all him, but it wasn't. He felt guilty because of the hidden laptop, but he just wanted to protect his dad. Bless him.'

'So Dylan's now saying he had nothing to do with the cyberattack?'

'Yeah, but he feels responsible because he thinks Salty did it and he covered up for him.'

'What did they use the hidden laptop for?'

'Just chatting, as far as we can tell. The police think this Salty was grooming Dylan and monitoring him.'

'Did Dylan ever meet Nicole?'

'The police asked that, but he says no.'

'They say she's not dangerous enough for a proper manhunt.'

'Fuck's sake.'

'They're trying, I suppose, but no one even knows her real name.'

'So what's this plan you've got?'

I brace myself to be kicked out. 'I don't think the police will track her down anytime soon, so I want us to go after her.'

'Us?'

'No one knows where to find her, so we can start in the most obvious place.'

'Where's that?'

'The dark web. Can we see if Dylan's IT skills stretch to tracking her down?'

She teases a tangle from Barbie's hair and purses her lips in contemplation. 'What does Joe say?'

'He'd better stay out of it until the police have cleared him.

I'm not supposed to have contact with him, and we don't want the police saying he's coercing Dylan.'

'Best he doesn't find out then, not yet. He'll breach his bail conditions by having any involvement with Dylan, so we'll have to get on without him. How's Dyl supposed to track her down?'

'He could show me those dark web skills that Salty taught him.'

Tara bites on her lip. 'I don't even know what the dark web is. I should be more tuned in, given what he's been up to.'

'It's an encrypted network, so it's untraceable. It doesn't come up on search engines and people using it can't be traced.'

'So how can you trace Nicole?'

'With bait. It's known as catfishing.'

She looks at me through narrowed eyes. 'It won't land him in more trouble, will it?'

'No, because he won't have contact with anyone. He'll help me navigate it so I find the right places to search. He can treat it as a research project and not interact with anyone. There's a lot of dodgy stuff out there, so he can't do anything unsupervised.'

'I don't have time to watch over him.'

'Can I be with him?' I pick up a stray Barbie stiletto and fit it onto the nearest barefoot Barbie. 'It means I can still have contact with him even though Joe's not around. I can sit in his bedroom or bring him to the flat and make sure he's okay. He'll help me put feelers out. I'll do the rest, if you and Dylan are okay with it.'

'He gets frustrated when things don't work out. This gives him a chance to fix it.'

320

'I'd like us to fix it.'

'I didn't know you were an IT expert,' she says.

'I'm learning.'

'We'd best go and find out if he's up for it.' She tosses Barbie aside and we leave Harper glued to the TV.

'Dyl?' Tara shouts up the stairs. 'Lauren wants to ask you something.'

The bedroom door stays closed. I tap on it and it opens a crack, the room veiled in darkness. No sign of Dylan.

'Hi, Dylan. Can we come in?' I ask.

'Go on in,' Tara says behind me.

I suppose that him opening the door a crack is an invitation of sorts, so I push it open some more. The curtains are still drawn and Dylan lies on the bed with Dora, his face turned to the wall. I perch at the end of the bed and Tara leans in the doorway.

'Hi, Dylan, how are you?'

''Kay.'

'I want your help with a secret mission.'

He flicks his fringe from his eyes and looks at me.

Blackmail is one of my income streams. I hack the messages of prominent men with reputations to protect. I might target an American businessman and find out his secrets – using prostitutes, having an affair, sexually harassing staff – and then I send a ransom demand. It's a high enough figure to be worth my while, but not so high he can't transfer the funds quickly into a bitcoin wallet. I say 'quickly' because the price goes up if he wavers. It's the perfect scam, since he can't risk spilling his dirty secrets by involving anyone else.

I didn't blackmail those two. I let the smart home cause a rift, cranking it up until she cracked, he left her or the police dragged him away. The sound system helped me get inside Lauren's head. Her paranoia was useful to play with. She doesn't know that hackers are paranoid too. You can channel it into ass-kicking or you can be a victim and let paranoia be your bitch. If Lauren got out in the world more, she'd realise paranoia is a good thing, keeping you alert to danger.

Dealing with those two face to face was harder than my usual scams. It's not my style, but I get off on risk, like when I stole the paintings. I watched her run terrified into the house, then I swiped the artwork and removed all trace of me on CCTV. The police interview had me on edge, but danger gets the blood pumping. I knew if I answered their questions and made it out of the country on a fake passport, they'd never find me.

CHAPTER FORTY-SEVEN

'I want us to track down Salty.' I sit on the end of Dylan's bed. 'He's connected to Nicole who set up the smart home with your dad. They might be the same person or they're working together. My IT skills are rubbish, so I thought you might help.'

"Kay.'

'Nothing dangerous, though, Dyl,' Tara chips in. 'Just some online searching, yeah?'

'Yeah.'

'Remember how your dad said there are black hat hackers, who are the online criminals?' I say. 'And the white hats are trying to stop them?'

'Yeah.'

'You can be a white hat.'

Tara looks confused. 'What's a white hat?'

'Cyber security. It's big business.'

'Hear that, Dyl? You could get a job in cyber security when you leave school.' Tara picks up his favourite black hoodie with a white skeleton design, and drapes it over the back of his desk chair.

'We don't know their real names and we don't have photos of them, which makes it hard. But maybe we can plant some bait.'

'Bait?' Tara asks, hands on hips.

'Let's say Nicole is also Salty. The police have checked and there's no obvious record of someone doing this particular scam before. She tailored it for us, knowing that Dylan's dad wanted a smart home. She saw that as a way in to ruin our lives. We won't find her through searches or through asking for information, so we'll have to be cleverer.'

'How you gonna do that?'

'I reckon that Nicole makes a living from IT scams. She knows what she's doing and she must make decent money. For starters, I thought Dylan could suss out the right places to go on the dark web to ask for IT help with a scam.'

She shrugs as if to say, *what do I know?*

'We'll probably get a load of dross, but I'll deal with it. What do you think, Dylan? Are you in?'

'Yup.'

We fist-bump spontaneously. It's the first time he doesn't mind me touching him.

'What's gonna happen?' Tara asks. 'Do you advertise for someone to hack a smart home?'

'We'll have to be subtle. Nicole's too sharp to be taken in. We need something she'll want to do justice to.'

'Like what?'

'I'll pose as someone wealthy who suspects her husband of

cheating. She wants to catch him out via their smart home and spring some kind of twisted revenge. But he's savvy, so she's looking for the best IT brain to deal with it, and is prepared to reward them generously.'

'Twisted.' She nods in approval. 'Won't she want evidence of who you are?'

'I'm thinking this person could be from some kind of super-wealthy closed community where it's hard to find out who's who, like a foreign royal family where the women have incredible luxury but not much freedom.'

'You'll never pass as a Saudi princess,' she scoffs.

'I don't intend to. This is just to flush her out. Dylan, let's work together on this. Can you take us into the dark web so we'll scope out where to go?'

'Yup.'

'The police still have his tablet as evidence,' Tara says. 'Far as I'm concerned, they can keep it.'

'I'll get my laptop from the car. I won't leave it with you, Dylan. You'll only do the searches when you're with me.'

'Dyl,' Tara says, 'you don't do anything without me or Lauren involved, right?'

He stares at the ceiling.

'Look at me, babe.'

He looks solemnly at her.

'Promise me you won't go on the dark web unless one of us is actually in the room with you.'

'Promise.'

She goes downstairs to check on Harper and I go out to the

car for my laptop. Tara's loading the dishwasher when I come back in. She nods to me and I go up to Dylan's room and watch him surf the dark web. Even if we don't pull this off, it's brought me closer to Dylan, both of us missing Joe and taking back a bit of control.

After two hours of roaming the dark web, Dylan has a firm grasp of the project, even if it's a long shot. He would have carried on, but I leave with the laptop. Tara and I remind him not to connect with anyone online. He has no computer, but Nicole or Salty might find a way to supply him with another one.

Nicole was either motivated by revenge or paid by someone else motivated by revenge. Karl Winter might be dead, but his wrongdoing lives on. I piece the clues together, my mind making frantic connections. He engineered the revenge porn, Dino said we were swingers, and emails suggest that Joe came on to Nicole. Sexual humiliation times three. Is that the thread running through it?

Karl Winter stalks me in my dreams, looking up at me through the CCTV. I wake in a cold sweat and try to bring my racing heart back to normal. *Fear and guilt are sisters.* It hits me with an electric bolt of realisation. Is that it?

Nicole – or whatever your real name is – we're coming for you.

My name's not Nicole. I call myself whatever serves my purpose. I stole the identity of a half-arsed techie too stupid to realise she'd been cloned. Her name was Nicole, which became my name. That's the thing with the online world, you can be someone else entirely and if you're good at it, you're believed. I do what I want online. I can be what I want.

Pulling it off in real life is a different matter. I needed a persona and remembered a cutesy girl from school who smiled a lot and said nice things in a breezy way. Everyone loved her except for me. I wanted to smash her face in, but I practised being that girl for Joe and Lauren. When the time came to be Nicole, I channelled the fuck out of that airhead. She became my disguise of choice, combined with my best Manic Pixie Dream Girl, who I've seen in films. Guys love that shit and no one's threatened by a wide-eyed girl with a sweet smile. Fucking losers should know it's not real.

Darkness lives inside me, but I made sure they didn't see it. I don't hide the darkness here. No one cares so long as the job is done. I'd raise more eyebrows if I came across as 'nice'. I won't do nice again.

Lauren wanted me as Dylan's role model. She'd no idea I already was. Then I caused havoc on Halloween night, throwing eggs and calling him names. In disguise, I'm small enough to pass for a teenager. Scamming them in person gave a bigger adrenaline hit than online. My shit-hot IT skills got me inside the house, but it turns out that I've a talent for real-life scamming. Fuelled by danger, I got off on the risk.

CHAPTER FORTY-EIGHT

Fear and guilt are sisters.

The words flit about my mind, those whispered words I heard during the attack. My subconscious worked it out in my sleep. Karl Winter was a dab hand at IT, and so is Nicole. They both used sexual slurs, but it wasn't sextortion since Karl didn't want money to keep the porn offline, he wanted revenge. This is the same. Nicole doesn't want money, she wants to destroy me.

First thing in the morning, I phone the detective sergeant who handled the Karl Winter case.

'DS Foster.'

'Hello, this is Lauren Geddes.'

'Lauren, how can I help?'

My heart thuds. 'Do you know if Karl Winter had a sister?'

I saw a flash of something in Nicole's eyes when I'd told her Anorak Man might have tampered with the smart hub. It didn't fit the kooky persona. I can still see it now, that look. She had the same eyes as Karl Winter, the same expression that one time when I couldn't put my finger on the resemblance. It's not a close likeness, but they could be brother and sister. Is that it? She's carrying on his disturbing legacy, blaming me and Joe for his death.

'A sister?' DS Foster says.

'Or someone close to him who would've been about eighteen when he died?'

'I don't know. Why do you ask?'

'Because a woman with extremely good IT skills tried to kill me. That's why I phoned last week. She faked CCTV footage of Karl Winter and orchestrated a cyberattack on our smart home. The DC on the case thinks there's some connection to Karl Winter, but the person who did it has disappeared.'

'The team investigating the crime can look into Karl Winter's family situation, but what makes you think she's a relative?'

'Because it's personal. It took her over a year of planning to pull off, plus a massive risk. My husband and I only know her in connection with the smart home, but either she's motivated by revenge or someone is paying her to get revenge.'

'Mm-hm.' She sounds sceptical.

If Karl Winter never had a sister, the police will write off that line of enquiry. 'Even if she isn't a close relative, the connection is too strong. There's revenge porn and a sexual tone to the campaign against my husband and me. It's too similar to be a coincidence.'

'Who's the DC? I'll check in with them.'

I give her DC Jones's name and direct line. 'Can you keep me posted?'

'I'll come back to you regarding any possible connection between this IT person and Karl Winter. DC Jones can advise on how it might relate to the case.'

I have to do something while the police confirm my hunch, so I go in search of confirmation. I take a drive to a place I've never wanted to go near. A local media report following Karl Winter's death said that his grandparents doted on him and never recovered after he died. The piece said they lived in Valley Drive, Durbeton. DS Foster said the grandparents are both dead, but someone still living there could have known the family. I set the sat nav and drive there.

An hour later, I pull up at a row of pebbledashed council houses. This is it. Valley Drive, but I've no idea what number to seek out. One of the houses has handrails and a ramp installed. It might have been done for an elderly couple and no one removed them. I ring the bell. No one answers and the greying net curtains don't twitch. I shudder at the thought of Karl Winter living here. Along the road a woman comes out of a house pushing a buggy, with a little girl in a red raincoat holding the buggy handle.

'Hello?' I come back down the path.

She glances at me and then returns her attention to negotiating the buggy and child through the rickety metal gate.

'I'm looking for a family called Winter. They lived here five years ago.'

'I've only been here two years.' She skirts the buggy around me, a toddler in it and the older girl still clutching the handle.

'There was an elderly couple who died, but their

granddaughter might have stayed on. She's in her early twenties now.'

'Nope. No idea.' She hunches into the buggy and pushes it away.

Nothing for it, I'll have to knock on doors. I start at the far end. No one answers. I glimpse a huge widescreen TV and a contemporary black leather sofa through the window. If they're at work, tomorrow's Saturday and I'll keep coming back.

The house adjoining it is more neglected, with a weathered mahogany front door and window frames to match. I knock loudly. No response. I go to leave and see a grey-haired woman in the garden behind the house.

'Hello?' I call to her.

She looks my way.

'Can I have a word, please?'

'What you selling?' She comes to the low wooden gate of the back garden. Her lavender zip-up fleece has leaves and twigs caught in it, her roomy navy joggers are muddy and baggy around the knees.

'Nothing. I'm looking for someone who lived on this road.'

'Who's that then?'

'A woman whose surname might be Winter. She's in her early twenties now. Her grandparents were called Winter and they lived on the road.'

'I used to know Molly and Derek.' She looks warily at me. 'Are you a reporter?'

She must know about the trouble surrounding Karl. 'No. Someone who might be their granddaughter did some work for me. She used a fake name and now she's disappeared. She might be Karl's younger sister.'

'Cause you trouble, did she?'

'You could say that. What do you know about her?'

'I know she was a bad 'un.'

'Was she ever in trouble with the police?'

'Not as far as I know. Molly and Derek covered up for her.' She huddles her arms around herself and looks at the darkening sky. 'After Karl died they packed her off to live with another relative. Last I heard was when she turned sixteen and disappeared.'

'What was her name?'

'Jade.'

'Jade Winter?' I hold my breath. My heart races. At last, I know who she is.

It starts raining, fat drops plopping down.

'Come inside, don't want to stand around in the wet.'

She hurries along the side of the house. Wanting answers, I follow her through the back door into a narrow, old-fashioned kitchen. She kicks off her Crocs and replaces them with moccasin slippers, and then puts the kettle on.

'Tea?'

'Please. Tell me about Jade.'

'Does she owe you money?' She eyes me warily and takes two floral mugs from a pine mug tree.

'No. She disappeared. What sort of trouble did she cause?'

'She wasn't right. Not ever. It's because of their mum, hers and Karl's. She had Karl very young. Then she got in with a bad lot and took drugs. Molly and Derek tried everything. They got Angela into rehab and she was clean for a while, until she took up with some fella from rehab and fell pregnant with Jade. She was all right until he left her after the birth and she went back on the drugs.'

'How awful,' I say as she pours boiling water into a stainless-steel teapot.

'They took Karl on when he was thirteen. Jade was a baby, and they said Ange needed space to bond with her. They were supposed to have Karl as a temporary thing. I guess they knew she wouldn't cope with two kids.'

'What about their dad?'

'Karl's dad didn't stick around. I doubt Molly and Derek even met Jade's dad. They skirted round that because it would've been quite shameful for them.' She pours the tea and slides one of the mugs along the kitchen counter to me.

'What was Karl like?' I'm nearly there, joining the dots of what went on.

'He was no trouble ... a loner, but a lot of boys spend too much time playing computer games instead of getting out in the fresh air on their bikes.'

'And Jade?'

'She had problems. Her grandparents covered it up. They couldn't manage a young child, what with Molly's bad arthritis and Derek's dodgy back, so they helped Ange the best they could. Then Jade was expelled from school and they took her on. She went to a special school. They said it was a school for gifted kids, but it was for problem kids. They couldn't handle the shame of it, what with her mum. I bet they worried she'd go the same way.'

'How old was she when Karl died?'

'Oh,' she taps her top lip and looks out of the window at the garden, 'about fifteen. They packed her off to relatives in Yorkshire.'

'That's a bit harsh.' I want to know everything she can tell me. I have to piece it together.

'I reckon they weren't abandoning her so much as protecting her.'

'Protecting her?'

'Karl's death sent her off the rails and they couldn't control her. That's just a guess, mind. They never spoke about her being any trouble, but it didn't need spelling out.'

This is it. It's making sense, that Jade is hell-bent on revenge for Karl. 'Did you see her again?'

'No. She went AWOL and broke their hearts. They weren't equipped to cope with the druggie daughter and messed-up grandkids. The trouble it caused. They tried, but they were no match for all the problems. Sad, really.' She cradles her mug and stares out at birds pecking at a feeder.

'Why was she expelled from school?'

'I don't know. She'd come and go, I'd hear shouting matches, mostly Jade mouthing off. They couldn't handle her but they didn't want the SS involved.'

'The SS?'

'Social Services.'

'Oh, okay. Do you know where Jade is now?'

'It wouldn't surprise me if she's in some bedsit, drugged-up to the eyeballs. But you say you know her, so you'll have a better idea than me.'

I nod and put my nearly finished mug of tea in the sink. 'Thank you for the tea, and for talking to me.'

She shows me out and I go back to the car. At last, I have something to go on. My tormentor is Jade Winter, aged fifteen when her older half-brother Karl died. That would make her about twenty now, instead of the twenty-three she told Joe. Did the grandparents bundle her off for fear of her reaction to the police and any media presence? With her grandparents' protection, she was young enough to fly under the radar, too young to be named in media coverage. But it's left an indelible mark which has stayed with her in the five years since. It's why she came after us – to exact revenge.

I think of the first time I saw Karl Winter, at the psychiatric unit of the hospital. He asked if I fancied a drink. He wore a soft yellow shirt with a dainty floral pattern and he looked harmless. I didn't want to say no when he was already down, so we went to the nearest pub.

We chatted over a drink in a corner of the deserted pub. He talked in eloquent therapy-speak about childhood trauma and his defence system against bad memories. He said his parents had been junkies and he hadn't had the best start in life. He told me he felt unsafe and would sometimes wake up in strange places that he didn't remember going to. It took a toll on relationships and holding down a job.

He had three drinks to my one, drowning his sorrows. I

guessed that he'd stay until closing. When I went to leave, he begged me to have another drink. I said I had to go. He asked for my number and I said I had a boyfriend. Joe and I were together at that point and planning our first renovation. Karl must have followed me, either that time or after my next session, because he found out where I lived. Or maybe he hacked the unit's online records.

He wanted more and I wouldn't give him more. He kept on, becoming frustrated and overreacting when I turned him down. His intensity scared me. I blanked him, but he kept on and blamed me for not helping him. And then he sent me a text.

Hi, I'm feeling low today and wonder if I could reach out to you? Need someone to talk to x

I couldn't ignore his message. I showed it to Joe, saying I'd look up some mental health resources, see if he could talk to someone.

'Lauren, it's not your place to do that. He's already in the system. He has access to mental health services.'

'He wants to talk. He's lonely.'

'He's playing you. You're too nice, and men like him take advantage.'

'But I can't ignore it. What if he's suicidal?'

'We'll point him in the right direction. Thing is, you're doing more harm than good.'

'How come?'

'Because he wants a relationship with you. You're always going to frustrate him by not giving him what he wants. It's no good for either of you.'

Joe intervened and texted Karl back. He suggested that Karl call his mental health contact for help and join a support group. Joe banned him from contacting me. It was days before we jetted off on our first trip to Ibiza. I felt awful for abandoning him to go on holiday. I hoped it would push him to seek help from people better equipped than me.

He took Joe's ban on contacting me to heart. A few months later I noticed him wordlessly stalking me. He became a shadowy presence in my life for three years. And now Karl is dead but Jade is still out there. I have to outsmart her and stop her coming back for me.

Karl understood me and didn't try to change me. But people tried changing him, putting him in a category and 'helping' him, not that it did any good. We were both fucked-up, and he couldn't help inflicting damage on others. There was a girl he fancied, way back. He'd hang out with her, to our nan's delight.

'Is Kelly your friend or girlfriend?' Nan asked when we were watching some shit on the telly and he came home from seeing her.

'Nan,' he groaned, as if to say don't embarrass me.

'Bring her over for some dinner,' Grandpa said.

When Kelly came over, Nan cooked a Sunday roast and apple crumble, and fussed over her. Grandpa was all jovial, he even slapped Karl on the back. Didn't take much to please those two. You'd have thought Karl had announced their engagement, but it was a big deal for him to have a girlfriend. He didn't expect much from life but he needed someone to be there for him.

I didn't get it – his craving for affection. Bit creepy if you ask me. I can't be doing with that clingy shit, but it did him good to have a girlfriend, someone kind who'd stick around. Nan and Grandad kept going on about how lovely she was. Then she moved away, brushed him off like an insect. It came from nowhere, although maybe it had been building. The bitch devastated him. Not so lovely after all, were you, Kelly?

He had some kind of breakdown after that and ended up in hospital. Then along came Lauren, who he met at out-patients. The bitch fucked his life up all over again. Me and Karl were treated like losers. Even at school, I never put up with that shit, but he did. I was the only person who understood, the only person he could count on.

I'm different; guarded. I learnt to hide my badness, to nurture it

338

in private. Lauren was on the right track when she phoned her police contact to ask if Karl had any brothers, thinking that's what she saw on CCTV. But he didn't have a brother, he had a sister. A sister who can superimpose an image of his head on my body when I posed for the CCTV. I deep-faked it, bulking up in a puffa jacket and wearing a beanie hat. My build is too slight to be him, but it's hard to get the right impression from a high-angled CCTV, and she was scared out of her tiny brain in the moment she glimpsed it. Then I deleted it.

After Karl's accidental death, murder, whatever, I drifted and fell in with the wrong crowd, which led to an even worse crowd. They were mostly wasters, but one was a tech drop-out with a Masters in programming. I learnt a lot from him. My IT skills found me a place in the criminal underworld. They have my loyalty and I'm protected in return. My skills are sought after, but not through the usual channels.

My biggest motivation has been to con the bastards who killed Karl. And they did kill him. Even if they didn't push him in the canal, they drove him to it. I did it for Karl, who's not here to defend himself.

CHAPTER FORTY-NINE

After I return from Valley Drive, DC Jones calls and asks to come and see me. Soon after, we're sitting in the flat and she leans forward to show me a photo of Nicole looking even younger. It's unmistakably her, but instead of spiky white hair, it's long and wavy in a dull shade of mouse.

'Is this the woman who posed as Nicole and installed your IT system?'

'Yes.' I decide against telling her I've done some investigating of my own.

'We believe she's the half-sister of Karl Winter.'

I mirror her grim expression. 'Can you find her?'

'She's living under an assumed identity, different to Nicole Cummings. She had a period of unemployment, then there's no trace of her beyond the age of eighteen. She hasn't used her National Insurance number, never applied to change her name, never had a driving licence or passport under her real name.'

I lean back in the chair.

'But now we have a photo, we can use age-progression software to show what she looks like now. We'll see if that brings up anything through international law enforcement. Given her advanced IT skills and ability to stay undetected, she might be involved in cybercrime, either here or abroad. It explains why she didn't need her NI number for work, if she's employed on the black market and paid cash, or she has a fake identity, or both.'

'What do you mean by seeing what it'll bring up internationally?'

'If she's operating abroad, there are specialist agencies dealing with cybercrime, so we'll make enquiries.' She stands up. 'I'll keep you posted.'

'What about Joe?'

'It changes the situation, given what we now know about her.'

'So you accept that she did this to us both, and Joe didn't mastermind it?'

'We need to assess it in light of the new information. We'll confirm it.'

'Can I talk to him? It won't get him into trouble?'

'There's still a process in place. I suggest you talk to his solicitor.'

The moment she leaves, I call Joe's solicitor. He's not there so I ask the receptionist to update him and do what's necessary to have Joe's bail conditions lifted. Then I google Jade Winter.

She doesn't exist online under her real name. Maybe she wasn't allowed to post anything before she was sixteen, and then she took on a new persona. Or she removed all trace of

341

herself. Sixteen is young to take off and build a new life from scratch with no work experience, family help and hardly any life experience. I caught a glimpse of her determination beneath the dipsy persona.

I phone Tara to share the news.

'Hello?' she snaps.

'It's Lauren.'

'Lauren, what's up?'

'I've found out the name of the woman who stitched us up. It's Jade Winter.'

'Winter ... wasn't that the name ...?'

'Yes. She was his younger sister.'

'Fuck me. Computer crime runs in the family, then.'

'Looks like it. The police have kind of agreed that Joe wasn't behind it. I've been onto his solicitor.'

'Thank Christ for that. Should Dylan knock off his dark web stuff?'

'She's still out there. She could do more harm. She might be posing as someone else, another Salty.'

'Right then. We need to nail the bitch.'

The doorbell rings. It's Joe. I want to launch myself into his arms. Relief surges through me, but ... but ...

'I'm sorry.' He comes towards me and cups my face in his hands. 'God, I've missed you. Can I hug you?' He doesn't wait for a reply and wraps his arms around me. He holds me close, dipping his head to touch mine.

I'm stiff in his embrace.

'You won't believe how many hours I've spent wanting you back,' he says into my hair. 'You're tense.'

I pull back, pressing my palms to his chest. He takes the hint and steps back to give me space, but the expression of longing stays on his face. I go to sit down and he follows, sitting at a suitable distance away.

He looks contrite. 'Is there any way we can start putting this behind us? I know I can't make everything okay, but I want to try and make it up to you. I want us to be okay.'

We're on shaky ground and I'm bruised from his dogged belief that my psychosis came back. 'We've a lot to resolve, starting with the way you put the smart home before anything else.'

'I know.' He looks down at his hands, his face tired and unshaven. 'I screwed up. I got carried away, but I'd no idea it would pan out this way. Any more news on her?'

'The police are distributing her photo to international law enforcement. What do you know about her?'

'Hardly anything.' He sounds weary. 'She always came to me for meetings, presented herself as awkward, but really good at IT and dedicated.'

'What about her personal life? What did she share with you?' I say it pointedly.

'Nothing. I never asked. We kept it to business. It's a bit creepy, isn't it, me as an older guy taking an interest in her personal life?'

'It *is* a bit creepy, Joe.'

He pauses at my tone.

'It devastated me when the police kept on about you having an affair with her.'

'Jeez, Lauren. That's not true,' he says in a hurt voice. 'You don't believe that, especially given what we know about her?'

'I'm being straight with you. I didn't know what to believe from the way you acted, making me the problem, not the smart home. The police kept implying you wanted rid of me. Other people did too. I know she's to blame, but I always assumed if things turned bad, you'd have my back and we'd look out for each other.' My voice shakes, my emotions close to the surface.

He goes to the window and drags his hands through his hair. It's longer than his usual neat haircut, curling at the ends. He turns back and gives me a look of pure longing. 'I do have your back. I wanted you to be okay. Nothing weird happened when I was around, so I thought your psychosis had flared up. That's what she wanted and I played into her hands. What can I do to make things right?'

'Lay off the technology for a start. And believe in me.'

He sits beside me, his face grave. 'I do believe in you.'

'You wanted every professional to think me paranoid – that policeman, Anja, Dr Reeve – as if you wanted it on record.'

He covers his face with his hands. 'Oh, honey, I'm so sorry.'

A tear escapes and trickles down my face. He smooths it away with his thumb.

'Let me make it better,' he says. 'You and me ... we're good together. I can't imagine life without you.' He holds my hand.

I stay impassive, my head turned towards the window.

'Can we try and find our way back?'

'Back?' Does he mean to Chilwood?

'Back to how we used to be. Because I'd like us to try. We're good together, you and me.'

We were good together, before Jade turned up.

'I won't let anything come between us again,' he says. 'Why's that blanket over the TV?'

'I don't want anyone watching me through it.'

'It's unplugged,' he says.

We exchange goofy smiles. Just having him close makes life bearable. I never believed he actually meant me harm, but the way he acted still hurts. He kisses me, tentative at first, a sweet, lingering kiss. We set it aside for now and go to bed.

'I've missed you,' I murmur between slow kisses and we start making right what's been wrong. He touches me in the way he used to in the early days of us, as if he can't get enough of me. It feels as if we've been reunited after a long stretch instead of days. Joe says every day is a whole year when you're locked in a police cell.

He falls asleep for a while and I watch him until he wakes up and smiles sleepily at me. Then he stretches and checks the time. 'Do you mind if I go to see Dylan?'

''Course not. He'll be stoked to have you back. But Joe . . .'

'Yeah?' He looks at me.

'I went to see Tara and Dylan, to ask for their help.'

'Their *help*?'

'Hear me out. I asked Dylan if he wanted to be a white hat, and look on the dark web for places where we might track down Jade.'

345

'Jeez, Lauren, is that wise given his track record? He's a kid. We shouldn't involve him.'

'He's already involved. Salty involved him. And he wanted to help.'

'But Christ!' He sits up and ruffles his hair. 'There's dangerous people on the dark web … dodgy stuff that someone his age shouldn't see.'

'He's not talking to anyone. He's only showing me where to look. We've been really specific about boundaries, and he's not allowed online without me or Tara supervising.'

'But the dark web's anonymous. What makes you think you can find her?'

'I found out who she is in the real world, so we might find her online. I want to lay some bait so she comes to us.'

'And Tara's okay with it?'

'In her words, she wants us to "nail the bitch".'

'Okay.' He rubs the stubble on his chin. 'I'll text her. Sounds like you should come too and we'll work out what to do next. But you don't have to be involved now I'm back. IT isn't your thing.'

'Jade's not getting the better of me. If we take her down, I want to be part of it.'

As for Joe and me, we'll see if we can be fixed. I haven't got over him doubting me, but looking at him now – the exhaustion on his face, the pain and determination – he's had a rough time too.

We drive over to Tara and Dylan, Joe looking more careworn. Not long after, we're drinking tea with Tara and talking about

Jade. Harper's at nursery and Dylan's sloped off to his room with Dora. Despite Tara's animosity towards me, it feels okay to be talking, since we've all been affected. I'd never have imagined sitting in her home, discussing a common goal. In trying to destroy us, Jade has brought us together. And not just Tara. After the police contacted Dale and Kim, they sent me an email checking I was all right.

'The thing with the dark web,' Joe says, 'is that it's not some massive criminal organisation. There are different specialisms, like ransomware, drug dealers, fake IDs, hitmen.'

'Drug dealers and hitmen?' Tara says. 'Should Dylan be mixing with people like that?'

'We're not looking down those avenues. Jade isn't a drug dealer or gun for hire,' Joe says. 'We need to scope out the best options for the specialism we're looking for. So are we clear on the objective?'

Tara shrugs and looks none the wiser.

'We're going to advertise for someone to hack a smart home,' I say. 'Advertise might not be the right term, but that's the gist of it. We'll make it anonymous, so the person placing the advert is a third party acting on behalf of someone wanting to use their smart home to track whether her husband's having an affair.'

'How far will we take it?' Tara asks.

'As far as it takes to flush her out,' Joe says.

I told Lauren I was tested for autism as a child, which was true. They came up with a different diagnosis: attachment disorder. My brother had it too, the brother Joe and Lauren killed. His 'disorder' manifested differently to mine. He could become obsessed with people, like Lauren, whereas I don't like people.

When the school expelled me, he was the only person who didn't make it my fault. I refused counselling after the first session. God, it was dire, stuck in a cramped, stuffy room while a dowdy woman tried to 'engage'. I stared at her dry auburn hair, the grey roots showing through. She could shove her fake concern of 'how does that make you feel' and 'poor you for suffering childhood trauma'. No shit, but talking won't fix me, same as talking about cancer won't fix that. Better to go off the rails than talk to some shitty therapist who wears cheap shoes.

'What can we do to sort this out?' Karl said.

'Blow up the school?'

'Or you could walk away from trouble.'

'Why?'

'It's better if you don't let things bother you so much.'

'But why should people get away with it? It's letting them win and I don't do that.'

Karl had so much therapy he could be a therapist. 'Why don't you find your passion, something that's all yours to escape into?' He probably regretted that advice when I told him what I did to Lauren.

Karl idolised her. He showed me a photo of her and said they went on a date, then she blanked him.

'Walk away,' I'd said, but he wouldn't.

'She's not worth chasing.'

He stopped talking to me about her, but I hate people thinking they're better than us. She expected him to go quietly, to be a problem that disappeared. But why should he suffer in silence?

Before leaving the UK, I ditched the contact lenses and coloured my hair back to honey-blonde. If they passed me in the street they'd struggle to recognise me in my Gucci black leather and diamonds. Got it, flaunt it; that's what my waster of a mum used to say. She preferred anything to us: drugs, the deadbeat men she welcomed into our lives. Even staring into space for hours on end was better than giving her kids any attention. She's dead now. Drug overdose. No one knows that I administered it. She was the walking dead so I put her out of her misery, gave us all a break.

I won't return to the UK anytime soon, if ever, not now I've got payback for Karl. Now he's gone, I'm better off alone. Trust no one and then no one can let you down. Those two paid the price for being trusting. Big mistake.

CHAPTER FIFTY

Three months later

We board the plane in the first batch of passengers, so Dylan can avoid sensory overload from the crush of people. He needed coaching to come away with us, and his medication takes the edge off. Joe reminds him about his app that makes stressful situations less bad. Tara waved us off in the car to the airport. 'He needs to break out of his little world,' she'd said.

Him and me both. Helping him through distracts me from my own twitchiness. The easy option was to leave Dylan safely at home. But he's determined, and we love his conviction to fly in a plane for the first time and go somewhere completely different.

If Dylan can do it, so can I. We had a joint session of hypnotherapy for reducing anxiety, and I like the sense that we're in it together. Joe squeezes my hand in reassurance, not that I'm scared of flying. Old habits die hard and I'm wary of public places and too many people. Passengers clog up the plane gangway and Dylan busies himself on his tablet in the window seat.

When the plane taxis along the runway, I turn to him. 'Hey, Dylan? Do you remember I said flying was my superpower?'

'Yes.' He blinks at me through his thick fringe.

'Taking off on a plane is pretty close to what it must feel like.'

The plane accelerates along the runway. Take-off is faster and more exhilarating than I expect, but I haven't flown for a while.

Dylan's eyes light up. 'The motorway – look! Look at the cars!'

Minutes later, Joe tries to interest him in the undulating South Downs Way where we used to live, but he's still fixated on the bird's-eye view of vehicles, now the size of ants. After we've left the UK behind, he has a brief fascination with low-lying clouds over the countryside – 'Like snow!' – before going back to his vehicle watch. I've never seen him so animated.

We might look like a family jetting off on holiday, but we're heading for a hacking town. I'd never heard of hacking towns, but they're all over Eastern Europe, dark web industries that trade in online passwords, email addresses and credit card details obtained by hackers. Our advert achieved nothing and we got nowhere in three months. Nor did the police. But Dylan followed a lead of his own.

When Salty groomed him, 'he' had talked about using a supplier of fake passports, so they could operate abroad and no one would know they'd left the country. I'm not sure how appealing that would be to a child who insisted on sleeping in his own bed every night, but Salty taught him well. Dylan tracked down every dark web peddler of fake passports but kept his word and didn't contact any of them. Joe and I did that. We used our cover story of looking for an expert in smart homes to help snare an errant husband, offering a finder's fee to be put in contact with the right person.

This time, we found a match. Amid the dross, came one reply:

I know a lady. Very good. Very confidential. The best hacker.
You will not be disappointed.

We hoped the 'best hacker' was Jade but after expressing an interest, our offer fell flat.

She say no. Is not the right person for the job.

We couldn't let it go, so the middleman took a fee for revealing where the female hacker operated from. That way we could try to convince her, with the proviso that we kept secret how we came by her location and identity. The hacker supplied a passport photo, but not of the fresh-faced Nicole we knew. In the photo, her silken caramel hair extensions framed a heavily made-up face, smoky eyes lined with charcoal and her sunny smile replaced with a crimson-lipped scowl. She went by the name of Elena, and our contact had her delivery address for supplying the passport.

She very in demand, he messaged when Joe and I transferred the payment. *I wish you luck and God bless.*

'Just as well we've sold the cottage,' Joe said. It cleared our debts and funded the mission to seek out Jade. We never moved back. A newly retired couple from London bought it, to our relief. They loved the seclusion and the tech, and they were welcome to it. I hope they get on with Mitchell. I let him know about the sale and he seemed pleased. 'Don't want it standing empty,' he'd said.

When our intermediary supplied the details, we talked about what to do. Other people would hand her intel to the police and let them do the rest. But in the time it would take to track her across national borders, hampered by bureaucracy, she could give them the slip.

It was Dylan who insisted we confront her, surprising us both, along with Tara. 'She pretended to be my friend,' he said. 'She did all this bad stuff. I want to tell her she can't treat us like that.'

'If the police catch her,' Joe said, 'you can tell the court in a letter. I think that's how it works.'

'But what if they don't catch her? I'll think everyone online is her, trying to trick me.'

Me too. We're not taking the law into our own hands. A private security expert is meeting us at the airport. He has the power to detain Jade under local laws. We can tell her what we think of her, then she'll be handed over to the police. It's the security man's job to keep us safe and deliver her to the local law enforcement. By then, we'd have called the authorities to let them know she's been apprehended. It's not the approved way, but she rendered us powerless and we're taking back control. I'll confront her, with Joe and the security expert by my side, and Dylan will film it on his phone. No violence, just letting her know she can't treat us this way.

The FASTEN SEAT BELT sign comes on. Dylan can't see cars now we're above the clouds again. He says turbulence is the best.

'We could have a frequent flyer on our hands,' Joe says quietly, still holding my hand. Dylan can't hear us through his noise-cancelling earphones. It feels like a turning point, our first trip away as a family.

'I can't believe we're on a plane together,' I say. 'We could do it again, for fun next time, go on holiday.'

We share a smile at the possibilities opening out, now we can step on a plane and go away together. The stress of what happened drove a wedge between Joe and me, but we're working on it.

When we land at Bucharest airport, Joe and I high-five Dylan. He's fourteen now, still very much a child. Our cover story is that he wants to visit Vlad the Impaler's home town, and the supposedly haunted Dracula's Castle in all its Gothic glory. He couldn't believe Transylvania was a real place until we showed him it on Google Maps.

I come here to work. Here's where the money is, along with the contacts. There's safety in numbers from all the scammers driving round flaunting their wealth. I work with the biggest players, even though I could form my own fraud ring. But there's protection from keeping in with the powerful criminals, since I'm an asset to them.

I got lucky here in the early days because of my English skills. The cleverer scammers wanted a native English speaker for a veneer of legitimacy. My emails weren't in broken English, and I had a knack for how far to push it and when to pull back and reel in the punters. At eighteen, I looked about twelve, so no one saw me as a threat. I learned fast and didn't stand out because cybercrime is a young persons' game.

I'd been working on my personal project since Karl's death. My grandparents tried to protect me in their useless, outdated way. They never mentioned what happened to him and treated me like a small child unable to process the truth. Grandad just kind of gave up and Nan died of a heart attack two years later.

The world was a bad place for people like me and Karl. The dark web became my stomping ground. I honed my IT skills to use against those two who killed my brother. Karl was all I had. He was the only one who knew me. He got it. We'd been through the same shit at different times. Those bastards took him away and they had to pay one way or another.

When I heard that someone wanted me to mastermind a smart home sting, my antenna went up. I'm not so well known for smart homes that a mystery person would headhunt me for a job. I thought the authorities had caught up. My instinct was to run. Then I did some checking, which wasn't that difficult, given my network. I found out it was them so I decided to fuck with them some more, give them a wasted journey. Nobody gets the better of me, especially not them.

CHAPTER FIFTY-ONE

Mihai meets us from the airport with smiles and handshakes. He runs a security business in the capital, and I'm reassured by his solid, imposing build. We couldn't do this without a local expert acting as the intermediary.

Joe found him online and did his best to work out if he was legitimate enough to help us. Joe gave the impression he worked in cybersecurity, and we took a leap of faith to procure Mihai's services.

'We do normal security,' he told Joe in his cheery way. 'We also know cybercrime. In Romania, the two go together.'

He accepts Joe's account of us confronting a black hat hacker who has masterminded an audacious scam. He drives us away in a black Mercedes and talks non-stop, with Romanian pop playing in the background. He says his clients include cybersecurity teams from major banks, trying to defend their systems. He acts as a muscled tour guide, showing security experts the scale of the problem. The cleverer hackers target banks, searching for intel on mergers and acquisitions for insider trading, so they can make a killing on the stock market.

'They have the job title of *data analyst*, ha ha ha.' Mihai laughs his rich, exuberant laugh.

He will meet Jade tomorrow in an office borrowed from his associate and we'll be in the next room, ready to confront her. Then local laws permit that she can be detained until the police arrive. It's unlikely she'll prove too much for all of us, but Mihai will have a man posted beside the door to stop her from running off.

He asks if we would like to pull over for a break and some food. Dylan perks up, probably expecting a Mars bar at a service station. Instead, we take a detour to a farmhouse B&B and the moment we stop, Mihai lights up a cigarette. He guides us to a wooden table outside and after a brief conversation between him and a waitress, we're brought a rustic salad with warm sourdough bread and soft local cheese.

Mihai jokes with Dylan about Dracula, seeming unfazed by the task ahead. He talks about bears living in the forest. I'm not sure Dylan believes him as it sounds like a folk tale. Back in the car, Mihai points out Lutheran churches and snippets of history about the Saxon villages we travel through. We pass lush meadows and the only traffic is horses pulling carts. At last, we reach a busy city centre, nearing the end of our three-hour drive to the foothills of the Alps. Our destination is known as Hackerville.

Joe and Dylan marvel at the top-end Mercedes, Audis and BMWs driven by blingy young men in a stark contrast to the centuries-old neighbourhoods we've passed. We stop at a red light and Joe asks how the men in their flash cars earn their money.

'They are thieves! They do crime on the internet,' Mihai says cheerily.

Joe's in the front seat and cranes his neck back at Dylan, whose eyes are on stalks. His look says, *don't get any ideas, matey.* It annoys me that Mihai laughs about it, but perhaps he sees us as scammers, since we're luring Jade out of hiding on a fake pretext. We've done our research on the town that's known for online fraud. Mihai points out developments of secure apartments, luxury shopping centres and nightclubs, along with car dealerships cashing in on cybercrime.

'Business is booming,' Joe says.

'Hackers have the nice offices. Like Silicon Valley, yes? Open-plan and beanbags!' He drives us towards the tourist end of the city, saying Jade won't have any reason to come here. Her work is in one of the anonymous high-tech buildings in the centre and she'll probably live in an equally anonymous apartment.

'No hiding. They work in a glass office.' He lifts a hand towards a glass-fronted office block that could be an insurance firm.

An electric current of danger runs through me. Jade might be in there, or Elena as she's now known. We're so close after all this searching, but are we doing the right thing? I'll talk to Joe tonight. If we both have cold feet, it's not too late to back out and call the UK police instead. 'How did you find her?' I ask.

'Not everyone is a hacker,' he tells us. 'This place has a reputation; bad reputation. Some people do not send money here. They have a firewall, yes? The firewall is people in other places. They take the money and charge commission. Sometimes cash not bank transfer.'

'Not bitcoin?' Joe asks.

'Not all people trust bitcoin. You spend bitcoin on Amazon, yes, but not everywhere. Drivers transport money from other places so nobody trace it. They also deliver the fake passport. The money is good for drivers, because they are money mules. I find someone low down who wants the easy money.'

It's late afternoon when we arrive at the hotel. 'Don't go to the Silicon Valley,' Mihai says in his final briefing. 'Stay in the tourist area, near to the hotel. She don't come down here. I see you tomorrow at ten in morning. We go surprise Elena. She English, but she have admirable Romanian name.' More laughter and then he shakes our hands and lumbers back to his car, lighting up a cigarette.

When we've checked in, we go to the hotel bar and the friendly young barman recommends chilled local rosé. Dylan has a Coke and we clink glasses. The barman recommends a nearby restaurant where we can eat tonight.

'You could almost forget why we're here.' Joe knocks back the wine. 'It feels so normal – having a drink in a European city with my two favourite people.'

'Aww,' I say. 'You're my two favourite people too.'

Dylan surveys us from under his fringe as if we're an alien species.

'Could you get used to travelling, Dylan?' I say.

'Yes.'

'Where shall we go next?'

'Florida.'

'Oh, okay. The theme parks?' I ask.

'Yes.'

'We can do that,' Joe says. 'They're doing some amazing things with technology—' He checks himself and squeezes my hand to say he's trying not to be tech-obsessed. It would be unrealistic to expect a complete digital detox, but we've agreed to no more smart homes.

'If that's your plan, you can come and meet me in the Florida Keys when you're finished. I'll be at the cocktail bar on the beach.'

'It's a date,' Joe says, then tuts at his phone and listens to a voicemail.

'Let's get some air before dark,' I say, when he deletes the message.

'Do you mind if I return this call? It's just one thing to sort out, then I'm all yours. We can go in half an hour or so.'

My head's throbbing from a day of travelling and hours of Romanian pop music. 'I need a quick walk, then a soak in the bath. It'll be dark soon. Dylan and I can go. Is that okay, Dylan?'

''Kay.'

The two of us leave Joe and stroll a little way along the river towards the old town. If I've learnt anything in the past few months, it's to live my life without hiding away and to reduce my reliance on Joe.

'That must be the restaurant the barman mentioned, over there.' I motion towards a little restaurant further along. 'Let's wander over and see if we can read the menu.'

Nervousness creeps up. Is Jade in some lair downtown, tapping away at her laptop? I have the number of the UK police contact in my phone, along with the number of the local police here. We've covered everything we can, but now we're here it seems hare-brained. We don't have to see it through. I'll speak to Joe when I get him alone.

Dylan and I go to the edge of the river and peer into the free-flowing water. 'I bet it's freezing in there.'

'Yes.'

'I'm proud of you for how far you've come,' I say without looking at him. 'A few months ago, you'd never spent a night away from home and I was scared to go anywhere new and different, and now look at us.'

'Yes.'

Something catches my eye across the river. My blood runs cold. *It's Jade staring at us.* Am I hallucinating? No, it's really her.

And she knows we're here.

My bag's already packed. I have a new passport from a trustworthy source this time. I'm done here. I'll go somewhere warm and execute the occasional blackmail when funds are low. I'm in charge of my life and can do whatever the fuck I want without any losers getting in my way. By the time I've finished with scared little Lauren, she'll wish she'd stayed tucked up at home. The pathetic loser wants to exorcise her demons but tough luck, bitch, because I'll exorcise her.

CHAPTER FIFTY-TWO

Jade locks eyes with me. I'm frozen in the moment. She must still be tracking us to know that we're here. She turns and stalks away. Dylan's still looking into the water.

'Dylan, call your dad now. Run to the hotel and bring him back here.'

He looks sharply at me, uncomprehending.

'I'll phone him in a minute, okay?' I say over my shoulder as I go after Jade.

''Kay.'

Adrenaline pumps through me. I race along the river, Jade in my sight, but only just. In a flash of anger, I realise she's getting away. We can't confront her now she's seen me. It's now or never. My only chance. I have to confront her right now.

She's smaller than me and no danger without her computer. She knows it too, that's why she's taken flight. If I can just tell her I didn't mean Karl any harm, convince her to call a truce.

Face to face, she might back off, since she can't hide behind her laptop screen.

I have to move fast. I sprint over a bridge to her side of the river and pull out my phone to call the police. No signal. Dylan's gone for Joe, but they won't find me without a phone signal.

'Jade!' I shout, out of breath.

She hunches forward, striding ahead. She knows I'm chasing her. We approach a rundown area. Jade ducks down a side road. Breathless, I've nearly caught her.

'Jade, it's Lauren.'

She doesn't look back. So close now.

I draw level. 'Remember me?' My heart pounds.

She looks straight ahead, her expression hard, and turns down another side road.

'Jade, we know about you. About Karl. I met someone who used to know you both.'

She turns to me, her face savage. I'm shocked by her transformation. 'Who?'

'She told me all about the two of you, about your mum, your poor grandparents.'

'Fuck off, bitch. You don't get to judge me, you of all people.'

'Oh, but I do.'

She turns and keeps going to the end of the road, taking a left into an alleyway that backs onto the river. I won't follow her. It's dark now. She'll be gone in moments, taking off in the night and she'll never be found. It's all ruined.

'Your brother died,' I call after her. 'He made my life a misery with his revenge porn and then you trashed it all over again.'

She spins around, her eyes feral. 'It's your fault for leading him on.'

'I didn't. I only went for a drink with him. There was never anything between us.'

'Too good for him, were you?'

'It wasn't like that. I tried to be kind and look what he did in return.'

'Karl didn't do any of that stuff to you.'

'Yes, he did. The police tracked it to him.'

'*I* did it.'

We stare at each other.

'*What?* But that's ... but hang on, you were a schoolgirl ...'

'A schoolgirl with IT skills. My misspent youth.' Her voice is a snarl, a cruel sneer on her lips.

'But that's sick. Did he make you do it?'

'He knew nothing about it until the police came for him.'

My head spins. I picture the mousey photo the police showed me. All this time, I feared a man with devious sexual intent and the real trouble came from a schoolgirl.

'But why?'

'Everyone screwed us over. Thinking we were no good. He'd taken a photo of you. I sneaked a copy and used it for the deep fake. When I told him, he said to knock it off. Said he'd been arrested over it. I told him the police couldn't prove anything because he didn't do it.'

'Jesus.'

'And then he was given hell and died, all because of you and your nasty husband. All Karl wanted was a bit of understanding.'

366

She squares up to me. 'When he died, the police and papers acted like he deserved it. I promised I'd get revenge. It kept me going: finding ways to bring you down. When I learnt something new about surveillance and cybercrime, I'd think of how to use it against you.'

'But I wasn't responsible for what happened.'

'Shirking responsibility is your thing, isn't it, Lauren? Locking yourself away, avoiding people, hiding from the world. You brought this on yourself.' She turns and slips deftly down the route alongside the river.

I lose sight of her, but I can't let her go, not when she's this angry. She'll come back and do more damage. Did Dylan see me take this path? Still no phone signal. If I follow at a safe distance, Joe will guess what's happened and might come this way. Dylan will be with him. He's safe. I turn the corner and—

She floors me with an almighty punch to my face. I crumple against the wall, disorientated, realising too late that she led me here to ambush me. I go to recover myself, pull myself up to run, fight back, whatever I can. But she shoves me to the ground, kicks me in the stomach and grips my arms from behind.

'No!' I gasp for breath, trying to get traction with my legs. I can't scream. She's knocked the breath from me. My throat's constricted in fear. I manage a yelp that's too feeble to carry. She hauls me to the water. Pain sears through my arms. My face scrunches from trying to pull free, digging in my heels, too close to the river, my feet sliding on the muddy bank. She's so determined, she'll drown me. *Have to fight back. Happening too fast. Oh God.*

She hauls me into the river, kicking me down. The absolute shock of it as I plunge beneath the icy surface. Water engulfs me and Jade keeps a tight grip on one of my arms. I go under, my body paralysed from the cold. Can't fight back. Is this it? Will I die? I break through the surface of the river, gasping for air. Water blurs my vision, pouring down my face and into my gaping mouth.

She grips my arm tight with both of hers. Her booted foot forces my head back underwater. It hurts so much I think my arm will dislocate or she'll break my neck. I tuck my head down, desperate to dodge her foot and push it away with my free arm. But she grabs that arm too, holding my wrists firm. Fuck, she's strong. If I can only pull her in, but her boot comes down on my head again, forcing me underwater.

I struggle frantically against her iron grip. Trying to find a foothold on the side of the bank, I ram my feet into the sludge, but they slip back out. Fighting for breath, I instinctively gasp despite being submerged and I gulp in river water, spluttering it back through my nose.

Then my arms are flung backwards and my body arcs towards the surface. Released from her grip, I strain for air, take an urgent breath. Where is she? My eyes focus on the riverbank through the blur of water. Dylan's wielding a big chunk of wood, sheer terror on his face. She's grappling it from him.

'No!' I propel myself forward and scrabble up the slippery bank, weighed down by sodden clothes and boots. Have to be quick. No time to lose. She grabs the log and whacks him in the ribs. Dylan doubles over and she shoves him hard. He tumbles backwards into the water with a forlorn cry.

I haul myself onto the bank, scrabble through the mud and grab her leg, yanking it with all my strength. She falls on her face. I try to stand, but she kicks out, landing a blow to my head. Dylan's discarded log is almost within reach. I lunge for it and drag myself onto my knees the same moment as she stands.

The log's a makeshift battering ram. I shove it into her with all my might. She doubles over with a deathly groan and I land a sideways blow to her head. She crashes headlong into the water. Dylan's at the riverbank, trying to get out. Have to save him. I messily haul him out, both of us gasping for air.

I squelch onto the bank, nearly dragged back, clothes heavy with water, limbs stiff from the cold. I'm desperate to pull Dylan away from the edge, can't bear that he might slither back in or Jade could pull him in. But he's lying there spluttering up filthy river water and Jade is face down in the river, arms splayed, not moving.

A siren sounds, becoming louder. Footsteps running. Joe sprints into view and stops when he sees us.

'Here!' he calls to whoever is behind him.

I want to throw myself into his arms, but I throw myself back in the water, to Jade. I turn her lifeless body over and pull her back. Joe crouches over Dylan, and two police officers are on the bank, one radioing for help, an ambulance perhaps. They reach out for Jade and haul her on the bank to attempt resuscitation.

Joe pulls me to safety and I collapse, retching. My body shakes uncontrollably from shock and exertion. Joe holds my shoulder and rubs my back.

'You're safe,' he says in a soothing voice.

I think he's saying it to me, but when I look up, Dylan's in a motionless heap, tears rolling down his face. He's caked with mud, the same as me.

'It's okay, Dyl. You did good,' I say, my voice croaky.

'He followed you,' Joe said. 'He had enough of a signal to call me. He saw you go in the water.'

I'd wanted him to go back to Joe and safety, but he came after me instead.

'I didn't see you.' I look up at Dylan, not expecting a reply, but he registers me with the wet blink of his eyes. He opens his mouth, shuts it again, and then takes a breath.

'It's my superpower.' He wipes at his face with his muddy, sodden coat sleeves.

'Huh?' Joe looks at him.

'I'm invisible.' He doesn't take his anguished gaze from Jade's lifeless body, along the riverbank, the officers still trying to revive her.

EPILOGUE

I lay down my paintbrush and grab my sandwich to take out to the shared space. Laughter carries through the door of my tiny studio in the artists' workspace. The others are in the midst of a raucous conversation.

'Lauren, come and hear this.' Hannah pulls out the chair beside her, her face animated, wanting to tell me what's so funny. The woven threads of her jumper are in gorgeous autumnal shades. She sells them at craft markets and has promised to make one for me.

Joe's name flashes up on my phone. 'Hang on,' I say to the four of them around the table, and go out to the courtyard.

'Hey,' I answer.

'Hey, how are you?'

'About to have lunch. Everything okay?'

'Not really. I might have forgotten to lock the back door when I let Dora out first thing. I'll be in Hove till four so I won't be back before you.'

'Oh, okay,' I reply. 'I'll send the little guard dog in ahead of me. She can sniff out the bad guys.'

Joe can't help worrying about me, but it's no big deal to forget to lock up once in a while, not now. Life has taken some working out, but we're settled in our no-frills terraced home close to town, with streetlights and life going on around us. We renovated it with a faster turnaround, minus the showy touches. It's all we need and I like the cosy feel. Dylan's sensory room is the only part of the smart home to survive the move. He's staying over tonight.

He filmed Jade punching me to the ground. When she dragged and kicked me into the river, he leapt into action. The police accepted that he wanted to save me and that I acted in self-defence. At least he wasn't the one to harm her in those terrible final moments. I'd never forgive myself if Dylan took any blame. He only tried to save me by fending Jade off.

Joe and I were floored by her revelation that it wasn't Karl's fault. He'd stalked me and wouldn't let go, but he didn't mastermind the revenge porn or hack my devices. I can't imagine how consumed by hate she must have been to keep her obsession burning strong for five years.

Jade never regained consciousness. It still threatens to overwhelm me sometimes, the enormity of what she did, and how I put a stop to it. The tragedy of their wasted lives is the hardest thing to accept. But Joe has a knack of seeing those darker thoughts of mine coming, and he pulls me back before I'm submerged again.

Brooke and I are emailing again. It turned out that her email account was hacked too, her later messages doctored by Jade. She'd received fake emails from me, claiming police incompetence and swearing allegiance to Joe. The subtlety of Jade's handiwork meant neither of us suspected the hack.

I go inside and Hannah takes charge of the huge, chipped enamel teapot. She pours tea and the four of us talk about her mission to go to the Isle of Wight Festival with me. I'd told her I last went six years ago and it's one of my aims to make it back there. I meant at some point in the future when I'm more comfortable going to packed places. She has this great rush of energy that sweeps me along and her joyful exuberance prompts me to say yes to things. When I agreed, she whooped and said we're going next year in her VW campervan.

We're back talking to Dale and Kim in Santa Monica, who to my delight have a four-year-old daughter. We've put the disagreement behind us and are making plans to meet up and visit the Californian theme parks.

Joe's helping me practise standing in crowds without panicking. We went to a gig at our local pub on Saturday night where I did a lot of deep breathing and kept hold of his arm in case I lost him in the crowd. The sky didn't fall in, so that's a start.

'If we keep this up, you might even enjoy it,' he said, 'like the old days.'

And I did enjoy it. Beyond the nagging fear, I liked the warm buzz of anticipation, the heady atmosphere when the band struck up, singing along with a beer in my hand, and then walking home, ears ringing and chatting to Joe about something that's not home or work-related. The series of small steps is freeing me up, including renting a studio with kindred spirits. That's one of my better decisions.

ACKNOWLEDGEMENTS

A huge thank you to the people who turned my manuscript into a book and sent it out into the world, including:

Camilla Bolton, literary agent extraordinaire, for her sound judgement, expertise and brilliance. Thank you also to everyone at Darley Anderson.

Rosanna Forte, for her masterful editing, calm voice of reason and bolstering emails.

Thalia Proctor and Jon Appleton for their copyediting prowess.

Also at Little, Brown, thank you to Millie Seaward, Brionee Fenlon, Lucy Malagoni and Charlotte Stroomer.

Special thanks to my family and friends for their encouragement and support, including:

Dawn Warrington, first reader who I can count on for a reality check.

Felicity and Chris Ward, who live in a smart home set up by

Chris, and answered my questions, as did Charlie Worsley. All inaccuracies are my own.

David Blunden, who helped immensely with planning this book.

My mum and brother, Gill and Graham.

My writing-minded friends for continuing to put up with me, including Becky and Ninesh Edwards, Chris Moore, Simon Forward and the Grey Havens.

You're all great.

An honorary mention to the dogs who inspired the complex character of Dora, including dachshund wonder-dogs Margarita, Peggy, Dolly and Archie, along with Milo, Phoebe, Chester and Dylan. Lastly, Ricky and Friendly, rest in peace, special boys. x